WITHDRAWN FROM
KILDARE COUNTY LIBRARY STOCK

Dermot Bolger, the novelist, playwright and poet, was born in Dublin in 1959 and is one of Ireland's best known writers. His fourteen novels include *The Journey Home, Father's Music, The Valparaiso Voyage, A Second Life, Tanglewood, The Lonely Sea and Sky* and, most recently, *An Ark of Light*. However in addition to these novels, Bolger has spent several decades writing shorter works of fiction, which, although widely published in anthologies and broadcast by BBC Radio 4, have never been collected in book form. They have all now been extensively rewritten for *Secrets Never Told*, which is his first ever collection of short stories. His debut play, *The Lament for Arthur Cleary*, received the Samuel Beckett Award. His numerous other plays include *The Ballymun Trilogy*, charting forty years of life in a Dublin working-class suburb; an adaptation of James Joyce's *Ulysses*, staged by the Abbey Theatre and, most recently, *Last Orders at the Dockside*, also staged by the Abbey Theatre. A poet, his ninth collection of poems, *The Venice Suite: A Voyage Through Loss*, was published in 2012 and his new and selected poems, *That Which is Suddenly Precious*, appeared from New Island Books in 2015. He devised the bestselling collaborative novels, *Finbar's Hotel* and *Ladies' Night at Finbar's Hotel*, and edited numerous anthologies, including *The Picador Book of Contemporary Irish Fiction*. A former Writer Fellow at Trinity College Dublin, Bolger writes for Ireland's leading newspapers, and in 2012 was named Commentator of the Year at the Irish Newspaper awards. www.dermotbolger.com

D0528110

Praise for Dermot Bolger

'Bolger is to contemporary Dublin what Dickens was to Victorian London: archivist, reporter, sometimes infuriated lover. Certainly no understanding of Ireland's capital … is complete without an acquaintance with his magnificent writing.'

Joseph O'Connor

'He has been prying open the Irish ribcage since he was 16 years old … Pound for pound, word for word, I'd have Bolger represent us in any literary Olympics.'

Colum McCann

'Joyce, O'Flaherty, Brian Moore, John McGahern, a fistful of O'Brien's … Dermot Bolger is of the same ilk … an exceptional literary gift.'

Independent UK

'A fierce and terrifyingly uncompromising talent … serious and provocative.'

Nick Hornby

'Dermot Bolger creates a Dublin, a particular world, like no one else writing can.'

Sunday Independent

'The writing is so strong, so exact, so much the right colour for each moment and episode… triumphantly successful – bare, passionate, almost understating the almost unstatable.'

Financial Times

Secrets Never Told

Also by Dermot Bolger

Novels
Night Shift
The Woman's Daughter
The Journey Home
Emily's Shoes
A Second Life
Father's Music
Temptation
The Valparaiso Voyage
The Family on Paradise Pier
The Fall of Ireland
Tanglewood
The Lonely Sea and Sky
An Ark of Light

Young Adult Novels
New Town Soul

Collaborative novels
Finbar's Hotel
Ladies Night at Finbar's Hotel

Poetry
The Habit of Flesh
Finglas Lilies
No Waiting America
Internal Exiles
Leinster Street Ghosts
Taking My Letters Back
The Chosen Moment
External Affairs

The Venice Suite
That Which is Suddenly Precious

Plays
The Lament for Arthur Cleary
Blinded by the Light
In High Germany
The Holy Ground
One Last White Horse
April Bright
The Passion of Jerome
Consenting Adults
The Ballymun Trilogy
1: From These Green Heights
2: The Townlands of Brazil
3: The Consequences of Lightning
Walking the Road
The Parting Glass
Tea Chests & Dreams
Bang Bang
Last Orders at the Dockside

Stage adaptation
Ulysses (from the novel by James Joyce)

Editor
The Picador Book of Contemporary Irish Fiction (UK)
The Vintage Book of Contemporary Irish Fiction (USA)

Secrets Never Told

Stories

Dermot Bolger

NEW ISLAND

SECRETS NEVER TOLD
First published in 2020 by
New Island Books
Glenshesk House
10 Richview Office Park
Clonskeagh
Dublin D14 V8C4
Republic of Ireland
www.newisland.ie

Copyright © Dermot Bolger, 2020

The right of Dermot Bolger to be identified as the author of this work has been asserted in accordance with the provisions of the Copyright and Related Rights Act, 2000.

Print ISBN: 978-1-84840-770-1
eBook ISBN: 978-1-84840-771-8

The story 'Martha's Streets' quotes from *Ulysses* (1922) by James Joyce. The story 'What Then?' includes a passage from the poem 'What Then?' by William Butler Yeats from the collection *New Poems* (1938). The story 'The Unremembered' quotes from the poem 'For the Fallen' by Laurence Binyon which first appeared in *The Sunday Times*, 1914.

All rights reserved. The material in this publication is protected by copyright law. Except as may be permitted by law, no part of the material may be reproduced (including by storage in a retrieval system) or transmitted in any form or by any means; adapted; rented or lent without the written permission of the copyright owners.

This is a work of fiction. All incidents and dialogue, and all characters, with the exception of some historical and public figures, are products of the author's imagination and are not to be construed as real. Where real-life historical or public figures appear, the situations, incidents and dialogues concerning those persons are entirely fictional and are not intended to depict actual events or to change the entirely fictional nature of the work. In all other respects, any resemblance to actual persons, living or dead, is purely coincidental.

British Library Cataloguing in Publication Data. A CIP catalogue record for this book is available from the British Library.

Typeset by JVR Creative India
Cover design by Anna Morrison, annamorrison.com
Printed by ScandBook, scandbook.com

New Island received financial assistance from The Arts Council (An Comhairle Ealaíon), Dublin, Ireland.

New Island Books is a member of Publishing Ireland.

10 9 8 7 6 5 4 3 2 1

For Helen, with love.

Contents

The Last Person

Jack had been too nervous to enjoy any of the launches of his four previous novels. Twenty years ago the first one was overshadowed by an unexpected BBC television interview, only confirmed that evening when the American novelist meant to be featured had his flight diverted. His publicist's anxiety about Jack speaking too fast on the programme had made him talk more slowly than a commentator at a state funeral.

At his second launch he was so overawed by the inflated praise of the initial reviews that he remembered little beyond the endless queue for signings and how, at the meal afterwards, the managing director of the publishing conglomerate assured Jack that he would shortly become huge in America.

Jack had barely noticed who attended his third book launch. Just married to Ellen, they had been too anxious to slip away to a coffee bar in Soho with his agent to discuss the film deal brokered that afternoon. They had skipped the offer of a fancy meal and wound up in his agent's house, casually sharing an oven pizza while watching midweek FA Cup replay highlights. Jack could still remember the agent's five-year-old son sneaking out of bed to sit on Ellen's knee and Ellen sharing a secretive smile with him, a hint of anticipation about how hopefully one day their own child would be snuggling down in her lap. He hadn't bothered to discuss money with his agent while watching football that night. There was no need. When the film got made his new family's future would be secure and his career would look after itself.

It might have too, if the movie had actually been produced or if a different publishing conglomerate had not swallowed up the respected literary US imprint due to release his novel there or if his original supportive editor in London had not been given five minutes one Friday to clear out his desk, with a large severance cheque being the only mail forwarded on to him.

Jack remembered his fourth book launch for the fact that the editors present were merely fulfilling outstanding contractual obligations, the speech was made by a mid-ranking executive whose name he didn't know and, when it ended, the exhausted publicist (who herself was sacked in a reshuffle two weeks later) never thought to call a mini-cab for Jack and Ellen.

This was the nature of publishing: you arrived with exaggerated hype and wound up going home on the tube. He had travelled by tube to numerous Grub Street writing gigs during the lean decade since that fourth novel appeared. His publicist at his new publishers was trying to make a virtue out of this decade of scraping a living by teaching creative writing workshops in poorly paid residencies or in prisons. Jack had been out of the public eye for so long, she enthused, that he was like a debut novelist all over again or, better still, a man of mystery who was breaking a decade long silence.

In truth this silence almost broke him: four novels rejected until he turned to an idea that he had spent twenty years shying away from; a plot so good that, with his natural fluency, he had written this new novel in just three months. Even before tonight's launch it had already sold in eight languages, with an auction currently ongoing for film rights. The early reviews were calling it his best novel since his debut twenty years ago; possessing an energy that had been missing from the books in between which, while beautifully written, still paled in comparison.

This unanticipated success was nice, but nicer still was the newfound sense of not feeling like a failure in his children's eyes. Not that they or Ellen ever complained when the money dried up. His fellow writers had never ceased to treat him with great respect as an equal, but many of the novelists he started out writing alongside had long ago left him far behind in terms of reputation and riches.

Still, so many of them were here tonight at this drinks reception and book signing; all so genuinely pleased at his belated success that he was genuinely moved. In truth he had never bemoaned his fate or made excuses or felt envy towards his more successful contemporaries. He was even more surprised and moved by the number of well-wishers who were present: anonymous readers who had especially loved his debut novel and told him how pleased they were that the long wait for a true sequel to it was over. They made it sound like a shared wait, as if during the years when he imagined that he would never again see his name in a bookshop window they had been keeping him afloat in their hearts and thoughts without him ever knowing.

Tonight was a good feeling. Last month his new agent had sealed a deal for two more new novels yet to be written. Hopefully there should be more launches to come, but just now he planned to take the time to savour this evening of celebration which nobody here could possibly begrudge him.

Or so Jack thought, until a slightly dishevelled figure entered the bookshop. At first Jack barely noticed this man browsing the fiction shelves, seemingly barely aware that a book launch was occurring. This man never looked towards him and even when he picked up a glass of the complimentary wine Jack merely regarded him as someone hoping to cadge some free booze.

But increasingly Jack's eye kept being drawn back to him because by now there was no mistaking his identity. Two decades had aged Cillian. His jeans looked frayed and as he turned Jack knew that he would be only wearing a light T-shirt beneath his long coat. This was all Cillian had ever worn, no matter how cold the weather. Cillian's features had become rugged but he still possessed such rude good health and looks – like a disposed king in a Tolkien novel – to make Jack suspect that certain types of rich and supportive older women were still capable of briefly falling in love with him.

It was twenty years since they had last spoken, back when Cillian wandered in unannounced to Jack's first book launch, when Jack was still coping with the pressures of suddenly being a published author. But their first meeting had been four years before that, when Jack was living in Sheffield in his early twenties, gathering only rejection slips and so despondent about his chances of ever being published that he was toying with giving up writing. Back then he haunted local bookshops, trying to unobtrusively flick through literary magazines that he was too poor to buy, but anxiously searching for the editor's name and the postal address so he could send them unsolicited short stories. These submissions had invariably led to three months of daily disappointments when no reply came, followed by a crushing despondency when his short stories came back with the standard rejection slip. Alone in his flat, Jack would try to gleam some solace from any handwritten phrase that an editor might add to the printed slip, desperate to find the encouragement to somehow continue.

The gist of what editors were saying back then seemed to be that Jack was no genius but he possessed some talent. He would never be great but with hard work one day he might be good. Cillian was his polar opposite. From the start Jack knew that Cillian was great: he just didn't know if Cillian possessed the work ethic to ever simply be good.

Cillian was from a remote west of Ireland village, which by the age of ten he had outgrown. He was expelled from secondary school and only allowed to sit his state exams in an empty classroom so as to gain the points to enter university. He left Ireland within a year of starting college in Galway for reasons that were never fully explained – although there were dropped hints of married women and jealous husbands, stung by infidelities and unsecured cash loans – and, almost by accident it seemed, wound up studying English in Sheffield University. But, as with everything else he started, Cillian quickly allowed his studies in Sheffield to slide because the classes were insufficiently challenging for his razor-sharp brain. Instead he had spent his days staying warm in Walkley Library. This was where he first met Jack, who at that time was equally broke and also drawn to dawdle in that public library because it was centrally heated and the staff asked no questions, no matter how long you stayed.

Both young men had wanted to be writers but if Jack was progressing like a snail, Cillian was like a cartoon Roadrunner, quick-witted enough to outfox anyone. At first Cillian's sheer intelligence terrified Jack. While Jack could only sneak glances at the small literary magazines sold in The Independent Bookshop on Surrey Street, Cillian had read them cover to cover. His paramour – a mysterious but nameless older woman – seemingly made a discreet purchase there, for Cillian's delectation, every time she also made a discreet purchase, for her own delectation, from the lingerie section of Coles upmarket department store opposite City Hall.

Cillian revealed few details of his benefactor, but whenever they adjourned to the greasy spoon café that became their meeting spot, Cillian would dogmatically dissect each magazine at length, telling Jack how mediocre the contributors were: a stale potpourri of stillborn poems, trite stories and bitter book reviews that primarily reflected the reviewer's own thwarted ambitions. As proof of this, he would quote passages of bad prose or verse that he had memorised after just one casual reading, deftly switching between a mesmerising array of comic regional accents during his recitation. Such total recall was a mark of genius and it seemed as if Cillian had been marked out as a genius from birth.

While Jack was struggling to start his first novel, Cillian was half way through his ninth. Cillian's problem was that he was also still only half way through the other eight. Having brilliantly original ideas was no problem for Cillian; his problem (or so Jack thought at first) was boredom. Midway through writing a novel he would figure out the ending. From then on he lost interest, too preoccupied with the next brilliant idea to occur to him.

That seemed to be the problem with being a genius – the grind involved in actually completing any story somehow seemed a bit beneath Cillian. But now, as he studied this shabby middle-aged figure in the bookshop all these years later, Jack knew that Cillian's problem was never a surfeit of genius; it was a pathological terror of being found out. From the moment they first met as young men Jack had accepted Cillian as a genius: erratic and cocksure but undoubtedly destined for greatness. The problem was that he had such an impossibly high, self-invented reputation to live up to that, if he had ever actually published a novel, then no matter how brilliant it was, it could still never have matched the expectations Cillian had built up in his own mind.

In comparison Jack was a dunce, with any tiny measure of success seeming like an overachievement. Watching Cillian approach him now in the crowded bookshop Jack desperately hoped for some well-wisher to appear, but he knew that nobody could intervene and save him from this encounter. Cillian picked up Jack's new book from the pile on the table and scanned a paragraph with the quizzical look of appraisal that Jack remembered well. Then he nodded as if he had read enough. He put it down and stepped forward.

'It flows well,' Cillian said. 'Whenever you found a good story you always had the facility to let it unfold.'

It was typical of Cillian to launch into conversation with no greeting, as if they were picking up the threads of an on-going chat. If Cillian had made Jack uneasy at their last meeting at Jack's debut launch, now he felt ten times more unsettled, with all goodness dissipated from the evening. Jack's initial success might have petered out, but at least for a short spell he had been someone. Cillian remained exactly himself, a fossilised genius uncontaminated by either success or failure. Jack suspected that he was still the only person to have read a word of Cillian's own fiction. Strangers glanced towards them, curious as to whether Cillian might be a famously eccentric writer or professor. Even in frayed clothes he carried himself with such a distinguished, commanding air that he stood out.

'I tried to let the story tell itself,' Jack replied, guardedly.

'That's wise,' Cillian nodded as if instructing an apprentice. 'Feel your way into the narrator's voice and don't force it. The story is already formed in your subconscious. You just need to be half diligent clerk and half medium.'

'How are you doing?' Jack asked.

'Working on different things,' Cillian said. 'I had an idea for a libretto that I sent to Europe's only half-decent composer, but I don't know if it reached him. When you phone his office you get blocked by minions.'

'Are you writing fiction?'

Cillian shrugged, wearily. 'I've a couple of experimental novels finished, but it's finding the right editor to send them to.

You need to put them in the hands of someone you respect. The critics are worse: all morons.' He paused. 'Not that they're wrong about your new book. I've read every review. For once they can recognise true originality.'

It was said with such warmth that Jack wondered if the barb was only in his own mind, his conscience gnawing at him. But from the start Cillian had been uncharacteristically kind about Jack's work, urging him to ignore rejection slips, making him believe he had a future in writing – not as great as Cillian's – but a future nonetheless, as a really fine second-rate writer.

Cillian had proven kind in other ways also. When Jack's money ran out in Sheffield, forcing him to give up his flat and return to live with his parents, Cillian – who was normally secretive about his private life – had offered him the use of his own tiny bedsit for Jack's last few days in that city.

It was the boxroom of a redbrick house where Cillian had not paid rent for weeks, as became apparent when the furious landlord appeared. Other tenants also made it clear that Cillian – and anyone who was a guest of his – was barred from the communal kitchen where food had regularly been stolen. Not that Jack knew any of this on the night Cillian gave him a spare key and then disappeared off to sleep with the latest in his list of femmes fatales who believed they could help to make something of his genius.

'Use anything whatsoever in the room that you want,' Cillian had said, handing him that spare key. 'It's no use to me, I'm throwing everything out.'

This remark puzzled Jack when he got there. Apart from two T-shirts and a spare pair of jeans the room was bare, making Jack realise how penniless Cillian was. The only other item was a suitcase under the bed. With nothing else to do, Jack had opened it and sat up all night, reading his way through the opening pages of nine discarded novels – some bizarre, some blackly funny but two of them utterly breath-taking for their extraordinary plotlines, their manic characters and entangled, tortured relationships.

These books were unfinished, as if Cillian had lost the patience or courage to continue, but if Jack ever conceived of any idea this good he would work doggedly to mine its potential. "Use anything you want … it's no use to me … I'm throwing it all out." Those words haunted him, refusing to go away, even after Cillian's landlord ordered him out after just one night. They stayed with him during the following ten months when Jack lived with his parents in Leicester, writing to Cillian twice at that address but getting no reply. They were still haunting him when a sympathetic publisher returned Jack's first completed novel, saying that, while superbly written, it lacked a spark, but to stay in touch; with the right debut it might make a good second novel.

It hadn't been deliberate plagiarism when he had begun to rework the first of Cillian's two abandoned novels that he most liked. It was an exercise, an attempt to play with a different voice. It wasn't plagiarism because soon the characters took off in directions that Cillian could never have taken them because Cillian would never risk the possibility of failure by taking them anywhere.

Even when sending it to the publisher, Jack had planned to call it a novel inspired by an idea of Cillian's or even a co-written novel, but a fortnight later the publisher replied, recommending an agent whom Jack should quickly appoint to protect his interests because he was about to be offered a three-book deal.

Saying anything then would have scuppered his career before it even started. Jack had returned to Sheffield to spend an entire week trying to locate Cillian at all their old haunts.

But he had found no trace of him until he appeared, just like this, midway through Jack's first book launch, saying nothing but wearing the same sardonic smile.

Not that all of Jack's books were based on the discarded ideas in Cillian's suitcase. Novels two, three and four were entirely his own work: those novels that critics had politely welcomed while waiting for Jack's next great work until his publisher lost patience and pulled the plug.

Now twenty years on it was hard to decide just how much of Cillian's other discarded plot lay at the core of this fifth novel and how much Jack had concocted in his mind over the past decade. During that time he kept resisting the urge to write this book until, finally in despair, he began to rework it as an exercise, a way to play with a new voice, not anticipating this unexpected late success.

'The reviewers got the gist of it,' Cillian said now. 'That's all you can expect with critics.'

There was no criticism of Jack in Cillian's voice, no judgemental accession. Just like at his debut launch, the judgement lay in Cillian's very presence, in the unspoken way in which he was letting Jack know that, without him, Jack would not be here, surrounded by well-wishers. Jack looked around this launch party, which suddenly felt fraudulent. Cillian followed his gaze.

'Is that your wife and kids?'

'Yes.'

'They must be proud. I hope the book does well. With kids you need money. That's why I never had any myself: too much responsibility. I prefer to travel light.'

'Listen, Cillian ...' Jack began, '... I owe you something. I can't get your name on the cover, it's too far gone. But I have royalties due. I'm more than happy to help you out.'

'What help do I need?' Cillian shrugged dismissively. 'You mind your wife and kids, bring them somewhere nice. You owe me nothing: I don't know what you're talking about.'

'Is there anything I can do for you ...?' Jack looked around wildly. 'Would you even just like a copy of the book?'

Cillian put a hand lightly on his shoulder. 'I'll buy one,' he said quietly. 'I've bought all your books. I've rejoiced in your success. You've worked hard, so enjoy it.'

'Let me at least sign the book for you.'

Jack immediately regretted these words. He knew the reply already; the same reply Cillian had given him at his debut launch twenty years before.

'No, you're grand,' Cillian reassured Jack before turning to disappear into the night. 'When I get home I can sign it myself.'

One Seed of Doubt

People told her that the first year of widowhood was the worst, but those same people spent that year constantly dipping in and out of her life, bestowing sympathy, dinner invitations and pots of homemade jam. On the first anniversary of David's death Evelyn received so many solicitously compassionate calls that she eventually turned off her phone, just to allow herself an hour of not being a widow to be pitied, when she could try to lose herself in the convoluted plots of soap operas she had enjoyed since girlhood. These friends and acquaintances meant well but seemed to act in unison, circling her in a collective whirlwind of empathy until – after David's anniversary – they migrated *en masse* to whatever warmer climes sympathisers disappear to when they feel they have done their bit and that it is time for her to buck up and accept the reality of life on her own.

Evelyn was on her own. Yet she felt oddly relieved now that her phone rarely rang because many people who had dutifully stayed in touch were friends of David's whom she only knew through whatever gossip he used to share with her when coming home from the badminton club. He had kept himself superbly fit for a man of fifty-eight by playing two club games on mid-week evenings and a league match most Sunday mornings.

From the start of their marriage Evelyn was determined that they never become one of those boring couples who live in each other's ear. Neither asked the other to give up friends or interests. Evelyn always respected that David was an integral part of the badminton club he had joined during his college days: a committee member and team selector; an encourager of shy new members; a subtle diplomat when testosterone-fuelled zealous players clashed; a reassuring dispenser of first aid if anyone got injured. She had recognised how the club was his home from home, as vital an outlet for him as evening art classes and book clubs were for her. Her hobbies were not David's hobbies. But this made their marriage stronger because they only truly shared one passion: an all-consuming love for each other that overrode all outside interests. Once they closed over their apartment door, everyone they separately knew was excluded by their inexhaustible joy at being alone together.

Opposites attract. From the start they were opposites in everything except their love for each other. They were even opposites in their attitudes to death. Not that they often discussed death but each held clear views on what should happen if they died first. Evelyn hated the thought of being buried. She had made him promise to scatter her ashes in the remote wood where they daringly made love on their first night away together and where, a year later, he proposed to her. David's demands were less specific. He didn't mind where he was buried but wanted a grave with a simple tombstone; a possible place of solace for her if she ever wished to visit it.

These late-night discussions – always in bed and strangely, generally after sex – were abstract speculations about an imaginary future. To Evelyn it had seemed impossible to contemplate a future without this man who felt like the secret other part of her soul. But now this was the reality and she found no solace in the thought of visiting his grave which she purchased in a daze, amid the frenzy of dozens of hurried similar decisions, ranging from the heartbreak of picking what clothes to bury him in to the banality of selecting finger food for the mourners who thronged the pub after his funeral. All these decisions had been forced on her after David's car was struck by a drunk driver who confessed in court to having no recollection of the crash and managed to survive with nothing worse than a hangover. Indeed rather than being a source of comfort, the prospect of confronting David's grave had filled her with such dread since then that she only found the strength to visit it once, four days after his burial when the plot was still a mess of caked mud and decaying flowers.

She sensed that she would never find solace there, merely a reinforcement of his absence. But, having got through the dreaded milestone of his first anniversary, Evelyn knew that it was time to revisit the grave. She would never become a dutiful widow, making fortnightly visits with fresh flowers. She did not intend to turn her grief into a crutch, but neither would she shirk responsibility or shield herself from pain. Evelyn had paid to have him interred in a lawn plot section. This was meant to be seeded, with the grass on the grave cut four times a year. She told herself that it was time to ensure the cemetery was fulfilling its pledge and his grave didn't look unkempt, but Evelyn knew that she was making this visit to confront her phobia about going there. If she was to somehow start making a new life for herself, this was one more step in the acceptance of loss. And maybe she had a duty to see if she just might derive solace from standing there, as David had hinted, because at unexpected times he had revealed a spiritual side of his personality at variance with his pragmatic work as an insurance actuary.

Deep down Evelyn knew that she would find no lingering sense of him in that cemetery. His essence was held firm in the unalterable memories carried in her heart. But her visit was not as distressing as expected. She steeled herself, determined not to be overcome by emotion. In fact her main feeling was panic when she stupidly got lost, as if expecting the cemetery to look the way it had a year ago when she was steered by a throng of sympathetic people, with undertakers leading the way and gravediggers keeping a respectful distance. Since then this section of the cemetery had quickly filled up. When she finally located David's grave, Evelyn realised that she had passed it several times already. She knew this because a man in a tweed jacket was kneeling at a grave four plots down from David's. She had previously noticed him, due to his small fold-up chair with a lunchbox and flask placed beside it. The man had become conscious of her aimless wandering through the rows of graves, and seemed about to rise from tending to a row of flowers planted tight against a headstone when she finally spied David's name on limestone.

Evelyn stood in front of the grave, stunned by that starkly carved name and how the unembellished inscription revealed nothing of the man she loved or the grief she was enduring. The strong gusts of wind that had blown up since dawn seemed to have overturned flower pots and scattered bouquets of flowers. One small bouquet had even blown onto David's grave. Evelyn bent to examine it, so intent on searching for an accompanying card that might identify what grave it came from that she didn't hear the man in the tweed jacket approach. His voice startled her.

'I always tell people how cut flowers, suffocated in plastic like that, are a waste of time. They never last more than a few days. Bring a small potted plant instead. With the rain we get, plants blossom for weeks on end. They add a bit of colour and workmen cutting the grass are generally respectful and put the potted plants back when they're finished. This new part of the cemetery has a ban on planted flowers but I cheat.' He pointed towards the carefully tended grave behind him. 'I claim squatter's rights to six inches next to my wife's headstone. I grow a row of flowers there, but keep it neat with a line of stones. It bends the rules, but the workmen turn a blind eye. They know me to see. I'm here most days.' He gave a self-deprecating smile. 'It's not that I've nowhere else to be, it's just that there's nowhere else I want to be. The workmen are probably sick of the sight of me, but they're friendly. Most people are. A cemetery is a surprisingly friendly place. Not that you'd disturb people ordinarily. If you see raw grief you move away, give space where space is needed. But other times people are happy to exchange a few words. It shows there's none of us on our own, even when we're left on our own. I'm a people watcher. It's a bad habit. My late wife always scolded me for it. You're a teacher, aren't you?'

Evelyn laughed. 'I took early retirement two years ago at fifty-five. It was that or lose my pension entitlements, though I regret it now. Is it so obvious?'

The man laughed apologetically. 'Only to an ex-teacher. I spent forty years hammering the rudiments of geography into boys' skulls – a singularly unrewarding task. I knew from the way you carried yourself when walking through the headstones, unsure where you were going but trying to look like you knew exactly what you were about. A teacher's trick. Always look in control. Kids are cruel. They sense any hint of weakness.'

Evelyn smiled in wry agreement. 'I was thirty years teaching English.'

'Do you miss it?'

She reflected. Everything about her life before David's death seemed distant. 'I miss teaching Philip Larkin's poems. I don't miss the simmering civil wars in staff rooms. I miss watching First Year classes come in and wondering which quiet student will shyly open up and become interested in what I'm saying.

There's always one student who is a joy to teach and makes you put up with the unbearable ones.'

The man shook his head ruefully. 'Trust me, those students rarely surfaced in geography.' He went to move off and paused, shyly glancing at her face and then the photograph of David on the gravestone.

'There's not much family resemblance.'

'Between me and him? Why should there be?'

'No. I mean between you and her.'

'Me and who?'

'His wife. You look nothing like her. That's why I wondered if you were a relation on his side.' He paused, perturbed by a look on Evelyn's face. 'Sorry, I'm being intrusive. My late wife said I talk too much and when you spend three hours a day in here there's not many people to talk to. It's none of my business. I apologise.'

Embarrassed, he turned to walk away. It took all of Evelyn's self-control not to grab his shoulder. Her heart pounded but she needed to employ the guile learnt as a teacher. This was laughable, yet it wasn't funny. The obvious thing was to correct his mistake but this would reduce him to mortified silence. It reminded her of dealing with students who needed to be subtly manipulated into revealing information about classmates who were bullies, situations calling for tact and a steely duplicity. Evelyn was amazed at how calm she kept her voice.

'Don't go yet,' she said, 'Tell me about his wife. I don't really know her.'

It was his turn to look confused. 'I don't understand.'

'David and I were work colleagues. Some teachers tell you everything about their lives. David was the opposite. He parked his private life outside the staff room door.'

The man glanced again at David's photograph.

'He was a teacher?'

Evelyn nodded, barely trusting herself to speak. She was a logical person. It was vital to not let her imagination run wild. There was surely some obvious explanation for this misunderstanding. But if it was so simple, why did she feel a sense of dread?

'His wife never said so. There again, she rarely says much. They must have been well matched, playing their cards close to their chests.' He picked up the cheap bouquet which Evelyn had imagined as having accidentally blown onto the grave and rested its half-dead flowers against the headstone. 'I tell her that potted plants last longer, but maybe he used to buy her flowers like this. They never get too withered anyway because she replaces them every ten days or so.'

Evelyn wanted to say that David would never buy such cheap flowers. Instead she reached out a hand to steady herself by leaning on the headstone.

'How do you know she's his wife?'

The man shrugged, puzzled by the question. 'She never denied it and I just presumed because he's barely dead a year and in that time nobody else ever came.' He glanced at Evelyn. 'You say you taught in the same school?'

Evelyn nodded, realising that she was trapped inside her own lie. The truth was too complex to explain and Evelyn was suddenly conscious of no longer being sure of the truth. She'd always presumed there was nothing about David she didn't know, but now felt inexplicably robbed of such certainty. This was her husband's grave: the tombstone carefully picked from the online catalogue, the photo she had e-mailed to the stone mason because it best encapsulated the essence of what David meant to her. Now she was being made to feel like an imposter, not by this retired chatterbox but by an unknown woman who had somehow usurped her role.

'You say she visits every ten days or so?'

The man nodded, circumspect, fearing he might have blundered into a family dispute. 'I've only spoken to her for a minute or two, just to let her know she's not alone in her grief. And I'm not here every day. I visit my grandchildren or play golf if my knees allow. I'm not short of friends, I just get ambushed by grief in ordinary places where we always went together. Coming here is my way to feel close to her without breaking down in tears in supermarkets.' He was anxious to terminate their conversation. 'I'd best head off. It's nice to meet you. I'll tell her that one of his colleagues was in if I see her. I'm sure she'll be glad that someone else remembers him.'

'She won't know me.' Evelyn felt panicked. 'It's years since David and I taught...'

There was no need to continue the deception; the man was scurrying back to his wife's grave. Evelyn wasn't sure what she had expected to feel during this visit. But now she felt robbed and numb and unable to address any imaginary words to her husband, from a fear that maybe she hadn't truly known him. Until this moment there was always such intimacy between them that not even death had changed it. Now everything felt soiled and made no sense. She needed to make sense of it. Most of all she needed to remain here until she heard the retired teacher depart because only when totally alone was she able to seize the wilted flowers left by an imposter.

When he finally left, Evelyn found a bin and didn't just dump the flowers in it but tore apart every petal, reducing the bouquet to shreds before she walked to her parked car and wondered which of her friends to call. The answer was that she could phone nobody, because who could she tell when what little she knew made no sense? She cursed that man for his interfering overfamiliarity. Without him she would have mistaken those flowers for having accidentally blown onto the grave or being left by an acquaintance from David's badminton club, casually paying their respects on his anniversary. However there was nothing casual about a stranger impersonating her. It seemed so crazy it was almost comic, yet there was something deeply perturbing and even malevolent about this territorial intrusion. Evelyn had managed to get past his first anniversary, but now instead of moving forward to create a future for herself, she was being forced to look back at an incomprehensible past she was no longer certain that she understood.

Nosing her car out into the evening traffic she knew she would not sleep that night. She would sit alone on her unlit balcony; the only sound being the clink of melting ice cubes in the gin and tonics she would raise to her lips, as so often in the early months after his funeral. Back then people had offered support, but Hallmark produced no sympathy cards for infidelity. Or, more accurately, Hallmark produced no sympathy cards for uncertainty because Evelyn didn't even know if David had been unfaithful. This was what she found truly agonising; the limbo of being unsure of what was real anymore. This other woman might even be a figment of that man's imagination. Was he an embittered fantasist who enjoyed wrecking stranger's heads? Evelyn didn't think so: he seemed singularly bereft of imagination. Indeed Evelyn could not remember any geography teacher with a spark of inventiveness. After one encounter she felt she knew him back to front. What she couldn't fathom was the identity of this other woman, this interloper on her grief.

In the following days Evelyn found it impossible to exorcise a seeming inexhaustible rage. She understood how the different stages of grief – denial, anger, bargaining, depression and acceptance – could occur in any order and last for any indefinite period. Evelyn thought she had managed to get through her initial fury at the drunk driver who killed David, sensing it would destroy her if she didn't force herself to let go of that wrath. But what she now felt was a new, incalculable rage. Even if this stranger was an eccentric with no connection to David, she was still a malicious cow for intruding into that most private of spaces. But Evelyn knew that her anger at this woman masked a deeper anger at herself for having been so unquestioning; at David for maybe having secrets; at friends who possibly consoled her at his funeral despite knowing about a secret liaison they kept concealed. The other woman had not just stolen Evelyn's sense of David, she had robbed Evelyn of her sense of trust in anyone.

After being someone who never visited graveyards, Evelyn became unable to stay away. She didn't go every day but every few days, late in the afternoon when she hoped the obsessive grave-tender was gone. Each time she visited David's grave it was with trepidation and a flood of relief when she found no trace that anyone else had been there. But on the fourth occasion she discovered a cheap bouquet, identical in every way to the previous one, except that the flowers looked so fresh they could only have been placed on David's grave that day.

Until that moment she could still try and convince herself that this was a misunderstanding, but now the ache of betrayal was unstoppable. She had been played for a fool, possibly for years. She was certain of it and certain that someone was still playing her for a fool, staking a claim to her husband as publicly as an explorer planting a flag. This was the grave that Evelyn had bought to have her husband interred in. Nobody else had any right to stand here. This time Evelyn didn't wait to find a bin before tearing the bouquet apart, scattering flowers everywhere. The retired geography teacher could clear them up if he wanted too. She felt such a helpless fury that she would have torn him limb from limb too, if he appeared from nowhere, dripping affability and spurious good will.

There was nothing spurious in Evelyn's feelings towards this other woman. They did not include good will. If she thought she could just visit this grave she was in for a shock. No matter how long it took, how many afternoons of waiting, Evelyn would track her down. She felt no guilt at her determination to confront this woman. It was she who had intruded on Evelyn's marriage, leaving Evelyn feeling robbed of every precious memory of life with David. Suddenly innocuous incidents became retrospectively imbued with suspicion. The badminton tournament in Cork two years ago where David needed to stay on for an extra day because he so unexpectedly made it into the semi-finals in the over fifties category. The evening he phoned to say that his car was broken down and he needed to spend hours waiting for the AA to charge the battery. If his car battery was so unreliable why hadn't David replaced it afterwards, rather than vaguely mentioning his intention to buy a new one without ever bothering to do so?

Then what about the evening walks that David had started taking on his own? He had claimed that the additional exercise helped him to sleep, but while he would not have had time to meet someone during such strolls, had they been his way of conducting nightly phone conversations with this other woman – this stranger who gave him exactly what? Was it just sex? Evelyn could remember no dilution of their love life in the final years, no unfulfilled kink he might have alluded to; no sense of disenchantment with her. They had not been less intimate in recent years, but merely intimate less often; a combination of ageing and busy lives and overfamiliarity perhaps. They hadn't always needed the whole rigmarole of sex to create a sense of total intimacy. In the same way as they evolved a verbal shorthand to convey details about their working days with just a roll of the eyes; they had been able to conjure a familiar sexual closeness with just the feel of her hand across his bare chest in bed or a kiss on her neck in the dark when he spooned into her, his hot breath close to her ear as she drifted asleep.

They had known one another inside out, able to second guess each other's needs and thoughts. But could it be that they never properly knew each other at all? David was probably never aware that on some nights she had longed for more than cosiness and soft kisses on her neck; she had been swamped by inexpressible longings for him to make her feel like a truly irresistible woman. Maybe – behind his seeming contentment – he too had secrets never to be told, moments when something in their relationship was missing for him? Or maybe the one thing he had wanted from this stranger – the one thing Evelyn couldn't give him – was a sense of unfamiliarity. In the grip of middle years, with the landmark of a sixtieth birthday looming only a few years away, maybe his infidelity had just occurred once on one night when he needed the challenge of seeing how far he could still push himself, just like that time when he seemingly defied age and played out of his skin to reach the semi-finals of that badminton tournament in Cork.

But if it was simply a one-night fling – a frisson of risk and desire on both sides – why would this woman regularly visit his grave with cheap flowers? Evelyn was unfamiliar with the grammar of adultery, but surely its first rule involved secrecy – discreet rendezvous in hotel bedrooms with both parties leaving separately. Surely similar rules existed for its aftermath. If so, nobody had coached this other woman in the etiquette of adultery; she was choosing to play a different, public role. Having robbed Evelyn of whatever peace of mind she had managed to restore over the past year, she now seemed intent on stealing Evelyn's identity as a widow.

Over the following fortnight Evelyn realised that cemeteries were a curious contradiction, neither quite a public space nor a private space either. You might feel alone by a grave but it didn't mean you felt unobserved. Evelyn felt like an intruder whenever she ventured into the cemetery. She was careful not to stray close enough to David's grave to have to engage with the retired geography teacher who was a near constant presence. She stood out in this part of the cemetery for being one of the few visitors who did not seem intent on transforming a place of sombre remembrance into an allotment. Families attached gaudy balloons to headstones to celebrate birthdays. Cans of beer or toy cars marked out the graves of boy racers. Plaster-cast angels littered the resting places of young women. Despite David's wish to be buried she knew that he hated graveyards. He never put any stipulation on her to visit his grave, unless, as he once said, she found solace in doing so. His wish would be for her to remember him purely for who he was.

But Evelyn felt robbed of any true sense of him. She was grief-struck and bewildered, because how can you still mourn a man who possibly betrayed you. But even if losing her sense of him, this didn't mean she was able to let him go. Since his death she had slept with his pyjamas under her pillow and carried his wallet around so that at any time she could open her handbag to discreetly touch its worn leather. But these touchstones had run dry. She could not even trust the precious keepsakes in their apartment; every item was soured by the possibility of betrayal. The only place left where she might pin him down was this grave. It might yield the key to his past, in the shape of a woman who had been his mistress or lover or whatever term they had used in David's secret life.

There was no guarantee of this fake widow continuing to visit his grave, especially if the retired teacher told her that another woman had turned up. But Evelyn had no other way to trace her. She had examined every notebook of David's, every text message on his phone – even pulling up the bedroom carpet in case a slip of paper was hidden there. She had no choice but to keep haunting this cemetery, hovering awkwardly at random graves from where she could keep watch on her husband's headstone. She came to recognise the regular mourners. There were far more than just the retired teacher who studiously ignored her presence. She didn't know what he made of her but she barely knew what to make of her own behaviour: her compulsion to be here, her anger at this other woman, at David and at herself for being unable to let go. She grew to resent the recently widowed women who visited with fresh flowers and uncomplicated narratives of loss. The rational side of her brain told her to stop haunting this place but rationality would never win out. She had a rendezvous to keep with a rival who might never reappear, but, if she did, Evelyn was ready for her.

Not that Evelyn knew what she would do if this woman turned up. Some nights she fantasised about charging through the tombstones to scream at her if she placed flowers on a grave where she had no right to trespass. But increasingly Evelyn hoped that this stranger would never reappear so that, after a month of loitering in the cold, Evelyn's obsession would dissipate. Some former teaching colleagues began to contact her again, suggesting lunch or theatre dates but Evelyn remained aloof on the phone, too absorbed in her cat and mouse game. One colleague even scolded her, saying that if Evelyn had a new man in her life, it was no excuse to act defensively and shun old friends who would be delighted for her. Evelyn had let the call end in silent acrimony, making no attempt to defend herself. While she hated hurting anyone's feelings, the truth was too bizarre and shameful to share – not that Evelyn knew the truth, trapped in this purgatory of unknowing.

Her purgatory ended one wet Wednesday afternoon when nobody with sense would visit a graveyard and even the retired teacher had folded up his chair and departed. Evelyn would have left too if she'd anywhere else to go, but she hadn't. In the same way as she had let friendships lapse, she had let the state of the apartment and her own appearance lapse, taking up smoking a quarter century after having stopped. The woman who appeared was so plain and unremarkable that Evelyn initially paid her no attention. It took several moments for Evelyn to realise that she had stopped directly beside David's headstone. Perhaps affairs were always conducted by the sort of person you were least likely to expect. The woman was younger than Evelyn, but had David really risked their marriage for someone who looked utterly unlike his type? Her clothes were too garish in an attempt to appear youthful. Her hair style looked like it had not changed in twenty years: an outdated perm held in place by so much lacquer that she resembled an extra from an old episode of *Inspector Morse* – the red herring secretary with the sordid past who gets murdered moments before the first ad break.

Evelyn's plans to confront her evaporated. She felt sickened, beseeching God that this woman had merely paused to get her bearings before seeking out whatever grave she really intended visiting. This seemed a possibility at first; the woman barely glanced at David's headstone and appeared to just loiter there, lost in thought. Then Evelyn realised that she had become aware of being watched. She glanced several times in Evelyn's direction. Evelyn panicked, fearing she had been recognised, that David had perhaps shown his lover her picture. This woman might have been among the congregation at his funeral. She could have regularly stalked Evelyn in supermarkets with Evelyn oblivious to her. Evelyn stared down at the random grave she stood at, shaking and suddenly fearful that the stranger would approach. The tables would be turned, with any element of surprise lost, if David's mistress made the first move.

Having been shamed and exposed, Evelyn expected her to skulk away. She kept her gaze averted for long enough to give her time to escape. But the woman seemed emboldened by being watched. When Evelyn looked again the stranger was kneeling on a handkerchief, having placed another cheap bouquet of flowers on David's grave. She remained there for several minutes, a solitary figure in the rain, the epitome and embodiment of grief. Then she rose, casting an accusatory glance across at Evelyn before walking away.

Evelyn watched her depart, too shocked to know what to do. When the woman disappeared she ran across to examine the anodyne bouquet that contained no note to yield a clue to this stranger's identity. With the woman gone Evelyn felt emboldened again and furious. She began to run, cutting a ridiculous figure in the cemetery if anyone was watching but caring about nothing except her need to find this woman. Evelyn emerged through the cemetery gates, convinced that she had lost her, then saw the woman standing at a nearby bus stop. The woman was too busy watching for a bus to notice her. Evelyn raced frantically towards the next bus stop in the distance. She almost stumbled when glancing back to see a bus pull in at the stop where the woman waited. It took all of Evelyn's energy to reach the next bus stop just in time to put out a hand and stop it.

Evelyn was glad there was so sign of the stranger downstairs. Feeling in control of this pursuit again, Evelyn sat panting in the back seat, aware that the stranger was unlikely to glance back and see her when coming down the stairs at her stop. The journey took so long that Evelyn began to fear the woman might not be upstairs but it was impossible to check without giving herself away. Eventually they reached the docklands, with Victorian warehouses and narrow red-bricked terraced streets demolished to make way for bland apartment blocks. This was where the woman came downstairs. There was no time for Evelyn to get off at the same stop, but she rang the bell as soon as the bus pulled away.

Disembarking at the next stop, Evelyn hurried back along the street, anxious not to attract attention but aware that every second lessened her chance of finding David's paramour. She felt lost in this soulless streetscape of apartment blocks with gated entrances and ethnic eateries at ground level. The small dockland pubs she recalled from her student days had been swept away. The gates of one apartment complex opened; a security guard silently emerging on a Segway before the gates closed behind him. Evelyn looked around in despair. Only then did she spy her prey. The woman was seated alone in the window of an Italian restaurant, where a sign advertised early bird prices. She was the sole customer at this hour, the young waitress obviously recognising her from how she nodded when coming to take her order. But they seemed to exchange no more words than necessary. The woman stared out the plate glass window while awaiting her meal but in the opposite direction to where Evelyn stood. This gave Evelyn the chance to scrutinise her: this home-wrecker; this marriage-destroyer; this woman who seemed to be trying to hold back time in the old-fashioned way she dressed, like a teenager from a quarter century ago who had morphed into a middle-aged woman. Her odd dress sense might have caught Evelyn's eye if they casually passed on the street, but only momentarily. There was nothing memorable about her. Evelyn had expected someone who radiated a sense of seductive mystery, but in the harsh light of the café window this woman looked utterly plain.

This made it even more disconcerting. Why had David risked everything for someone so ordinary and – on the outside at least – uninteresting? But she must have catered to some latent secret need. Or was she a lonely person in his office to whom David had charitably reached out, offering an innocent companionable drink after work, unaware that she would entrap him in an impulsive fling that he could never escape from. No. It was too easy and neat to simply blame the other woman. Something had been going on, perhaps for years, about which she knew nothing. The only way to get answers to the questions tormenting her was to confront this stranger, woman to woman, without losing her composure.

Evelyn watched the waitress serve a plate of pasta which the woman picked at disinterestedly. After a short while she pushed aside her half-finished meal. The waitress reappeared, obviously knowing from experience – perhaps nightly experience – that this was all she would eat. The woman nodded to the waitress but no words were exchanged when the waitress returned with a small coffee. Evelyn felt panicked in case the woman finished the coffee with the same speed with which she had toyed with her food. But the waitress's dismissive glance when walking away convinced Evelyn that she would linger over her coffee for as long as possible, dawdling here because she had nowhere else to be.

Evelyn found the courage to push open the door and enter. She meant to approach the woman's table and take the chair opposite her but lost heart. With so many questions, she could not sufficiently order her thoughts to know what to ask first. Evelyn picked the window table furthest from the woman but sat facing her. The waitress approached holding the menu but Evelyn just asked for coffee. The woman had glanced up indifferently when Evelyn entered, then stared back out the window. But something about Evelyn perturbed her because she looked back, trying to place Evelyn and conscious of Evelyn's gaze fixed on her.

The waitress returned with Evelyn's coffee but stepped away once she placed it down, sensing the unspoken tension between her two solitary customers. The other woman arched her eyebrows inquisitively as if inviting Evelyn to proffer a comment and then dismissively looked away. But unease was etched into her countenance, followed by a quiver of recognition. The woman looked back; her gaze different, vulnerable and shaken. Squirm and suffer, Evelyn thought, shocked at the vindictiveness surfacing inside: I have you where I want you. Evelyn knew she didn't need to approach; this would be a sign of weakness. Guilt and entrapment would force the woman to approach Evelyn instead. After an uneasy silence she rose and walked over to take the other chair at Evelyn's table.

'I know your face from somewhere today but can't place it. Have you followed me? What gives you the right to follow strangers?'

'We're hardly strangers,' Evelyn replied quietly. 'We've too much in common.'

'Like what?'

'A taste in men.'

'I don't know what you're talking about.'

'There are differences of course. We built a home and a life together. I don't know if he pretended that he'd leave me, but he wouldn't have. We fitted each other like a glove. I don't know how long something was going on, but David would only have turned up on your doorstep with his bags when I found out, because I'd have sent him packing with his tail between his legs.'

The woman looked at Evelyn cautiously and then glanced at the waitress who pretended to clean a counter while listening to every word. She lowered her voice, forcing Evelyn to lean forward until their heads almost touched. Anyone would think their posture was conspiratorial, old friends confiding intimacies.

'Do you know my name?'

Evelyn shook her head. 'David, unsurprisingly, never mentioned it.'

'I haven't a clue who you are either. I only know you're half cracked. You've no right to intrude on my life. Whoever you're looking for, buzz off and find her, because it isn't me. You understand?'

'I understand what intrusion feels like. I'll not accept lectures from my husband's mistress.'

'Your husband's what?' The woman laughed. 'You're married to a fantasist. Go home and bring him to a head doctor.'

'There's nothing any doctor can do for David and you know it.' Evelyn opened her handbag to take out the memorial card she had designed with such love and care. The woman stared at the photo, casually at first and then with a shock of recognition. She looked around, desperate to flee from Evelyn's scrutiny. Flustered, she summoned the waitress.

'Keep the change,' she told the young girl, pushing a banknote into her hand. Hurrying back to her own table to grab her coat, she needed to pass Evelyn again to reach the door. Uneasily she glanced down. 'I'm sorry, desperately sorry.'

'You can't just walk away from me,' Evelyn replied.

The woman was close to tears. 'Stay out of my life. I promise to stay out of yours.'

Then she was gone out. Evelyn knew she had been scared away from ever revisiting David's grave, but this wasn't enough. She needed answers. Leaving money for her coffee Evelyn hurried after the woman and caught up with her as she punched a code into an electronic gate which led into the courtyard of an apartment complex.

'Is this where you brought him?' Evelyn asked. 'I need answers.'

Flustered, the woman turned, ignoring the electric gate which swung open.

'How well did you know your husband?'

'I thought I knew him as well as I know myself. Obviously I didn't.'

'Had you a good life together?'

'That's none of your business.'

The woman nodded. 'That's truer than you can possibly know. I see you're grieving but I even envy you your grief, do you know that?'

'You wouldn't if you knew how it feels.'

'Don't get me wrong; I'm not belittling your grief. What I envy is how the world gives you special status as a grieving widow. It makes allowances, bestows respect. It doesn't look through you like you're invisible.'

'You made your own bed by starting an affair with a married man.' But Evelyn's tone softened, aware of how wretched the woman looked. 'Maybe you never knew David was married and only found out when you saw his death notice. I don't know what draws you back to my husband's grave, but I need to know — even if the truth hurts. Can you understand that?'

The woman stepped back to let a neighbour pass through the gate that was closing again. 'I'd ask you in, but I've not much to say. There's stuff about me you don't know, but it's stuff you'll find out for yourself now that you're a woman alone. You'll discover it when you start feeling lost in a crowd. Everyone is there with someone else but you're alone and you make all the couples uncomfortable. It means you start to only go to the pictures in the afternoon, with the other odds and ends left on the shelf after everyone else magically paired off. I eat the early bird menu in that restaurant, not to save money but so I can be gone before loving couples saunter in holding hands or yummy mummies so engrossed in their perfect lives that they're oblivious to their screaming brats driving other diners crazy.' She paused. 'People don't like seeing women our age on our own. I'm sorry to break the news, but you'll discover it soon enough. Have you tried internet dating?'

'I'm in grief,' Evelyn said. 'It takes all my willpower to just get out of bed.'

The woman nodded. 'Save the computer dating phase for when you have energy. You need lots of energy to don your smiling face and walk into yet another coffee shop, trying to stay positive even though you know your hopes will almost certainly be crushed again.'

'Did you meet my husband on a dating site?'

The woman sighed. 'You're not listening to what I'm saying. I gave up dating sites long ago, along with meet-up groups, event volunteering and doing endless evening classes. I put away my smiley face because I got exhausted taking it on and off like a mask. But we still need some sort of mask, don't we? Men have it easy. If they buy a fishing rod and stand by a river, passers-by consider them paragons of patience. If a woman stands by a river, everyone considers you a suicide case. You can get a dog and convince yourself the stupid mutt understands every word you say, but my apartment has a "no pets" clause in the contract. So where do you go if you're someone like me? Where will people see nothing odd in you being alone? Obviously I have a job but I only job-share now, week on and week off. I'm so long in the civil service that I really don't need a full wage. But I still need to stop the four walls of my apartment closing in on me. If I go to parks I get hassled by drunks and sad cases. You can only walk around the shops for so long before store detectives start to trail you. I used to love going swimming three times a week: nobody says boo to you there, but I had to stop and haven't got back into it. It's only recently that I discovered the one public space where nobody even looks at you.'

She stared at Evelyn, one lonely woman to another, allowing the implication to sink in, though it took Evelyn a moment to understand what she was saying.

'You never actually knew my husband, did you?' Evelyn said at last.

The woman gave a shrug, both apologetic and defiant. 'I don't know any of the men whose graves I visit. But I like to pretend that I gain a sense of them, based on the photos and inscriptions on their tombstones or how often relatives leave flowers. Though once I realise a grave is being tended to, I stay away.' She reached out to awkwardly touch Evelyn's jacket. 'Trust me, if I'd known that you visit your husband's grave I'd never have chosen it, but there was no sign that anyone went there.'

'Whether I go or not, it's still my husband's grave.'

The woman nodded. 'I don't deny it. This is just a habit I got into after I saw a woman walk into a cemetery with a bouquet of flowers. I watched through the railings and everyone she passed left her in peace so as not to intrude on her grief. They gave her space to be herself, no awkward questions or glances. I didn't plan anything as such but on impulse I bought a bunch of flowers and entered the cemetery. I can't describe the sense of freedom, walking down avenues of graves with everyone assuming that I knew where I was going; nobody seeing me as lonely or an oddball or threat. It became something to do. On quiet afternoons during my weeks off I could become a widow simply by buying a few flowers. Nobody bothered to notice that I was a widow without a grave.'

Evelyn suddenly felt cold and exhausted, aware of how long it was since she had eaten or enjoyed a proper night's sleep.

'Are you saying you picked David's grave to visit at random?'

The woman shrugged again, embarrassed. 'Like I say, I wasn't getting in your way. You never visited.'

'How do you know?'

'He told me.'

'Who?'

'The busybody who spends half his life like a faithful hound at his wife's grave. Cyril his name is. There's nothing worse than over-helpful men desperate to talk. Cyril never mastered the art of privacy. He put two and two together and came up with forty-six.' She paused and looked at Evelyn. 'I never intrude by placing flowers on a grave that already has flowers. In that part of the cemetery most graves have all kinds of things placed on them during the first years, from plaster angels to cigarette packets. People visiting a cemetery often pause to look at any graves that stand out. I only stopped at your husband's grave because I was curious. It was so bare and neglected.' Her gaze grew almost accusatorial. 'Be honest. You neglected it from the start.'

'I couldn't bear to visit. Being there hurt too much. Even being at home hurt, but at least home was private.'

'A cemetery should be private,' the woman said. 'Ordinarily nobody speaks to you. That's the beauty – nobody questions or invades your privacy. You can walk for hours holding one bunch of flowers and you only look odd if you walk back out the gates with them. That's why I'd normally pick some neglected grave to leave them on. The first time I paused at your husband's grave I had no thought of placing my flowers there; I still intended to use them as a prop for another hour of walking. I stopped out of momentary curiosity, but I lingered a few seconds longer than I meant to, lost in thought, minding my own business, until this Cyril fellow appeared behind me. I'm startled, especially when he starts consoling me, asking me how I'm doing. He thinks I'm you and I'm caught off guard, so it seems simpler to play along. Not that I ever claimed to be David's widow: I just didn't deny it. But if you pretend once then you're trapped. Do you understand?'

'I understand how vast the cemetery is,' Evelyn insisted. 'There are a dozen walks you could take to ensure you never went near David's grave again.'

'I know.' The woman nervously took out a packet of cigarettes and lit one, her hand shaking. 'I know every route in that cemetery. But older parts date from Victorian times and feel very isolated when I'm on my own. I didn't want to get mugged. A protective instinct always steered me back towards the more recent graves where a few people were moving about. The problem is that any time I came within sight of your husband's grave Cyril jumped out of his chair, his hand raised in greeting. He's a permanent fixture, lurking there waiting for anyone to talk to. Once he saw me I'd feel trapped into going over. And besides, I needed somewhere to leave my flowers.'

'It didn't always have to be my husband's grave,' Evelyn insisted.

'I know it was wrong.' The woman took an anxious puff of her cigarette. 'Afterwards I never felt good about myself. But the crazy thing is that when standing at the grave it didn't seem such a terrible white lie. I never shattered Cyril's presumption because what harm was I doing? By giving a lonely man the chance to be solicitous I let him feel good about himself. Sometimes it almost felt like my good deed for the day.'

By now Evelyn wasn't sure which of them was more anxious to terminate this conversation, both standing there, feeling foolish. 'You're making yourself sound like Mother Theresa.'

The woman stared at Evelyn. 'Trust me, I'm no saint. A lonely woman can always find company at a price, or at least until she loses her looks. That price is generally your pride.

Lying married men, so anxious to get away that they're already rooting for their car keys, half way down your hallway, before they're even finished ejaculating. But I gave up all that stuff. I'm settled into my own loneliness. Sex only enters my life when I watch people having affairs on *Coronation Street*.'

'You must have friends.' Evelyn suddenly feared that she was staring at her own future, drifting towards a time when every couple she knew gradually forgot about her.

'Of course I have friends,' the women replied defensively. 'I'm no social retard. But they are nine-to-five friends; work colleagues. Some friendships go right back to when I arrived from Galway to start in the civil service. But one by one they got married or settled down with a partner or got separated from a partner whom they still bitch about. Most of them have broods of kids they drone on about. I zone out when they start discussing their domestic tiffs because I've nobody to quarrel with. I can't yap on about attending parent teacher meetings with the same anxiety as if I was visiting a cancer specialist. Can you even begin to understand this?'

'What makes you think I don't understand loneliness?' Evelyn asked. 'I've lost my husband.'

'That means you had a husband to lose,' the woman shot back. 'It means you had a life and you'd still have the pieces of one to pick up if you weren't out here letting your imagination run amok on a wild goose chase. You don't know how it feels to be utterly isolated. I'll be brutally honest. I only visited your husband's grave when in that cemetery because I knew that Cyril would probably be there, dove-eyed and sympathetic, dying to ask how I'm doing. Can't you see? I wasn't visiting your husband's grave: I was really visiting Cyril. Cyril gives me a life, even if only for a few minutes. He doesn't look through me, he looks forward to seeing me. I was crushed that he wasn't there today. I wouldn't have even bothered leaving the flowers only I saw a figure watching me in the distance and felt I had to go through the motions. I'm no fool. I know full well that the life I pretend to lead at that graveside isn't my life. But it's the only human contact I have and, let's be honest, you haven't actually been using your life.'

'Have you any idea how your actions wrecked my head?' Evelyn asked. 'I've driven myself demented, trying to figure out who you are, re-examining my life with David for any clues to infidelity, lying awake imagining all kinds of things. What you've been doing is crazy.'

'I'm not crazy.' The woman stubbed out her cigarette and again keyed in the gate code. 'I'm desperate and lonely. Desperate people do irrational things. If I caused you distress, I apologise sincerely. But I can't do any more than promise never to go back. Now, if you don't mind, four apartment walls are waiting to greet me.' She reached out her fingers one last time to brush against Evelyn's sleeve. 'Forget about me. Everyone else has. When I die it will be like I never existed. I see how you're torn apart by grief, but that's something, isn't it? If you didn't love David you wouldn't care who stopped by his grave. Think of your grief as a blessing. It means you can be certain that you loved and have been loved in this life. That's something precious.'

'David was precious,' Evelyn said quietly, near tears. She felt a calmness spread within her, the equilibrium of certainty slowly return. She could begin to grieve again. Everyone assured her that grief eventually passed. 'He was a good man, a loving and faithful one.'

'I don't doubt it.' The woman nodded with sympathetic understanding. 'I'm mortified that I caused you distress but I know nothing about him. He was just another stranger's name on a tombstone. I'm genuinely sorry for your loss.' The woman tried to smile. 'And I've learnt my lesson. Next time I enter a cemetery I promise it will be in a wooden box. Now stay busy. You have friends. Forget about me. Get out and start living your life.'

Evelyn couldn't resist the impulse to touch the woman's shoulder. She felt relieved and oddly empty. 'You stay active too. Go back and do your swimming again.'

The woman nodded. 'I must get back to it. It's just that I'm very competitive and some strokes are difficult to do properly since I broke my wrist.'

'How did that happen?'

'My own carelessness.' The woman smiled at the memory. 'I took a stupid tumble when playing badminton.' She nodded in farewell. 'Treasure those memories of a wonderful man.'

The electronic gate was starting to close. The woman slipped quickly into the courtyard before it fully shut. Within seconds she disappeared from sight. Evelyn stared in through the gate, desperate to call her back. There was one last question she urgently needed to know the answer to: in what club did this woman play badminton? Evelyn had felt that she got her husband fully back during the moments when this stranger was telling her story, but now realised that she couldn't be certain. What if the woman's story was invented? What if they had actually met playing badminton? If so, this stranger hadn't picked out his grave at random. Surely David had never strayed and not with this sad creature, but Evelyn had no way of knowing. The problem with doubt was that it was like a little crack in a dam. No matter how hard you placed your hands against it you couldn't totally stop water from seeping in. Maybe the fault wasn't in David. Maybe it stemmed from her need to find a bigger explanation to explain away her grief, her inability to let go, her need to hold onto David even if only through suspicion and anger. Evelyn remained standing at that gate as darkness settled in over the city. She was unable to tell which lit apartment window marked the room where this stranger sat and she felt unable to face the emptiness awaiting her at home. Their paths would never again cross. This woman would never revisit David's grave and Evelyn would never find her way back here. Her knuckles turned white from how tightly she gripped the bars of the gate, but she felt broken, wounded, unable to let go as she stood there for hours, hoping against hope that the woman might reappear. She was left with a crack of doubt that was spreading into every memory of their life together and once that crack was there it would never disappear.

Coffee at Eleven

It was a tiny daily routine that was special to them both, though only in recent years had they come to appreciate the uninterrupted quietude of these fifteen minutes spent together. Breakfast was different, when she would always cook a fry to fuel the morning tasks – tasks that took him longer as he grew older. Dinner at one o'clock could also be hurried; one ear cocked to the news while he fretted that the weather might turn, or about the jobs on the farm that needed to be completed before the onset of dusk in winter. But they shared an unspoken agreement that neither of them rushed this new ritual of having coffee together in the kitchen at eleven each morning.

Perhaps it was foolish to consider it a new ritual, as they had allowed themselves this small luxury for the past nine years. Before then John had simply left his tractor engine running in the yard when grabbing a quick mug of coffee if time allowed. But ever since Julia's health scare – his inexpressible terror at her diagnosis and their trips for chemotherapy to Waterford Regional Hospital, where he would grip her hand tightly before the nurses banished him to wander aimlessly around Ardkeen Shopping Centre until it was time to collect her after the treatment – John no longer allowed anything to interrupt this quarter of an hour spent together in mid-morning.

He stomped his boots now on the cast iron scraper that had stood for a century outside the kitchen door. Julia would be inside, listening to the radio and plugging in the new Nespresso coffee maker he had purchased last month in Kilkenny City. Until Julia's cancer scare they only ever drank Nescafé Gold Blend instant coffee. Indeed when John first came from Kilgara in Roscommon to work for Julia's father forty-five years ago he had distrusted the unfamiliar taste of coffee – not that he was offered it much or invited to enter this kitchen. But now they had developed sophisticated palates, sampling Colombian, Kenyan and Fairtrade Guatemalan beans – although John basically liked anything from Tesco with a Number 3 strength on the label. What he loved most was watching Julia make the coffee, because at times when driving her home from those chemotherapy sessions, he had feared that a day might come when they would never be able to do anything as simple as sip coffee in amicable silence.

He associated posh coffee with her illness. Left alone to wander through the shopping centre near Waterford Regional Hospital, he had plagued shop assistants with queries about items he never intended to buy, just to drown out the fears in his head. One day he spent so long questioning a young girl about a De'Longhi Magnifica coffee maker with an integrated grinder that he had noticed her grow uncomfortable, suspecting him of gaining some sexual thrill by detaining her in conversation. Embarrassed by his behaviour, he had purchased the machine, even though he thought it over-priced and suspected that neither he nor Julia would know how to work it. When collecting Julia he had presented it to her, claiming to have bought it because he was too shy to be seen buying her flowers. It had vanished into a kitchen press, with John needing to put it away for Julia because she lacked the strength to lift it herself. Months later, after they had been through hell and back and Julia received the all clear – with instructions to just come back for bi-annual check-ups – he entered the kitchen to find that she had taken it down and laid out the good china, ready to serve him his first cup of proper homemade coffee. This was the moment when these fifteen minutes each day had become precious. Every two years since then, on the anniversary of Julia receiving the all clear, he had presented her with yet another sophisticated coffee-maker, ignoring her protests that the last one was still functioning fine. It was one of the few luxuries he allowed himself and saved him from enduring the mortification of entering a florist's where he wouldn't have a notion about what flowers to ask for. The coffee served from each new-fangled machine was a reminder of bad times never mentioned; an unspoken acknowledgement that they remained still as much in love as on the evening, decades ago, when they faced down her father's strenuous disapproval.

Giving his boots a final bang he entered the kitchen where she was humming while setting the table. A Dublin politician was talking rubbish on the radio but she had it on so low that it didn't disturb the ambience. He loved to watch her like this – perhaps because in the early years of marriage he was still too shy to look at her properly. She was slightly older than him and past the first flush of youth when they married, but although others might not see it, for him she had grown more beautiful with age, blossoming fully into herself despite the grey hair that she was wise enough not to hide with some coloured rinse. She was aware of being watched now, secretly pleased by his new habit. She looked at him and smiled.

'Are them boots of yours clean?'

'Spotless.'

'I believe you. Thousands wouldn't. What's the weather doing?'

'It will spit rain later, but I'll be long finished the high field by then.'

'You were wise to make an early start with the spraying.'

'I'm too old to enjoy lie-ins, or maybe my bones aren't old enough.'

She smiled. 'When did you ever take a lie-in?'

'You've a short memory,' he teased. 'What about Ballybunion? We had three great lie-ins there.'

She laughed with playful mockery. 'Ballybunion was thirty-five years ago and it was our honeymoon, or what little we had of one.'

'Do you remember the guesthouse owner tapping on our door to announce that if we weren't up soon we'd miss her grand cooked breakfast?'

'And us pretending not to hear, giggling like children under the sheets. I thought it must surely be love to stop this fellow missing out on a cooked breakfast.'

'It was to put the busybody's nose out of joint, with her dying to grill us about our seed and breed. But it was love also.'

Julia kissed him softly on his balding head, leaning forward to place biscuits on the table. 'You old romantic.'

'That was me, all right; the strong silent type.'

They could laugh about their honeymoon now but there had been nothing funny about that first night or the frantic first lie-in: both of them pent up and nervous; knowing what they should be doing but too shy to know how to make it happen. It had felt too pressurised in that bed which creaked so loudly they feared the entire guesthouse would hear. It needed to happen unexpectedly the first time: the pair of them lying like teenagers at twilight in the grass overlooking the remote Nuns Beach and suddenly daring each other with their eyes, acting out of character but caring about nobody else. They never did anything so risky or immodest again, but never needed to, as if that first time laid any demons to rest. Julia ruffled what remained of his hair now, perhaps sensing what he was thinking about, because they often seemed to know each other's thoughts without need for words.

'Strong and silent is right,' Julia said. 'You needed to be strong in your early days here, my father working you from dawn to dusk. And you were so silent it took me three years to get a sentence from you longer than "Yes, Miss". I often wondered if it hadn't been such a scorching day with tar melting on the road would you have found the courage to finally knock at this door and ask if you could trouble me for a sip of water.'

'I wasn't thirsty.' John teased her with a joke they never tired of. 'I feared for your safety. You kept leaning so heavily against the lace curtains every time I removed my shirt to work bare-chested that I thought you might fall through the window.'

'That's not true and you know it,' Julia replied with a soft laugh.

'Then how come the imprint of your fingers are still on that parlour window all these years later?'

Julia went silent. John had touched a chord he hadn't meant to. He stroked her fingers lightly. She smiled but couldn't hide a trace of sadness.

'Maybe I took the odd peep out, wondering what might unlock the heart of our silent farm labourer.'

'A coffee might have gone a long way, though your father would have had a heart attack at the thought of us fraternising.'

'Daddy liked you well enough.'

'As a labourer willing to work all hours. He liked me less as a potential son-in-law.'

'He came around to the notion.'

'With smelling salts.'

'He was a strange man,' she said. 'King of his castle. You knocked along well enough after we married.'

'If the grandchildren ask about him, you always say, "He was nice, but his father was nicer." That's one thing I've always loved about you. You are so gentle that even when you fillet a man you hide it inside a compliment.'

'I suppose Daddy wanted to ensure I was looked after. And his farm.'

'I often wonder who I'm looking after it for now. Thank God our pair had more sense than to try and make a living from this place. Maybe we should sell up.'

Julia smiled. 'One day I'll call your bluff and suggest we buy an apartment in Kilkenny City. I can see you stalking the corridors at dawn, desperate to find something to poke with a pitchfork. I was born in this house and please God I'll die here. And do you think our grandchildren would troop over so often from Zurich without these fields to run in? You're like a child yourself when they arrive, terrifying their mother by letting them clamber up onto the tractor with you. What was the phrase you taught little Celeste last time?'

'I taught her nothing; she overheard.'

'Announcing in an eight-year-old serious Swiss accent: "Health and Safety my arse." I thought her mother would drop her teacup, but Dominique just burst out laughing. They love the freedom here, she says. It's funny, at their age I never associated this house with freedom.'

Again that faint trace of sadness. John desperately wanted to make her laugh. '"Health and safety my arse." Maybe I should wear that slogan on a T-shirt next time they visit.'

She scoffed at him affectionately as she poured his coffee. 'How would they see it? You don't even take off that old black coat when we're having our coffee.' She paused and pointed out the window. 'And we mightn't get to have it in peace. Someone's after driving into the yard.'

John did not recognise the car drawing to a halt. This perturbed him, though it would never do to let whoever was driving this black Skoda Octavia with Cork number-plates sense his unease. It was no farmer anyway; only a fool would keep a car so clean when any fall of rain on the narrow roads nearby would leave it filthy with mud.

'He's probably a lost tourist making a three point turn. Cheeky but better than anyone landing in on us.'

'Wishful thinking,' Julia said. 'He's parked there, staring into space. I think he knows that we're watching. It couldn't be anything to do with the children, could it?' Julia asked, suddenly uneasy. 'You know how they sometimes send policemen if there's bad news.'

'The children are grand.' John looked longingly at his steaming coffee. 'If he knocks at the door he's a beggar, but he thinks that if I'm forced to go out to him he'll have me on the back foot. Put a saucer over that cup.'

'Be polite, John,' Julia urged as he made for the back door. He looked back to reassure her.

'I'm polite to everyone. Start your coffee before it gets cold. I'll find out what he wants and help him on his way.'

As expected, he saw Julia place a saucer over her cup also, waiting for him. Entering the yard he approached the car leisurely, giving him time to size up their visitor. At least he wasn't a scam merchant in a white Hiace who would call him boss while scanning the yard for anything he could come back to rob. Fellows offering to fix imaginary faults on shed roofs. John was well versed in getting rid of such callers. He wasn't shuffling brochures so he probably wasn't a salesman. Nor was he a Department of Agriculture inspector; he looked long past retirement age. He might be one of those elderly tourists who traipse around looking at old churches that can no longer display collection boxes without them being stolen.

Or could he be an elderly doctor, press-ganged into working as a locum and calling about one of the four elderly bachelors still clinging to their small holdings further up the road? Sometimes

Julia scolded him gently for not minding his own health, saying that these old men took advantage of his kindness on winter nights when he ventured out in the rain to bring his four neighbours into Bennettsbridge. There John needed to nurse a solitary bottle of stout while allowing them to bore the barman stupid until closing time. But although Julia teased him about being a glorified taxi driver, she was proud of his decency towards their old neighbours who relished being able to go for a drink without fear of losing their licences or meeting boy racers on the hairpin bends nearby. Without their weekly outing these men would go daft with loneliness, never knowing if they were about to be attacked by robbers every time their dogs barked. One night he came home with news that Joe Flaherty had taken to sleeping with a loaded shotgun. Julia had laughed, saying 'Joe is so shy it took him seventy-eight years to share his bed with anything.' John would sooner let those bachelors repeat their old jokes every Tuesday night than call in some morning to find one of them dead and feel that he had done nothing for these men who made him feel welcome here at a time when larger landowners barely bid him the time of day. In all likelihood it was John who would find them dead, being the only neighbour who called in. Social workers occasionally visited, but social workers were strangers and those men had their pride and would tell John their health problems before contacting any outsider. Therefore he ruled out the possibility of this stranger being a locum doctor who had just attended to one of them.

The visitor was dressed in black. Could he be a mourner looking for a funeral? But if anyone had died locally John would know. John preferred Protestant funerals. He still felt a touch of wonder when entering Protestant churches with plaques to the Great War dead – churches he had been forbidden to enter in his childhood. Not that people paid attention to such rules now: neighbours piled into either church indiscriminately, or simply into funeral parlours if someone wished to be cremated without any priest or rector whispering sweet nothings. John's neighbours were good and he tried to be good in return, driving his tractor up the narrow road when it was impassable during floods to bring those old bachelors their weekly shopping of white bread, cooked ham and Jameson whiskey. For all the talk of people being clannish, nobody made him feel like an outsider anymore. It was a respect he had needed to earn but he had earned it. Julia and he never put themselves forward to serve on committees, but he was respected. If anyone had died within thirty miles he would have been phoned. Therefore this intruder was seeking directions to no funeral.

Something about how the man remained seated after switching off the engine convinced John that – for whatever reason – he was seeking him. John discreetly wiped his palms on his coat as he reached the car. He was friendly but wary of what friendliness might cost him. This man was collecting for something – money for charity or signatures on a petition. He looked like he had held a responsible job and such fellows always needed a crusade to compensate for the void of retirement. The man looked oddly familiar, but John suspected he would have to go back years to place his face. The only place John wanted to go back to was the kitchen where Julia awaited. He rarely wanted to go anywhere near the past. The present should be enough for any man, especially one blessed with a wife who loved him and two children with the foresight to grasp the education John never enjoyed, education he had gladly funded, knowing it would lead them to successful lives elsewhere: his son a scientist in Switzerland and his daughter doing well as a barrister in Dublin. The man looked apologetic as he lowered his window on the driver's side, knowing that his intrusion was unwelcome, despite John's cordial manner as he leaned in to ask if he could help the stranger.

'Are you lost by any chance? It's easily done on these roads. Can I help with directions?'

'I'm not lost now, although you weren't too easy to find.' The stranger studied John's face. 'You don't remember me, do you?'

'To tell you the truth,' John replied, playing for time, 'I'm a holy terror for names.'

'It's Desmond, if that helps.'

Behind his apologetic laugh, John tried to recall every Desmond he ever met. He needed to be careful not to get over friendly until he placed this stranger. If forced to invite him inside, it could be hours before the man got around to revealing what he actually wanted. If it was a donation for some cause John could fob him off in the yard. Twenty euro might be a small price for not having to bring him indoors. 'Do you mind me asking, Desmond, but are you related to anyone locally?'

The man shook his head in this cat and mouse game. 'I was never in Kilkenny until I set out to find you, John.'

John was on his guard now. Whatever this man wanted, it was more than twenty euro.

'Did we meet in Dublin? You're not one of the financial brokers my son encouraged me to see some years back?'

The man smiled. 'Do I look like a financial broker?'

'Those brokers are probably in hiding after the advice they gave. I kept my powder dry but some farmers lost the run of themselves, investing in property in countries whose names they could barely pronounce.'

'You know what they say about a fool and his money?'

John didn't like the man's tone. Those farmers had been no fools, but men trying to plan for their families' future, being badly advised by men in suits selling promises. The man noted his disinclination to reply and reassured him.

'Don't worry. I'm selling nothing and you're no fool. This is a fine farm. That's how people described it when I sought directions, though they got confused at first because I asked for the Cunningham Farm.'

John nodded. 'Locals still call it the L'Estrange farm. It's good to see the old surnames live on.'

'A good Protestant name.'

John held his gaze, perturbed by such an unwarranted reference to religion. 'And we raised two good atheists from it.'

'And have you grandchildren, John?'

John eased his hand off the driver's door and took an almost imperceptible step back; his tone mild but making it clear that the small talk was over.

'The fact is, if you know me you wouldn't need to ask and if you don't know me, it's not really your concern.'

The man looked suddenly nervous. He was clearly in poor health. It was like he had needed to summon up strength to enter the yard and now the effort was showing.

'I apologise,' he said. 'I'm being overly inquisitive. I've no right to ask. I just always hoped that life would work out well for you.'

John refused to be drawn. There was something increasingly disconcerting about these features. An instinct told him that he didn't want to place them.

'I also have a field half-sprayed and I'm anxious to beat the rain. So is there anything in particular I can help you with?'

'This isn't about helping me, but helping you. You still don't recognise me?'

'If I'm honest I could use a clue and I haven't all day.'

'It's nearly fifty years ago but back then you never called me Desmond or even Father Desmond, though I said you could. In Roscommon – though I wasn't much older than you – you called me Father Coyne.'

It felt cold in the yard now. The black car and black clothes: no wonder John mistook him for a mourner. But no dog collar: his shirt open at the neck.

'What can I do for you, Father?' The feigned friendliness in his tone was tinged with caution.

'You needn't call me Father. I prefer Desmond.'

'I prefer Father.'

'You've done well for yourself.'

'I've worked hard for it.'

'I'm not surprised. You were always a good lad.'

'I'm no lad, Father. That's what the farmers who gave my father seasonal work called him when he was an old man, bent double from stooping in fields. I'm a man now and a busy one. Are you collecting for something?'

'Why would I be collecting money?'

'People in Kilgara always said that whenever a postal order arrived from England, the parish priest grabbed one shilling each time the money changed hands until every penny ended up in his pocket.'

'I was never your parish priest. I was the old canon's dogs-body.'

'Whatever you were, I don't know why you're here on my farm.'

Curiosity had overcome Julia or else she'd grown tired of waiting for him. She appeared in the kitchen doorway, hesitant before her innate sense of hospitality made her approach.

'I'm probably the last person you wish to see. But it would mean a lot if you gave me ten minutes of your time. Is this your wife coming out?'

'Do me a favour, Father. Start your car and drive away.'

'Do you know how hard you were to track down?'

'I know I never asked you to.'

Julia was almost upon them. She would insist on tea and cake and polite conversation. How had this man found him? John wasn't scared of him anymore, John hadn't thought about him for years. He had enough to be thinking about. The man leaned forward to address Julia.

'Mrs Cunningham, I'm sorry to land in on you. I'm an old friend of John's.'

'This is Father Coyne,' John said. 'He was the curate in Kilgara when I was a boy.'

'I was passing and just thought I'd look up my old parishioner. I hope I'm not intruding.'

Julia smiled in welcome. 'Has this man of mine not asked you in? I'll be insulted if you won't take a cup of tea.'

'That's up to John.' The priest looked at him. 'Am I intruding, John?'

John felt trapped. He glanced up at the sky.

'Well, the rain may hold off a while yet.' He stepped back to allow the intruder step from his car. 'We were about to have coffee in the kitchen.'

Julia only now registered the unease in her husband's eyes. If John had been a boxer, his opponent could have knocked him out and he'd still pretend to stand upright, with only a good referee able to tell he was unconscious. John didn't show emotion, unless you knew the signs. But he was tender, even when he disappeared into himself; a good man who felt things deeply. She would be lost without him.

'The kitchen is in no state for visitors,' she said. 'We'll have tea in the parlour. We rarely get an occasion to use that room now.'

It would be the good teapot and china, John thought as they made for the front door they rarely used. It would be John and the priest left alone, while Julia fussed over biscuits. God knows what this man felt he had to say to John because John had nothing to say to him. Julia noticed how slowly he walked between them.

'If you don't mind me saying, you don't look too well, Father.'

'Call me Desmond, please,' he insisted. 'I'm just a bit stiff. I'm not long out of hospital. I thought the drive wouldn't tire me so much.'

'It's rest you need. Let's get you inside. John doesn't get many visitors from his Roscommon days.'

'My brothers left for England the minute they finished school. If my mother had been alive they'd have written home, but when a mother dies ...'

'That was the way with families,' the man agreed. 'Tea would be lovely, Mrs Cunningham, but please don't fuss with food. I've no appetite since the chemo.'

Julia touched his arm gently. 'I thought you looked gaunt, but didn't like to say. I endured chemo myself so I know what you're going through.'

'I'm finished with the chemo, thank God.'

'Then your appetite will soon come back.'

Julia led them into the hallway where the visitor paused to catch his breath. 'My appetite had better hurry up. The doctors say I'm in remission but they really mean I've a stay of execution for a year or two at most.'

Julia opened the parlour door they kept locked unless the grandchildren were over from Zurich. The room smelt of must and respectability. Their visitor accepted the offer of an armchair. Julia look around.

'John, would you fetch the little table that is normally in here. I moved it into the back room when the chiropodist was here. Excuse us a moment, Father.'

John followed his wife down the hall and into the smaller back room where they watched television in the evenings. 'You've never mentioned a Father Coyne to me.' She pointed to the coffee table. 'He'll need that to put his tea on.'

'Why would I mention him?' John grumbled. 'I barely knew the man.'

'You must have known him once or he wouldn't have come. What does he want?'

'I wish to God I knew.'

'I'll put on the kettle and that will give you men a chance to talk.'

'I've nothing to say to him.'

'Well, he must have something to say to you.' She paused and looked at him closely. 'Are you all right?'

'Why wouldn't I be?'

'Because I know you.'

'Have I said a word?'

'You never do. You keep things inside. Sitting up here some nights in this room, lost in thought and the only way I know anything is wrong is the smell of whiskey when you finally come to bed.'

'How often does that happen?' he said, agitated. 'Once every few years and yet you store up those nights to use against me.'

'What has you so rattled? I'm holding nothing against you. I'm just saying that at first I thought you didn't show emotion, until I learnt to read the signs. You disappear into yourself at times.'

'I get indigestion and can't sleep. If I'm rattled it's because I'm flummoxed as to why this fellow has shown up and I'm keeping one eye out for rain.'

'Go in and talk to him. I'll not be long.'

John picked up the small table and reluctantly re-entered the rarely-used parlour. Without Julia, he felt a sense of panic at being trapped there. He set down the table, avoiding direct eye contact with the man. Sensing his unease, the visitor asked, 'I suppose you're wondering why I came, John.'

'The thought did cross my mind, Father.'

'I've said you needn't call me Father anymore.'

'I know, Father.' The title was no mark of respect, just a way to maintain a distance. 'But I've no reason to call you anything else.'

'We're hardly total strangers, John.'

'I've a new life, Father. It took me decades to build. You're a stranger to me. If you're collecting for some charity, Julia and I give to good causes in every creed or none. Name a sum and I'll fetch my cheque book. I'm sure you've other calls to make and I've jobs to do because this farm won't run itself.'

'Why would I come seeking money for charity in my state? I haven't long left. It's forgiveness I'm seeking. I've come to apologise.'

'For what?' John's stomach felt so bad that he wanted the Maalox Julia kept in the medicine chest. 'I don't know what you're talking about.'

'I think you do.'

'I do my own thinking these days, Father.'

'Then surely you've thought about the harm I did to you. The older I get the more I truly understand it. It's all I think about these days.'

John walked to the window. 'No disrespect, but I barely remember you. It sounds like you're confusing me with some-body else entirely.'

'John, we're talking man to man. I know my arrival is a shock and – trust me – it's not easy to stand before you. But it's doing neither of us any good to bury the past.'

'I've buried nothing.' John lowered his voice lest it lured Julia back from the kitchen. 'I remember neighbours looking down on my father who couldn't cope after my mother's death. A piss-pot poor village where even the teacher barely had an arse in his trousers, because he spent his wages drinking Jameson in McGrath's bar, spouting nonsense to liggers. I remember children in his class mocking half-starved children like me, but all of us powerless to stop his beatings when he flew into furies if hungover. He knew he could beat me harder than any child, because my father was nobody. I've not forgotten the welts he gave me, but their pain has faded. What hasn't faded is the sense of powerlessness. No one cared about me, least of all the Canon, stinking of brandy in the confessional. Even with my face battered, he just wanted to know if I had sinful thoughts of girls. I was too young to think of girls. I could only think about hunger and how to make myself invisible to stop the teacher using me as his punch bag.'

'Kilgara was bad, all right.'

John pressed his palm against the window. 'It was primeval. Then you arrived, unleashed from Maynooth, trying to change everything at once; togging out with the Gaelic team like you could be one of the lads, scoring points because fellows were too cowed to clatter you when challenging for the ball. Half the parish thought you were a saint and the other half – including the old Canon – thought you were Karl Marx.'

'I was little more than a child, but I was no child. Being a seminarian was a form of arrested adolescence. I left Maynooth knowing everything about theology and nothing about life.'

John's voice went cold. 'You knew more than your prayers, Father.'

'Do you remember my car?'

'I remember an extra collection taken at Mass for months to buy you the damn thing: the Canon reading out the sum every family contributed. The social hierarchy of the parish announced in pounds, shilling and pence. Using his tone of voice as a weapon to express approval or disapproval and then pity when he finally reached my father's name. We lived on bread and dripping so our name could make it onto that list.'

'I didn't even need a car. I could have borrowed the Canon's car when I got called out at night to visit the dying in Slatta or Derryvane. But he wasn't going to risk having a young upstart scratch his prized Austin.'

'You mightn't have needed it but you got it whether you wanted it or not.'

'I didn't know what I wanted back then.'

'That was no impediment to you getting it. There was great power in a clerical collar.'

'Far too much power.'

'I'm too busy to ever dwell on those times.'

The visitor rose. 'The powerlessness you felt was a terrible affliction. But absolute power is terrible too. Immunity, immaturity and loneliness are a dangerous cocktail.' He hesitated. 'Do you remember anything that happened in my car?'

'It smelt of leather. A clean smell. You gave me a lift once to a county final.'

'Do you remember what happened after the match, John? What occurred eight or nine times between us?'

'I remember that Kilgara Gaels won by a point from a late free kick. There was a schemozzle with fists flying and the mentors joining in.'

'Forget about the county final. Do you think I've lain awake for years and tracked you down to talk about a bloody Gaelic match?'

'Easy with the language, Father,' John said quietly. 'Julia wasn't raised with bad language. I doubt she even knows that priests curse.'

'At thirteen you didn't know that priests did lots of things. By the age of fourteen you did.'

John struggled to sound unperturbed. 'No disrespect, Father, but it sounds like you've come on a wild goose chase. You're mixing me up with somebody else. I don't know who, but I'd lay odds he has probably long forgotten about whatever you're talking about. Do you not think that maybe it's time you did the same?'

The visitor grew exasperated. 'For God's sake, John, this isn't easy but I'm trying to talk to you seriously. Can you even just look at me instead of staring out that window?'

'I'm trying to gauge how long before the rain comes.' John reluctantly turned to face him. 'I don't take orders anymore, Father. This is my house where you've turned up, unwelcome and uninvited.'

'I thought it better I call than have two policemen visit.'

'Why would the police knock at my door? I've done nothing wrong.'

'But I did. To you. No apology is enough. Chemotherapy leaves a man sick to his core, but its debilitating effect gives you time to think, especially when you're running out of time. Recent scandals in the church made me realise the evil I did. Part of me has been subconsciously awaiting my fate, a midnight knock from the Gardaí. Now I lie awake and know it's not the Gardaí coming for me; it's cancer as my judge, jury and executioner. I haven't long left, too short a sentence for what I did to you, but I'll willingly go to jail in what time remains to atone. As the innocent victim you must be compensated. You deserve more than the few bob in savings I can leave you.'

'I don't want your money.'

'Trust me, I've damn all. The diocese keeps priests on a tight financial lease. They work us until we drop, then swoop in to hoover up any cash. But if I'm convicted you can take a case for proper compensation against the diocese. I've no right to ask you for anything. But I'm asking one favour: for the right to be found guilty of the wrong I did. No judge can condemn me more than I condemn myself. You owe me nothing, but think about the innocent boy I destroyed, maybe you owe him the justice he deserves.'

'Christ, man,' John said, exasperated. 'Look around you? Can you see anything of the half-starved boy you once knew? I'm a year off qualifying for the old-age pension. Crucify yourself if you want, but why drag me into it?'

'Can't you see, John?' the man pleaded. 'You're at the heart of it. I can't confess to the police without a wounded party. There can't be a victimless crime.'

'Then find yourself a victim somewhere else.' John tried to keep his voice measured. 'Men like you were shielded, moved from parish to parish with barely a slap on the wrist. Why draw my name from your list, especially as I don't even remember what you're talking about?'

'I'm not denying that celibacy has been a battle, John. On occasion I came close to abusing again, desperate for some human contact. But I fought that impulse until my knuckles bled. You were my only victim, but you're one victim too many. I don't want to die with this on my soul, even though I've realised we have no souls and only face oblivion. But if I'm not answerable to God, I'm answerable to myself. To make a statement to the police I have to name you. They will come and ask you for a formal complaint they can act on. I want to cut through all that.'

'And do what?'

'Accompany me to the police station in Kilkenny City. If we both make statements, it's an open and shut case. Tell your wife where we're going or tell her nothing. I don't know if you ever told her, though for your sake I hope you did and you've talked this through with someone. Counselling is important. It's the way out of a life sentence.'

John stared at him in bafflement. 'Even if I admitted to knowing whatever you're talking about, do you think I'd burden my wife by discussing such a dark thing? When you arrived in Kilgara half the parish thought you were daft. Now you've lost your mind entirely.'

'I was weak and immature and lonely and almost as innocent as you were. The seminary never prepared me for real life. I did wrong and I want to put it right. You won't have to testify in court if I make a full confession. You just need to confirm my statement that I did inappropriate things to you and cajoled you into doing them to me. I know I was no kind of Father Brendan Smith, physically forcing you into doing things. In so much as you understood what was happening, I remember you being desperately grateful for any affection, not just for chocolate bars and lemonade but for being made to feel special. I'm not defending myself when I say I never used force. I used kindness, preying on your vulnerability. I never raped you, but even back then when people never spoke about such things, I knew in my heart that what I was doing was wrong.'

John's movement was so instinctive it felt primeval. He had never used violence against any man, yet found himself pinning the elderly priest's head against the wall with such force there was a thud. John didn't care if Julia heard the man gasp for breath as John's hands tightened around his neck.

'For God's sake, John let go!' he begged. 'Please… you're choking me.'

'Choking would be too good for you.' John wasn't just struggling to control this sudden rage, but struggling to grasp how deep inside him it was coming from. 'Are you listening to me for a change? Have I your full attention?'

The man gagged. 'John, please … I can't breathe.'

'This is nothing compared to what I'll do if you ever dare enter my house and say such a thing again.'

'Say what, John? I don't understand …'

'I'll take Julia's father's shotgun down from the attic and blow your brains out if you ever dare suggest you didn't rape me.'

'There was no penetration, John … you remember it wrong.'

'I remember everything. How you used my mouth.'

'Never with force.' The man was truly struggling for breath now. 'I gave you pleasure … and afterwards you wanted to give pleasure to me in return … I never made you do anything.'

'You never needed to. You were so powerful you didn't even need to say things aloud to make me do them. I was so scared of displeasing you, of being cast aside, of leaving stains on the shiny leather in your car that I'd have done anything to be with you. Yet I wasn't with you in that car. Part of me was so scared that I went absent in my mind, telling myself this wasn't happening. I've tried to make myself not remember. But I do remember and, years later, when I understood such things, I knew the word for it was rape. But raping me as a child isn't enough for you. You want to do it again.'

The man looked to be on the verge of passing out but John's fingers felt so knotted that he needed to struggle to make himself ease his grip. The visitor slumped into his armchair, his face red. John tried to control his own breathing and somehow become again the man who had been relishing sitting down with his wife for a quiet coffee just a short time ago.

'If Julia asks any questions when she comes in with tea and biscuits and kindness, tell her you've had an asthma attack. You left your inhaler behind and need to leave. You understand? She is the most fundamentally decent woman and I'll not have her upset.'

The man glanced up, trembling now, fearful that John might strike him. 'I'm trying to upset nobody,' he whispered. 'My sole purpose is to atone, to make amends and do what's right for you.'

'I'll tell you what's right for me. Drive out that gate and follow the road into Ballyragget. When you get past that town and away from any connection to me, drop dead at the wheel and try to kill nobody else in the crash.'

The man shook his head despairingly. 'If that's what you want I'd gladly do it if I could because I deserve to be punished. It's only now, seeing your rage, that I realise the damage I'm truly guilty of.' He looked up. 'Coming here like this wasn't my finest hour, was it?'

'You've done worse things.'

'I know only too well.'

John sighed. His seemingly inexhaustible rage had dissipated, replaced by such weariness that he needed to sit down himself. 'But whatever you did, it gave me no right to attack you like that just now. I'm not a violent man. I've never laid a finger on anyone.'

'I know.'

'You don't know me, Father.'

'I think I do. I think what drew me to you was that you were so lost you reminded me of myself.'

'That's all in the past.' John closed his eyes, so breathless that he feared the onset of a heart attack.

'I wish it was, John. But I look at you and I don't think it is. That's why I'm trying to bring you some closure.'

John opened his eyes. 'Closure is just a word that clever people use, Father. It lets them charge astronomical fees to listen to the innermost thoughts of wounded people. Cancer is the only closure you're going to get, and we both know it. Do you honestly think that if we went to the Guards, my name would be kept out of your court case, if you live long enough to have one?'

'The victim can't be named unless you waive your right to anonymity.'

'That's the point,' John said. 'I refuse to be your victim. I'm a farmer with close to two hundred acres and the respect of my neighbours. Neither of those things were easily earned. You won't make me a victim again. How could a court case involving you happen without folk in Kilgara putting two and two together? They'd ignite a heap of malicious rumours that would burn their way down here. I've not gone back there since I buried my father. But there were whispers from the day the canon got rid of you. Some folk in Kilgara would love to reignite those whispers. Imagine their glee at cutting the labouring boy masquerading as a big farmer down to size again? I'll not be sniggered at by men on bar stools.'

'Court reports can't mention my name if it might identify you. And once I'm convicted you can sue for damages. Even if you don't need the money, it would be something extra to leave your grandchildren.'

'My grandchildren won't be contaminated by this. Any money I leave them will be earned by my own sweat. Find your own way to live with what you did but just make sure you take it to the grave with you. Don't think you can taint my children or grandchildren with your actions. I'll not be used by you again for your own purposes. Do you understand?'

'John, you need help for this anger you're carrying inside you.'

John carried silent hurt about a hundred things. About the third child they never knew because Julia miscarried, already so old that the pregnancy was always a risk. Neither Julia nor he were stupid enough to believe their pain would be eased by paying a stranger to listen to their cares. They lived with it in their own way: not needing to discuss grief to recognise how they shared it. Nothing could change the past. How John's father died alone, a penniless drunk, drinking methylated spirits to block out the ache of rheumatism. How Julia's father quietly worked the land alongside John for ten years, with John knowing how he kept trying to leave the farm to his cousin, who refused to take it and see Julia disinherited for marrying him. John had remained civil to his father-in-law like he was civil to everyone. But he would not be civil if this priest crossed his threshold again.

'The child whose hand shook so much he couldn't open your car door doesn't live here,' he said with finality. 'I left him behind, but even if you found him he'd never forgive your weakness in preying on him. You may wish to carry your cross in public and be crucified, but the reality, Father, is that this is Kilkenny, not Calvary.'

There was the rattle of a tray. Either Julia had stumbled on the step up from the kitchen or this was her way to let him know she had been listening in the hallway. She entered and took in the strained atmosphere.

'I'm afraid this tin doesn't keep tarts so fresh anymore.' She looked at them both. 'Are you men alright?'

'Never better,' John said. 'You can't beat a good catch up, eh, Father?'

'That's true,' the visitor said shakily.

'You sound breathless, Father.'

'Asthma. And I left the inhaler at home.'

Julia put down the tray. 'But sure John can drive to the chemist in the village. Isn't that right, John?'

Her husband shook his head. 'Father Coyne can't stay. He got a call on his mobile.'

The shaken priest nodded. 'A sick parishioner in hospital; she may not last the night. I've a long drive back.'

'Surely they can send another priest given the state you're in.'

'She asked for me.'

'All the more reason for you to have some tart before you set off,' Julia insisted. 'You'll feel stronger with tea inside you at least.'

'I should get started and take a break half way there,' the man said. 'My back gets stiff from driving. I'm sorry to put you to all this trouble.'

'It was no trouble.' Julia turned uneasily to John. 'Will you not twist his arm to take some tea at least?'

Her husband shrugged. 'If Father Coyne wants to leave, let him. He always got what he wanted.'

'I want us to part as friends,' the man said. 'Are we friends, John?'

'I was never your friend, Father, only your parishioner.'

'Will you accept a handshake at least?'

John looked at the proffered hand. 'I never yet shook a priest's hand except after a funeral. It would feel as odd as accepting your blessing. I was in Kilkenny City with my two little Swiss grand-children last year when three old men in black went past and little Genevieve asked who they were. "Priests," I said. "What's a priest, Grandpapa?" she asked. After I finished laughing I gave her such a hug I nearly knocked the breath from her.' He paused. 'Sorry you've come on a wild goose chase, Father. Will you see him out, Julia? The poor man got me mixed up with someone else entirely.'

His voice sounded calm but in his heart he felt he would never recover his equilibrium again.

'I'll pray for you, John,' the visitor said. But John had already risen to stare at the clouds through the window.

'Pray the rain holds off, Father, and I get that field sprayed.'

'It was lovely to meet you, Mrs Cunningham,' the man said. 'There's no need to see me to my car.'

Julia glanced at her husband's clenched shoulders. The way his hands pressed against the window pane brought back echoes of how trapped she had once felt in this room.

'I'll see you as far as the door, Father,' she said quietly. 'The unexpected step there has done damage to its fair share of ankles.'

Julia made no comment on how John hadn't shaken the priest's hand. He knew that she would ask the priest nothing when walking him to his car and would remain in the yard to give a final polite wave as the car swung out the gate. Finally he heard her return. He was shaking, with his back to her, but Julia knew better than to approach at once.

'I never like tea at this time anyway.' She paused and asked: 'Are you all right, John?'

'If there's one thing I hate, it's people disturbing our morning coffee. Let's keep these few minutes special, in the time we have left.'

'Sure we've years left, John,' she assured him. 'We're both in good health, even if the doctor keeps warning about how much salt you sprinkle on everything.'

'Time is funny. It feels like another lifetime since I was a boy in Roscommon, yet at other times it feels like yesterday.'

'How long ago does it feel just now?'

'I can never understand people dragging up the past. What are my chances of a fresh coffee?'

'Let's have it in the kitchen.'

'I'd like that more than anything in the world.'

'Do you know what I'd like more than anything?' she said quietly. 'You to die before me.'

He looked at her in surprise. 'That's a queer thing to wish for. Would you not be lonely on your own?'

'I'd be lost and heartbroken, but people would recognise my pain and somehow I'd survive. You would only appear to survive on your own, because with me gone there'd be nobody left who can recognise the way you carry pain inside you.'

'Were you listening outside this door?'

'I wasn't brought up to eavesdrop,' Julia replied sharply, then added more softly; 'That doesn't mean I didn't overhear.'

'Then you'd have heard me tell him straight that he might have done it to me once but he wasn't going to do it to me twice and nor to my family either.'

'Do what?'

'Do you really want to know the whole damn business?'

She touched his arm softly. 'Haven't I known all there is to know for years? Not the details; I don't need to know your details, no more than you need to know mine. But on the day you finally found the courage to knock at the kitchen door and ask for a glass of water, I looked into your eyes and I knew, even if you couldn't see it, that we shared secrets as kindred souls. Let's go down to the kitchen. I never liked this room. It has too many bad memories.'

'I used to think your father didn't like me because I was Catholic and poor.'

'When did you realise the truth?'

John glanced back out the window, beyond the neat out-houses towards where the farm sloped uphill. 'We were fixing a fence in the rain in the high field, a few months after he noticed that you and I were fond of each other. Me holding each fence post in place, him swinging down his sledge hammer. I looked up and his face... I'll never forget the sudden fury in his face and his voice, "You'll not take her from me, you hear?" A wise man might have jumped to one side, because as that sledge hammer came down there was a moment when not even your father knew if he was going to strike the fencing post or smash open my skull. He hit the pole such a blow that I thought it would split in two and then he raised the hammer again and still I didn't budge from holding the wood, even though that second blow came within inches of my fingers. But during those few seconds – the closest we ever came to physical violence – I suddenly realised what I was stealing from him by marrying you and he knew that I understood more about him and his ways than he'd ever want any man to know. We finished that fence and walked back and never spoke a word about it until the day he died. I watched you nurse him with tenderness, in his bedroom and then, when we needed to move his bed down, in this parlour.'

'Aye,' Julia said. 'But you never saw me nurse him with love.'

John nodded. 'He knew that and knew that I knew. I don't know if there's a heaven but this parlour became his purgatory; him watching us watch him die here, knowing that no tears would be shed.'

Julia was silent for so long that it looked as if they had both turned to stone. Then she looked up. 'I cried at his funeral but not for him. I cried for the little girl trapped in this room. This parlour wasn't my purgatory after Mammy died. It was hell. That's all that needs to be said. Anything else goes to my grave.'

'Anything that happened in that priest's car goes to mine. Never a word to the children, do you hear?'

'What do you take me for? People are too free and easy with secrets these days. I don't remember any priest calling today, just a lost tourist seeking directions. Come down to the kitchen and I'll make fresh coffee. Do you think the rain will hold off?'

John followed her out into the narrow hallway. 'It can rain cats and dogs and the world can go to hell for all I care, once I get the chance to sit down for coffee with you.' He closed the parlour door and locked it. 'I'll throw away this key if you want.'

Julia chided him mildly. 'And where would our grandchildren play when they visit? To them it's just a fusty old room. I'll always open the window before they come to blow away the ghosts.' She looked down. 'Give me your hand, John, it's shaking.'

He let her hold it. They stood in silence until the shaking stopped.

'I'd better make the coffee strong,' she said affectionately. 'You'll need your strength to drive those old men into Bennettsbridge later. You let them take advantage of your kindness.'

'They're lonely,' John said. 'And I know what loneliness feels like. I knew it until the day I finally found the courage to knock on the kitchen door.'

Julia kissed his hand and let it go. In the kitchen she set the table with fresh cups. She said nothing, while John watched her in companionable silence, both knowing that nothing more needed to be said.

The Lover

Dublin, 1965

I met him first more than fifty years ago, not long after he returned from the Amazon jungle. The mark of that humid swamp was indelibly upon him, in his eyes, in the first streaks of grey in his beard, in his slightly haunted aura. What he bore witness to in the Amazon forever changed him. Not just the tortures and exploitation, the casual flogging to death of natives (more as a warning to others than for any minor misdeed) and the indifference of the other Europeans he met there who rarely raised their heads from the profit columns of company ledgers to take in what evils were occurring in their closeted domain. He could recognise the depths of such true evil because he was already haunted by similar images from his days of observing what passed for life in the private fiefdom of Leopold II, known as the Belgian Congo. For him there was no living creature viler than that King of the Belgians, who forced mothers to watch their children's hands being amputated if their families did not harvest a weekly quota of rubber when slaving on the King's plantations.

His detailed British Foreign Office report that revealed the atrocities of Leopold the Second was his first act of class betrayal: the moment when he cut himself adrift from the other acquiescent white men who had gone to work for rubber companies in Africa. Such men trained themselves to see nothing or were gradually corrupted by the intoxication of absolute power, the insidious addiction of the opened box of cruelty in plantations so remote that even God had ceased to watch over them.

If I'm honest, I don't know how I would have coped with the lure of possessing such dangerous power because I've rarely known any sense of power or control in my own life. But once or twice in a darkened bedroom, when a kneeling man cried out beneath me as I penetrated him, I did run my fingers along his naked back to encircle his unprotected neck, damp with sweat. Sometimes they stiffened and I sensed their unspoken desire that I might choke the life from them during that moment of freedom, when they could truly and finally be themselves, when they can feel only my cock inside them but could not see my face. There were occasions when I sensed their unspoken wish to die at the height of their climax, without having to leave some furtively rented hotel room and return home to face the deceptions and evasions that awaited them once they donned their clothes again and retreated back into the arctic wastes of the pretence and lies of their married lives.

But I was never a rough man who would take any pleasure in such games. Maybe occasionally I momentarily tightened my grip on their necks, simply to heighten their mounting passion and my own. But I have never surrendered to the romance of any death wish. Unlike the zealots that Casement hung around with at the end, I am an unobtrusive born survivor, possessing no cause and no saviour. However if they gave medals to my kind, then my chest could hardly hold all the decorations with ribbons and bars I would be due from the skirmishes and ambushes I've endured. My lapel would be even more adorned than the coats of some of my fellow old-age pensioners who proudly stand near me in this crowd, close to the gate of Glasnevin cemetery, waiting for what remains of Casement's bones to pass us by.

My primary wish was always to live and this is a wish I shared with Casement, because never once in the darkness of our love-making did I sense that he did not long to go on with living life to the brim. On the contrary, his life force was like a glow, the memory of which sustained me for days after I fucked him or he fucked me, exciting himself further by calling me his splendid, gallant steed. I could feel his inner strength in how he braced himself on those occasions when he yielded to my cock and even more so when our roles were reversed and he pushed me down; his passion so manic that it felt as if his cock was not just engorged by pounding blood but with the sheer essence of his being. I could still sense the aftermath of him inside me for days after we had hurriedly parted, walking quickly in separate directions as if strangers.

His strength came from the fact that he never lost his boy-ish innocence, despite having forced himself to watch every act of cruelty and genocide in the Belgian Congo and then in the Peruvian Amazon. He never flinched from keeping meticulous records, even when the other white men there realised that he was their nemesis, come to expose and shame them to the world. He had a royal commission to be there to report on the starvation and rape and casual murder of Peruvian Indians. If not, they would have killed him with the same ruthlessness as they killed the Putumayo: either quickly through floggings or hanging, or slowly through impossibly long hours of toil that no human being could endure. But instead they shunned Casement, out in their wilderness, and sat on their verandas to drink expensively imported Scottish whisky and dream of white women before slaking their lust with compliant, or non-compliant, black girls. The rubber traders did not think to have him followed in the evenings. That was their first mistake. They were too stupid to recognise the tell-tale signs I immediately noticed when I first saw him prowl along a country lane on the edge of Belfast in 1911. I say 'prowl' because everything about him that evening reeked of desire. Here was a toff who wished to fuck or be fucked to the hilt. I had known other rich toffs before, but generally they were primed to flee before I had barely finished tossing them off. Casement however was a man who held your eye with his slightly fanatical stare. I knew within seconds of seeing him that he was as bent as hell and he knew the same was true of me and that we were both only walking that godforsaken country lane because we knew how men who sometimes took the air there would disappear together into the ditch at dusk. On that first evening I needed to pretend not to recognise his face from the newspapers as a knight of the realm; to play along with the identity he invented for himself as a minor Colonial Office clerk. But over the weeks that followed, the chance encounters that ceased to be by chance, I gained his trust as he realised that about the only two things I refused to engage in were fisting and blackmail.

There were other men also meeting in other remote country lanes on those same evenings, drilling and plotting and taking lavish secret oaths. Up North his tribe were marching to prevent being governed by Home Rule from Dublin. But down South the tribe he had now thrown his lot in with, with his usual frenetic sense of infatuation, were demanding complete Irish independence. Like our kind who met in ditches, they were fired up by passion; but it was not a passion I could share because their version of freedom never included freedom for the likes of me to be myself. Casement, however, embraced them with a convert's zeal. The Republican Brotherhood was his other secret life. None of them knew – or perhaps in truth they simply never wished to know – about his other existence: the world where he came in my arse or my mouth. Even today outside Glasnevin

I can see how the crowds still don't want to know, here in this capital that will never be mine. From the morning the British authorities hanged him for treason – subjecting his corpse to an anal examination to let a doctor confirm the rumours they had already leaked to the press about his diaries to ward off pleas for clemency – his comrades here in Dublin have wished to only claim those parts of his life from which they did not need to avert their gaze.

Now they have their wish to fully claim him at last. Last week the British exhumed whatever remained of him under cover of darkness in Pentonville Prison: a few ribs, several vertebrae, his lower jaw and the skull almost preserved whole. Quicklime had eroded the rest. Now the coffin containing his few bones is slowly making its way across Dublin city, past these vast silent crowds in a solemn state procession. I don't know Dublin. I have never liked this city or wished to live here. But still I needed to come and be part of this occasion, like I have discreetly attended the funerals of other Belfast men, standing at the back so that I could pretend, if necessary, to be waiting for another service to begin.

All week the Dublin newspapers have been remembering the courage that made him highlight the plight of those enslaved Peruvian Indians; the bravery that saw him resign from the British Foreign Office to renounce his class and join the Irish rebels; the schoolboy zeal that saw him land in Ireland after having to abort his dream of bringing German guns to aid their short-lived uprising. But I was witness to a more commonplace courage within him on those first nights we met. Gangs of youths often trooped out from Belfast, eager to have sport by hunting us down in those remote lanes. One evening I needed to hide among briars that cut my skin to shreds as I watched two rival gangs of Taigs and Prods come together to kick a couple of lonely men whom they found together. I remember the faces in the mob so consumed with hatred for my sort that they momentarily put aside their religious differences. One night, when Casement began to obsess about the ways in which he hoped to unite Catholics and Protestants, I told him it was simple: just give them outsiders like me to track down in a national sport of hatred that would know no boundaries.

Poor Casement didn't understand hatred. After the British hanged him, he became a traitor and deviant for one tribe and a martyr and icon for the other. But for me he remains the man I first fucked in that remote Antrim field while placid sheep grazed, unperturbed by our silent exertions, and, in that twilight, white candles of chestnut blooms were still visible between the luxuriant canopy of leaves above us. Nobody passed along the nearby lane during our passion and neither of us spoke as I ran my hands underneath his shirt, my nails gripping his nipples, as I used whatever tricks I had learnt to make us come simultaneously.

That first time I could already sense how he had been touched by some foreign place, though it was much later before he talked about the Amazon. But he was always a hunter for love and love brought him to the strangest places. If those plantation owners had only followed him along jungle paths at dusk they would have found the ammunition to destroy him before he destroyed them. They would have seen him come in his extraordinary fashion as though you were his first love. They could have blackmailed him and buried his report. But despite their jibes and mock indignation, they would have lain awake long into the night, haunted not by the act that they had witnessed but by his sheer capacity for pleasure. Because, for all their whores and mistresses and wives, they could never achieve such naked bliss as they would have witnessed in the eyes of Roger Casement when he came.

The crowd here is now twenty deep as a man holding a small transistor tells us how the radio is reporting that his state funeral has reached Cross Guns Bridge. An old IRA veteran stands proudly among the crowd, explaining to people why he received each of the medals displayed on his chest. He is my age, his face as caved in and deeply lined as mine. But in his youth he must have been handsome, like I was once handsome enough to catch Casement's eye. I want to say, 'You gave him a sense of fellowship but I gave him a sense of pleasure. For long moments he was mine in a way he could never truly be yours. I was his only nation back then because we were equals and he was only free to be himself in my arms.'

Had he lived I wondered what he might have become? If the British had not executed him, then probably in time the new Dublin government would have, because he'd have never settled for this nation they settled for. He hadn't the responsibility of a wife or children to take the edge off his zeal. The comforts of public office or an honoured title would never have soothed him because he had given away such trappings. The last time we met he spoke feverishly about desiring freedom; but how can any man like us be free who fears a knock on his door, who dreads being discovered by a mob in a lane, who lives in trepidation of exposure and ruin? For long moments I gave him freedom and pleasure and I was not alone in this. Unseen in the Amazon jungle he was free to kneel in clearings to let young men who bore the marks of whippings on their backs fuck him tenderly or mercilessly, copiously relieving at least one white man of his burden.

I remember the luxury of twice spending an entire night lying naked in bed with him on the two occasions he risked taking a room in the Grand Central Hotel on Royal Avenue in Belfast, nights when I played along with the illusion of being a toff like him; both of us enjoying prolonging our sense of expectation by playing games of billiards as a tantalising form of foreplay, allowing a discreet five minute interval to pass between us each separately slipping upstairs. On one of those mornings he made a half-hearted attempt to convert me to the cause of nationalism, but generally he was happy to keep his two worlds separate.

Now the older I get, the more keenly I remember the feel of his hands and tongue. And sometimes I curse him because I know that I shall be remembered by nobody: no former comrades will ever stand by my grave. I have enough money saved for a headstone but no one will ever seek it out. My bones will lie undisturbed in Belfast, unlike Casement's, exhumed from the wet soil and quicklime of Pentonville Prison and brought here like religious relics, to lie in state for these past five days in Arbour Hill to allow crowds to file past. No pathologist will examine my ribs that were cracked when I was beaten up in a public toilet in 1936, or my fingers that were broken by a young man who came back to my flat in 1957 and demanded more money than I possessed. I gave the boy everything, yet he ransacked my home for more. But he never found the hidden ten shilling note that Casement gave me after our first encounter. I accepted his money because I was no fool but I never spent it, recognising that this was the closest thing to a love letter that he could ever risk sending me.

A young soldier has just fainted in the colour guard on the road in front of us, having been stood to attention for the past two hours waiting for Casement's hearse to pass. He lies exposed, his comrades unable to break from their rigid poses until two officers remove him from sight and order the remaining soldiers to close ranks. I look around at other old men like me in this crowd and suddenly wonder how many others of

Casement's kind might actually be here, unable to step forward and proclaim, 'I knew him, we shared love.' I can hear the sound of the cortège now, with his tricolour-draped coffin displayed on a gun carriage: a coffin containing so many secrets that are unspoken and so few actual bones. I don't notice that I am crying as the gun carriage passes until a woman touches my arm.

'You knew him?' she asks.

'Yes.'

'You look like a veteran. Did you fight side by side?'

I don't reply. Side by side was not his style. She takes in the absence of medals on my dark suit. Maybe she is going to ask something else. I push past, joining the throng who are now trying to manoeuvre in through the cemetery gates. The freshly dug grave has pride of place in front of the O'Connell monument. Their nation's shaman, De Valera, is there, half blind, peering at his speech printed out in big type, but I have no interest in whatever platitudes he intends to say. The tricolour is removed from the coffin. Men kneel bareheaded while women cover their hair. One of their priests speaks in Latin. These curious words that I cannot understand move me strangely because I can concoct my own meaning for them. For a moment at least I can pretend that this burial is in honour of all the boys like me whom Casement once lay with: those with names that he knew and those whose names were unknown. I can pretend that this empty coffin is meant for us all, that Casement has left space inside there, alongside his few loose ribs and the skull encrusted with fragments of shroud, for all of us who must by necessity remain unknown and unremembered.

Soldiers lift the ropes and the casket is lowered. Shots ring out and I stand up among the kneeling throng to lift my face to the sky. I can see white clouds over chestnut trees beside the Antrim field where I was first undressed by his trembling fingers. If only the comfort of a god really existed, or there was some promised land where our kind could be free, then Roger Casement would be there with his penetrating gaze, waiting with open arms to welcome me.

Martha's Streets

Martha's hand was so stiff that writing was now impossible, but she could still read very slowly by concentrating with a magnifying glass. Until she lost the ability to read she could still escape in her imagination from this nursing home in the outer suburbs; she could turn a page and be transported back to the streets of a city that belonged to James Joyce and belonged to her. She could still stand on the Dublin quays to encounter the passing faces that her father would have known. She could ignore pitiful sounds from the nursing home's Day Room, where the other residents awaited death or their dinner with equal meekness. She could hear again the calls of gulls and hawkers shouting across the Liffey at low tide.

The important thing about being ninety-one was not to get frustrated or to panic. Her bedroom light would be put out soon, although she had little chance of sleep. Strangers kept her awake, wandering through her room at night. The night nurse denied this and claimed that Martha was always asleep whenever she checked her. But that was because the nurses expected residents to sleep soundly, when every other patient here was drugged, except for Martha. She was the only one still with her wits left, the only one to cause trouble and make the staff laugh. Not that she was complaining because everybody was kind. Adjusting to life in this nursing home had proved difficult and, after being independent all her life, Martha did not intend to stay much longer. While she appreciated the efforts of other people on her behalf, Martha had her own plans to escape once she regained her strength. The nurse understood this and had even promised to help Martha pack when the winter ended. Spring was the best time to move. She would find a small flat in Rathgar or Drumcondra – it didn't really matter where, provided that it was located close to a small bakery and a public library. At this stage of life soft bread and intelligent books were all the nourishment that she needed – crime novels because they intrigued her and Samuel Beckett because he could still make her laugh. Not just his work but the comic thought of him, during the time when he acted as a sort of unpaid, unofficial secretary to James Joyce, hobbling around Paris because such was his awe of the great maestro that he even tried to wear the same size shoes as Joyce himself. Hopefully by next spring she would be hobbling around Dublin on her stick, still equally in awe of that same maestro. For the past year the nurse had been offering to help Martha pack whenever she was ready, while always encouraging her to rest up here for just another three months to gain strength for her move. But come next spring she would not be fobbed off in her determination to again find a small flat for herself with a windowsill where birds would be welcome to gather for the crumbs of bread she would leave for them.

At times she thought bitterly about how it was those crumbs of bread that had her trapped in this nursing home. But in less agitated moments she knew that she would be dead by now if one of her former Muckross Park College pupils had not seen a small report in *The Irish Times* about her court case. She had been summonsed to appear for consistently ignoring an injunction taken by an interfering new neighbour. He had objected to the noise of the birds congregating on the rooftop in expectation of the windowsill of bread crumbs that she had been leaving out for them three times a day for decades. The case seemed too minor for

The Irish Times to bother reporting. But after the judge described the noise of the birds as a commotion, the reporter was apparently intrigued by how Martha had quoted Joyce by heart in her reply. She had said that for her it sounded more like 'a duodene of bird notes chirruped bright treble, all harpsichording,' and that she loved to watch the way in which every bird that soared towards her windowsill 'held its flight, a swift pure cry, soar silver orb it leaped serene, speeding, sustained, soaring high, high resplendent, aflame, crowned, high in the effulgence symbolistic, high, of the ethereal bosom, high, of the high vast irradiation everywhere all soaring all around about the all, the endlessnessnessness.'

The newspaper had reported how she received a round of applause from the courtroom, along with a caution, which the judge said he was forced to hand down with reluctance. But the journalist also had the impudence to describe her as looking infirm and malnourished, although defiant. Father would have disapproved of such publicity. Father's definition of a life well-lived was a life where your name only needed to get mentioned once in *The Irish Times*, in circumspect phrasing among the death notices. But that court appearance, while unseemly, resulted in the miracle of how several of her former Muckross pupils had banded together to pay for this nursing home care. In her heart she knew that she would never have survived another winter in the unheated bedsit she had occupied for half a century off Baggot Street, crammed with books and cat food and memories.

Martha wasn't entirely sure how long she had been here or who exactly her fellow residents were. They spent their days dozing in the common room that Martha never entered. While there was bingo and singsongs some afternoons, Martha disliked communal activities and therefore knew little about them. This caused her guilt because she so much enjoyed meeting all their visitors. Each afternoon, wrapped up in cardigans and a woollen hat, she lay on the sofa that she had commandeered inside the porch where she could chat to everyone who arrived. Sometimes Matron fussed about the quantity of books the nurses needed to bring out for her. In reply Martha would quote Viktor Frankl, just like she had loved quoting him to her pupils: 'Without a sense of purpose, a man will either be despairing or dangerous to himself and others.'

At ninety-one she had such little time left that each day needed to have a purpose. This evening, despite her cataracts, she had managed to reread six pages from the Sirens chapter of *Ulysses*. Lost in Joyce's words she had relived the disconsolate moment in Leopold Bloom's life when he sat in the Ormond Hotel, knowing that his wife was preparing to be unfaithful with Blazes Boylan.

But she had also relived the moment in her own life when, at eighteen, she first read this chapter of the scandalous book which her older brother had managed to smuggle home from abroad. How many pairs of curious hands did this copy surreptitiously pass through before she had chanced to find it one afternoon behind a row of innocuous-looking books on a shelf in his room? She had been a Loreto-on-the-Green convent girl back then, hiding it in her school bag so that she could sit in St Stephen's Green after class, disguising this illicit copy of *Ulysses* with a dust jacket from Father Herbert Thurston's revised edition of Butler's *Lives of the Saints*. She still recalled the shock and excitement she had felt at how Joyce captured the language between the two coarse barmaids. She had not liked Miss Lydia Douce and Miss Mina Kennedy but instantly recognised those barmaids as flesh and blood women in a way that women simply were not in other books. Joyce allowed them to have thoughts that she had never imagined could be expressed in a printed book. Martha could still recall the moment a policeman had passed by her park bench in Stephen's Green, and her fear that he was going to turn back and confiscate the book, dragging her across to the Loreto nuns to proclaim that she was a brazen unchristian hussy found reading filth and pornography.

That was what Father considered *Ulysses* to be on the one occasion when it was mentioned at the dinner table. Father would have felt let down if he had known that, before her nineteenth birthday, she was already addicted to regularly rereading and seeking an ever deepening appreciation of it. But, then again, he had always felt somehow let down from the first moment that she began to think for herself. Let down by her desire to go to university, by her refusal to find a respectable man and marry, by her ambition for independence that went against everything he felt a woman should aim for. *Ulysses* had become her bible in those college years, proof that people could think and believe differently, that secret lives were running like a current beneath the facade of her native city.

Still she regretted those years when Father and she had grown apart. Not that he had ever ceased to love her, but his baffled disappointment was like a cancer that forced her to follow Joyce abroad to where she no longer had to feel the shadow of his disapproval. She was teaching in Madrid in 1961 when a message came from her brother that Father was dying in St Vincent's Hospital.

She had returned home to sit in strained silence at his hospital bedside, unable to find common ground with him. Returning to her mausoleum-like childhood home where Father lived alone, she had walked from room to room before, on a sudden impulse, looking behind the row of dusty books in her brother's old bedroom. There, wrapped in brown paper, was that same edition of *Ulysses*.

Next day she had brought it to the hospital and began to read to him - not from cover to cover because Father would have no time for Stephen Dedalus. But, over his protests, she began to read about Leopold Bloom's visit to the newspaper office crammed with hard-drinking Dublin men of the world, and the chapter where Bloom travels with other men to the funeral in Glasnevin. At first Father had been belligerent, demanding to know why she was poisoning his mind. But then his human curiosity had kicked in. These were his streets, his type of professional drinking men. He confessed that, as a young man he had once spent an evening drinking with Joyce's elderly father, a painful case who was always cadging whiskey and disdained all offers of porter, calling it swill only fit for jarveys. There were expressions in the book that he delighted in, having not heard them in decdes. 'By God, Joyce got that right,' Father would declare suddenly, almost despite himself. Or he'd open his eyes to say 'I knew the very bowsie he's talking about and knew his father too.'

In those weeks before he died *Ulysses* had given them a common world to share – the fictional world that Martha had immersed herself in and the physical Edwardian world her father had grown up in. The book had helped them come to know each other in a new way. But that was the secret of *Ulysses*. It became her calling card to the entire world. It was as good as walking into an unknown café and placing down a chessboard. Always someone came forward out of curiosity. At first people in Dublin were shocked to see her reading it, after she settled back here when Father died. But then young people started to approach her in Bewley's Café in the late 1960s, curious about the book that was still not sold in Irish shops back then.

The joy of the book was that it could be reread forever. As she grew older she kept reading *Ulysses* in airports and on foreign beaches where the young were more interested in each other's bodies than in an old woman in a deckchair. But always someone would stop to talk, an elderly fellow aficionado or a young girl, surprised to see it in the hands of an old woman. Occasionally the people who stopped bored her: Joyce experts frothing about a misplaced semi-colon in some edition, sucking the vitality from her father's people. Or that mad Italian man one time in Malta who mistook her reading the book as a sign that she might be interested in allowing him to act out some of the masochistic sexual games that Bloom had fantasied about in Nighttown. With ordinary readers, the people who quickly became her friends, she could laugh about such encounters. These readers were like her in being able to imaginatively move between two worlds, perpetually carrying the book in their heads. During business meetings or dutiful family occasions they could flee with Bloom from the drunken bigoted mayhem of Barney Kiernan's pub or walk into eternity with Stephen along Sandymount Strand.

In recent years, after even the last of her cats had died, the people in Joyce's book had become more real to Martha than the people on Dublin's streets who impatiently brushed past her as she spilled change at supermarket check-outs or the strangers who looked alarmed when she casually started up conversations with them on buses. She had lived too long, with almost every-one dead who had once known her. Looking in the mirror on some days she had barely recognised herself. The only people who never aged and who kept her sane were Joyce's quarrel-some, bickering and all too human characters.

Martha knew that she was drifting into senility because the people whom she saw wandering into her room at night were not just nurses or attendants but characters from his book – Blazes Boylan, the Citizen, Nosy Flynn or little drunken Bob Doran on one of his periodical bends. Some nights they shouted at her and on other nights they argued and gossiped amongst themselves, ignoring her presence in the bed. She was going daft and knew in her heart that she would never leave this nursing home. But her plans for her death were in great order and did not include allowing her body to fall into the hands of any clergyman. It would be wonderful though if the Muckross girls remembered her wish that at her cremation they would play a recording of the choral finale of Beethoven's Ode to Joy – composed when he was so deaf that someone had to pluck his sleeve before he turned to witness the crowd's rapturous applause at the premiere.

Martha planned to die as she had lived, with all artifice stripped away. Yet despite her preparations, there were certain nights when death's closeness scared her. When would the nurse turn out her light? She needed to get asleep before the intruders starting sneaking around her room. Tomorrow somebody might call to take her out in her wheelchair. And if no one came then there was Joyce's humour to sustain her as she could find the strength to painstakingly reread another few pages with her magnifying glass.

The bedroom door opened and the nurse appeared. The woman looked tired, but Martha hoped that with the other residents asleep there might be time to talk.

'How was your day, Martha?'

Martha looked back on the trials and frustrations of the day and yet how she had still accomplished her task of reading six pages of Joyce. 'Good,' she admitted.

'So are you still leaving us?'

'When spring comes.'

'Off on your travels. You've had a few, haven't you? I was never abroad myself. We'd miss you if you went off.'

'Would you?' Martha was touched.

'You're a dote except when you get into your moods. Where did that weird poster come from?'

Martha looked up at a photograph of an impoverished look-ing young man seated at a bare table with a pile of roughly cut sandwiches on one side and a heap of books on the other. He was ravenously eating while devouring a book at the same time.

'I saw it years ago in Spain and had to buy it. That's what books are, food for the soul.'

'I like a good romance to curl up with myself,' the nurse said. 'Something sexy that doesn't answer back. Here, let me tuck you in till you're snug as a bug in a rug.'

Martha allowed her to adjust the tight bedclothes. 'Do me a favour, open the window.'

'Aren't you always complaining about the east wind? And you know you can't leave out bread for the birds.'

'I know. Just for a minute. There's something I want to hear.'

The nurse shook her head in good-humoured exasperation. Still she opened the window and stood back to listen before shaking her head.

'You see? There's nothing to hear.'

'There is.' Martha closed her eyes to listen to the night's luxuriant silence, the infinite possibilities of unheard sound from which the deaf Beethoven had stolen his marvellous joy-ous finale. 'There's a whole symphony out there.'

The night nurse listened too, then closed the window. 'Maybe you're right and the rest of us are daft. I don't know. Goodnight, Martha.'

Martha didn't reply or open her eyes even when the door closed. She wanted to hold on to the still, majestic chords of the earth at peace and to hear, in faint whispers, the echoes rising from the distant Dublin streets, all those voices and thwarted lives that Joyce had captured. This intimate fictional universe that she loved and which would live in other people's minds long after her ashes were scattered on her father's grave, yards away from where Bloom had once stood as a slighted mourner in Glasnevin cemetery: both decent and decadent, imbued with all the human contradictions that made life worth living.

The Keeper of Flanagan's Hotel

There was something suspicious about the ponytailed man in the leather jacket, scuffed white sneakers and faded Rolling Stones T-shirt, booking in for the night. Decades of experience, long before he ever imagined that he would become the manager of Flanagan's Hotel, had imbued Johnny Darcy with this instinctive sixth sense. It also trained him to stay back, watching from a distance as Marieke, the young Dutch woman on reception, gave the guest a card to fill in. She reached for the key to 104 and put it on the counter.

The man appeared to be alone, with a single item of well-travelled hand luggage. He leaned forward and spoke, but Johnny knew from Marieke's thin smile that whatever joke he tried out on her wasn't funny. Since being sent over from Utrecht by the new owners-to-be, Marieke had proved to be resolutely her own woman, respectful and relaxed with Johnny, but not easily impressed by what passed for Dublin chat up lines. A younger Irish woman, fresh from school, might have been momentarily taken by this guest's manner because he seemed to be trying to cultivate a disreputable charm, like a rock star dressing down to remain incognito. Yet there was something vaguely familiar about him which Johnny found disturbing, even if he was not yet sure that his instincts were correct.

It was busier than usual for a midweek night: the bar crammed with an office do, the dining room busy with an American coach party and the lobby tables occupied by the curiosity vultures who always return for a last look when any old hotel is about to close for a major revamp. Such upheavals brought out nostalgia in people who had met in the bar for their first date or held their debs' ball in the ballroom or who, as children, spent their first ever night in a hotel here, when brought to Dublin if their father had a dog running in Harold's Cross. Over the years Flanagan's traditionally did better from greyhound owners than horse trainers.

But Johnny might have gone home by now – leaving Simon, the elderly night porter, to keep an eye on the usual flotsam – if some instinct hadn't made him sense the possibility of trouble, like a miasma in the air. This was the unseen part of a manager's job, knowing when to position yourself to be ready to intervene if necessary. Decades ago the hotel's original owner, Finbar Flanagan, had instilled in Johnny the importance of always being present until any risk of disruption dissipated.

Johnny's wariness was partly due to the stocky Dubliner booked into Room 107. Simon was the only staff member who recognised how this nondescript-looking man – who discreetly installed himself in the same room once a fortnight – was among Ireland's most notorious and camera-shy criminals; a teetotaller who specialised in smuggling counterfeit gin; a non-smoker who hated being around drugs, despite overseeing supply routes for cocaine into Ireland; a family man who, like Johnny, had married above his own social class. This gave them a curious, although never mentioned, connection, in that their wives both attended the same pottery evening class. Not that Johnny ever betrayed any sign of recognising him. Simon likewise never acknowledged the man's presence during his visits to enjoy clandestine threesomes, so unobtrusive that not even guests in the adjoining rooms were aware of them. Johnny knew better than to refuse his business, not just to avoid any risk of retaliation, but because the rumour that Flanagan's was his bolthole for such *ménages à trois* scared away small time drug dealers from the basement nightclub. They feared his wrath if a police raid occurred and his name leaked out as having been on the premises. One of numerous mental notes that Johnny never wrote down was to ensure that Room 107 remained unoccupied on any night when his wife had a pottery class.

Back at reception, the ponytailed man picked up the key to 104. Johnny noticed how he glanced up at the faded portrait of Finbar Flanagan's son, Francis Xavier, which still hung behind the desk. It was one of two pathetic details which Francis Xavier insisted on when a staff consortium bought the hotel from him: that his portrait remain on display and the hotel would still bear the surname of his father who had built up the business from scratch.

Simon appeared at the coffee alcove beside Marieke's desk and glanced at the ponytailed man picking up his bag. Johnny glimpsed his face as he turned. He looked older than the dyed ponytail suggested. He waited beside the lift as the doors opened and several Americans emerged to join others from the coach party seated in the lobby. Johnny looked away as if afraid of being caught, as the man entered the lift. The doors closed, leaving Johnny with only vague impressions: a glimpse of his face, the hunch of his shoulders, his nonchalant walk. He was also left with an irrational, almost paralysing sense of unease.

Simon brought down a heavy tray of coffee and biscuits to a table of elderly Americans. He stooped slightly under the weight in a way that would not have showed a year ago. But nothing in the porter's impassive face hinted at the pain he was in. This was another reason why Johnny Darcy was relieved that Flanagan's Hotel was about to close, with all staff laid off while the new owners rebuilt. Otherwise Simon would refuse to stop working until his cancer caused him to physically collapse. While Johnny was unafraid of harsh decisions, Simon was the one person here he could never bring himself to sack.

He entered the alcove that was Simon's private fiefdom. Other porters knew which shelves belonged exclusively to Simon. Staring at the coffee pots and the cheap biscuits waiting to be transferred into expensive looking tins, Johnny had a vivid memory from decades ago of making a secret den in here at Simon's feet. This was when Johnny and Francis Xavier Flanagan's daughter, Aisling, were both nine years old and Simon would indulge Aisling by playing along with her fantasy in which Simon was Batman's faithful butler. Aisling always played Batman during those games and Johnny, as befitted his lowly social status, was her obedient underling, the boy Robin.

Back then everything still glistened in the new-look hotel that Francis Xavier had built on the proceeds of a huge insurance pay-out when a mysterious fire destroyed the original hotel. This occurred shortly after Finbar's death, when some Trinity students, campaigning to conserve Dublin's architectural heritage, lodged an objection to Francis Xavier's plans to replace the original Victorian hotel with a modern building, designed by the architect Sam Stevenson in his favoured brutalist style. Francis Xavier even insisted on the hotel possessing a brightly coloured Navan carpet with the Flanagan family crest and his initials, 'FF', woven into it in Celtic script. Simon had wryly suggested to Johnny's father, who back then was assistant manager – that the initials should read 'MP', in honour of the most likely suspects responsible for the fire: Maguire & Paterson – Ireland's favourite brand of matches.

The fortunes of the Flanagan and Darcy families were interconnected since 1924 when Finbar Flanagan first opened his hotel, opposite what was then called Kingsbridge Railway Station, when Dublin was a traumatised city, sullen and shattered from the Civil War. His business might have failed were it not for its proximity to the train station and its reputation for discretion, built up by Finbar and by Johnny's grandfather, 'The Count' Darcy, who was employed from the start to be far more than just Finbar's head porter.

When he first watched the film, *The Godfather*, Johnny realised that his grandfather's job description should have been *consigliere*, although neither of these hard-drinking men would have known this Italian term. As a child Johnny recalled his disappointment at discovering that his grandfather did not actually possess a papal knighthood, like the tenor Count John McCormack. The title by which everyone referred to him was a nickname 'earned for services bestowed on Mother Church', as Finbar often said, enjoying a private joke which Johnny had been too young to understand.

The hotel survived in its early years by becoming a haven for rural curates on annual drinking sprees. Finbar and the Count ensured that the general public never glimpsed the residents' lounge and the handpicked staff – men who, like them, had taken the anti-treaty side in the Civil War – maintained a vow of silence about whatever occurred in this sanctum. In old age the Count had instilled in Johnny the diplomacy needed to succeed in hotel management, describing how clerical collars used to be inconspicuously slipped off on arrival in Dublin, during the short walk from the station. These collars were discreetly replaced by Finbar, after he ensured that the drinks bill was paid and the curates reasonably sobered up with black coffee before departure. The Count always remained on the platform to avoid any unforeseen hint of scandal as each ecclesiastical guest was dispatched back to their rural parish. When Simon started work here, at thirteen years of age, the Count began taking him with him to Kingsbridge Station, recognising how the boy possessed an intrinsic gift for secrecy that would serve him well in the hotel trade.

Johnny wondered what the Count would make of Flanagan's Hotel now, as he stared through the open doors into the public bar, where the office party was heating up. Pete Spencer, the younger barman there, was bitter at the prospect of losing his job. Johnny suspected he wouldn't be above fiddling people's change, if he could get away with it later tonight.

Simon returned to the alcove with his tray. 'Mean Yanks,' he muttered sourly, dropping a few coins into his box. 'How do they expect me to work my way through college on these tips?' This was Simon's long-standing joke. He took a sip from a glass in front of him. Johnny could not remember when Simon first commenced the pretence that the clear liquid in the glass perpetually half full in this alcove was water. Initially Simon was so discreet about pilfering vodka that only Johnny's instincts alerted him. Recently it became so blatant that the barmen complained. But vodka seemed as good a painkiller as any, and so Johnny played along with the deception.

He found it hard not to feel guilty about Simon, although thirty years ago the staff who formed a consortium to buy out Francis Xavier had offered to let the porter join them. 'All I want is a wage and no aggravation,' Simon had told Johnny's father who coordinated the takeover. For many years this had seemed a wise choice. With a single owner Flanagan's Hotel might have reinvented itself as a vibrant concern, but the elderly consortium's management style was too unwieldy to change with the times. Wages were always paid and near closures averted, but the hotel had limped along on weekend specials and hen parties. The hotel only began to turn a profit when the nightclub started after Johnny inherited his father's twenty percent share and borrowed money to gradually buy out each consortium member and modernise the business and convert the basement into a nightclub. The elderly men who sold their shares for a fair but modest profit could have never foreseen Dublin's hotel boom, or that Johnny would now be selling the business for a small fortune to a Dutch rock singer, Luuk de Vries, and his Irish wife who planned to transform it into a deluxe boutique hotel. Gerry, the older barman, still harboured hopes that Johnny might arrange for him to be reemployed when the hotel reopened. But new owners never wanted staff who knew more about the bar takings than they did. Luuk de Vries might be a rock star, but most rock stars that Johnny ever dealt were invariably cut-throat businesspeople behind their cultivated bohemian personas.

In four weeks' time all the staff, including Simon, would receive statutory redundancy. As Simon realistically hadn't long to live and nobody to leave his money to, perhaps this disparity in their fortunes didn't bother him, but Johnny sometimes suspected a resentment buried within him. Johnny was never certain what went on in the old porter's head, but he knew that every tip ever received was logged there, with guests judged accordingly. Simon took another sip of vodka, defying Johnny to comment.

'Ponytails,' Johnny said, hoping to lure a reaction from Simon about the guest who had booked in. 'I never liked them, even on ponies.'

Simon declined to reply as he leaned forward to listen to an American lady who approached with another coffee request. Johnny went to the reception desk and asked Marieke to show him the card the guest had filled in. The name given was Edward McCann with an address in Luton.

'I asked for a credit card,' Marieke said. 'He claimed he left it on his desk when packing this morning. He paid in cash and said it was just for one night. I've put a block on the phone in his room for outside calls and a note that room service must be paid for in cash. I asked if he stayed here before and he replied "yes, when it was under better management".'

'What did you make of him?'

The Dutch woman shrugged. 'He'll frighten some girl if he visits the nightclub later. She'll think it's the night of the living dead when the lines on his face show up in the strobe lights. He asked if hotel guests had free admission. If it was my hotel I wouldn't have admitted him without a credit card but it's not my hotel.'

'Not yet,' Johnny teased.

'Maybe Luuk will make me manager when this place reopens, like he has promised, but I can be sacked on his whim. Still maybe that's not a bad thing. Who wants to work in the one job all their life? This place will never be mine like it's yours.'

Johnny nodded. 'It's an odd thing, but I've never really felt this hotel belongs to me. Too many ghosts.'

'When did you start working here?'

'Aged five.'

Marieke laughed. 'You're teasing. Next you'll say you were a child chimney sweep.'

Jonny smiled. 'I was fourteen before I first drew a wage, but my earliest memory is of sharing an armchair in the lobby of the original hotel with my older brother. My mother was taking us to Mass and called in to see my father because she forgot her scarf and needed to borrow a linen napkin to cover her head in the church. I sensed we weren't meant to be here because hotels were only for important people and I remember thinking that it had a special smell.'

'Of what?'

'Glamour, sophistication. Two other children sat on a sofa and they seemed part of the glamour. Perfectly dressed, perfect in everything. A boy my brother's age who stared at me so arrogantly that I was terrified to touch anything and a girl my age who kept smiling across as if longing to play with me. But from my mother's anxiety I knew I wasn't allowed to. Then my father emerged from a swing door with a tray, wearing a dickie-bow like a film star. He saw us but couldn't approach until he'd cleared the breakfast plates. I remember him piling his tray impossibly high, but he had to leave two plates behind. When I stood up my mother was scared that I'd forget my place and approach the Flanagan children, but I just wanted to help my father. I picked up the remaining plates and walked behind him through the swing doors into the kitchen.'

'Into the hidden world within every hotel, the parts that don't reek of glamour.'

Johnny nodded. 'The world of my father and grandfather that smelt of boiled cabbage and burnt bacon. Chefs barking orders and grease and dirt everywhere. I was so scared I almost dropped the plates. Then I felt a hand on my shoulder. It was old Finbar Flanagan. It felt like meeting God as he took the plates and said I was a chip off the old block and should be paid a working wage. He put a small silver coin in my palm and said his family would always have a job for me here.' Johnny felt embarrassed at having revealed so much. 'I suspect De Vries is paying you slightly more. If he didn't intend making you the face of his new hotel he wouldn't have sent you over to keep an eye on me.'

She smiled back. 'He said he wanted me to learn from the best hotel manager in Ireland. I appreciate you letting me see what clientele the place attracts.'

'Hardly the clientele De Vries is after.'

'He'll fly in for a photo op if he persuades The Arctic Monkeys to stay in the Penthouse Suite, but this place won't survive without ordinary customers.' She glanced towards the bar. 'Rock stars bring column inches but office parties pay the rent.'

'You'll do well.' Johnny glanced at the portrait behind them. 'Hotels are about giving guests the illusion of glamour but never let yourself be seduced by such illusions.'

Marieke followed his gaze. 'I meant to ask about that portrait. He looks so self-satisfied it's like he made the artist paint him as monarch of all he surveys. I asked Simon if it was your father but he laughed.'

'Portraits weren't my father's style,' Johnny said. 'He preferred to remain behind the scenes.'

'From what I hear, he saved this hotel and guided it through tough times. It must have been a great consolation for him to leave it in such safe hands.' She stared again at the picture. 'Is this Finbar Flanagan?'

Johnny shook his head. 'It's his son. Normally it takes a dynasty three generations to destroy itself. The first to make a small fortune, the second to turn it into a big fortune and the third generation to blow the lot. Francis Xavier Flanagan managed to do the work of three generations in two. He'd no badness in him, but no self-awareness. Every beggar, ligger and hanger-on loved him. Simon nicknamed him "Dorian Grey in reverse". The portrait never aged, but the man grew more haggard by the day.'

Johnny looked away from the portrait. There was always something in those features he had feared. Not that Francis Xavier paid Johnny much attention when he was a boy learning the trade from the kitchens up. It was the same with Francis Xavier's son, Alfie, who – although only four years older than Johnny – treated him with the disdain that a self-important adult reserves for an inconsequential child. If Alfie's sister, Aisling – the girl he first saw as a five-year-old – hadn't needed a playmate, Johnny's father would never have been allowed to bring him in here so often as a child.

Marieke touched Johnny's sleeve in a discreet gesture of apology. 'That was a silly thing I said about people wasting their lives by working in one job. I meant no offence. You're obviously

cut out for this job. It's just that, even with my hotel management degree, I don't know if I'll want to do something different.'

'You should try all kinds of things,' Johnny replied. 'I often
wish I had.'

The woman laughed good-naturedly as if he was humour-
ing her. 'I can't imagine you doing anything else. This hotel fits
you like a glove. You'll miss it.'

'I won't.'

'You must have great memories. Simon says that all the big-
shot young politicians once drank here.'

'Before my time. I've just tried to keep the place going.
Hopefully I didn't do too bad a job.'

'You've been a great success,' she said. 'Don't be so dismissive of your achievements, or so defensive.'

'I'm not defensive.' His reply was sharper than intended.
'And my staff don't normally talk to me like that.'

'I'm not one of your staff, Johnny,' she retorted calmly.

'Touché.' Johnny smiled in apology. 'I hope I didn't sound
rude. I'm a bit distracted tonight. If I'm not careful I'll get myself
barred from the new Flanagan's before it even opens.'

'You'll always be welcome back. You made a big impression on
Luuk. He said that I would learn everything there is to know about
hotel management from you and absolutely nothing about you. But
he was wrong. I've learnt that you're the most defensive person I
ever met, without even being aware of it. You should be proud of
having transformed a rundown hotel into a successful business.'

'Somebody had to do it.'

'It didn't have to be you. Your life wasn't pre-ordained. You
could have done something else.'

'I was meant to do something else.'

Marieke sounded intrigued. 'Is there a side of you I haven't
seen? What were you meant to be?'

Johnny nodded towards Simon who was soft-soaping the Yanks he had just served, nudging his way to a bigger tip. Marieke followed his gaze and laughed.

'Don't try and tell me you were meant to have Simon's job?'

'Absolutely not,' Johnny said. 'It was understood that Simon was head porter for life. The man in that portrait had me marked down as Simon's assistant. In Francis Xavier's grand scheme my brother was meant to one day wear a suit like this, but only as assistant manager to him.'

'That's twice you've mentioned your brother. Do you see him much?'

'Charles died in Canada years ago.'

'I'm sorry to hear that.'

'It's okay,' Johnny assured her. 'We were never close.' He felt embarrassed again at having revealed so much. It meant he was definitely rattled tonight. 'I better do my rounds. A hotel manager should always show their face.'

He walked away, across the famous carpet that Finbar would never have approved of. Although his son always claimed that the 'FF' in the pattern represented his initials, everyone recognised them as a fawning act of sycophancy towards the ruling Fianna Fáil party. Finbar would have known that the politicians who had frequented the hotel neither needed nor welcomed such overt displays. It wasn't party allegiances that drew the Fianna Fáil Young Turks like Brian Lenihan, Donogh O'Malley and Charles Haughey to drink in the original hotel in the late 1960s. They had valued the discretion that Finbar and the Count were famous for, a diplomacy Francis Xavier Flanagan never grasped. The second thing Johnny took from watching *The Godfather* was that, after Finbar's death, Flanagan's Hotel resembled the Corleone family business if the Don had unwisely allowed Fredo to inherit it.

When the Royal Automobile Club awarded the hotel a 'Triple A' rating in 1967, Finbar – amused at being expected to display anything containing the word 'Royal' – had offered a whiskey to any drinker able to smash the RAC plaque with a single hammer blow. Instead the Count had set to work with a chisel, hacking off the three As, scratching in three Ps and offering a brandy to whoever guessed what this 'Triple-P' rating stood for. Brian Lenihan won the bet, coining a phrase that became legendary in Dublin: 'Popular with priests, politicians and prostitutes'. Not that the Count allowed just any lady of the night to occasionally loiter in dimly lit alcoves. Looks were less important than circumspection and the Count had such a reputation for insisting on no roughhouse games, and on girls being fairly paid that whatever occurred here remained known only to those in the know.

Attempts to distil such discretion into Francis Xavier were reasonably effective while Finbar was alive. Indeed nobody ever saw Francis Xavier drink whiskey until the final months of building the new Stevenson-designed hotel. Any snag list should have been left to be ironed out between the architect and the builder. But Francis Xavier was so enthralled by seeing his new vision arise that he made himself the effective – or ineffective – de facto project manager, presiding over late night discussions in a makeshift bar which he set up on the unfinished premises. Perhaps it was only a matter of time before he succumbed to alcoholism anyway, but nothing had prepared him for the heavy drinking in those months spent poring over architectural plans as if he was a general commanding troops in battle. Sub-contractors made it their business to call in and let him pontificate on inconsequential details of the fit-out, knowing that – as one of them told Johnny's father, who was press-ganged into serving drinks – the free bar had no official closing time because it wasn't officially open. While the insurance pay-out was enormous – especially because it covered numerous objects secretly moved into storage just before the fire – by the time the new hotel opened, its finances were already perilous. Drink took such a hold on Francis Xavier that it was impossible to stem the money haemorrhaging from his wallet.

Yet from a child's perspective, the weeks leading up to the reopening were among the happiest in Johnny's life. Or at least they were until his sense of himself was irrevocably altered by incidents during the final few days when Alfie Flanagan kept luring him into the newly installed lift. Those events left him confused and ashamed, clouding his childish innocence, although it took him decades to grasp their effect on his character. What he most clearly remembered about the days preceding them was his father's and grandfather's happiness at being re-employed by the Flanagan family, with the rebuilding completed. But while the hotel remained unopened, nine-year-old Aisling Flanagan had regarded it as her private kingdom. Because Johnny was allowed in to keep her company, they had explored each freshly painted bedroom, jumping on unused beds before chasing cartoon villains like the Joker down the long corridors in games where they became Batman and Robin. Chambermaids and workmen would shoo them away, but even in death Finbar was their protector. While Francis Xavier only really had time for his son, Alfie – groomed almost from birth to one day inherit the business – Aisling had been Finbar's pet, and such was Finbar's aura that nobody still dared to scold his favourite grandchild.

Johnny stopped now, midway across the busy foyer, momentarily fazed by the ping of the lift opening. How many thousands of times had he heard this sound without it causing these flashbacks? Again he pondered the features of that ponytailed guest and his territorial nonchalant walk when striding towards the lift. Why on earth were his palms sweating? He reached into his inside suit pocket and, as if it were an amulet to ward off evil, unobtrusively fingered the cardboard edges of the estate agent's brochure. The sale had been agreed months ago, yet he still carried this brochure around with him. But an innate discretion or reticence meant that he had never shown anyone in Flanagan's Hotel a single photograph of the eighteenth-century Palladian villa he had purchased, nestled in woodland near Enniscorthy.

After his wife Phoebe finished supervising the renovations, they would open for business this autumn. Eight deluxe bedrooms – each room named but not numbered – and seating for eighteen diners in the library overlooking the pond that they were having dug out. Eighteen was the correct number. Any more and the illusion of exclusivity was ruined. This new phase of his life would be about targeting discerning guests. Europeans were generally more willing than Americans to pay for the ambience of an authentic Irish country villa. European visitors better understood good wine and cognac, although rich Japanese guests had a fetish for obscure Irish whiskeys. He was in talks with a leading distillery about them bottling a small run of eighteen-year-old whiskey, to be called after the villa and exclusively sold on the premises. Nothing sold better than instant antiquity.

Phoebe was surprised when he insisted that the villa trade under her family's name. 'Let's call it Darcy Manor,' she'd protested. 'God knows, you slaved long enough under somebody else's name.' But this was the point: Darcy's seemed like an echo of Flanagan's for him. They would call it Mount Conyngham: a classy Protestant name with no baggage. Johnny didn't want to bring any goodwill from here with him to Enniscorthy or to write blurbs about the Darcy family having three-quarters of a century of experience in welcoming visitors. He wanted to put a full stop on the past and start somewhere new. He wanted anonymous guests who stayed up late beside log fires, discussing business in a babble of foreign tongues, while a floodlit fountain gurgled soothingly outside. He'd had a lifetime of coach parties. He wanted American Express Platinum cards and a twelve-and-a-half percent built-in service charge with no Simon cadging tips. He wanted gold embossed menus printed on Conqueror watermarked paper, discreetly coated in a protective layer of ultraviolet, unlike the cheap Edge Seal lamination used here. He wanted diners who studied the fish dishes first and not the prices.

In another month his long years of service here would be over. Why should he even care if his suspicions proved right about who had just booked into Room 104? Finbar's advice on the day he started here had always stood him in good stead: focus on the task in hand and let the rest look after itself. Johnny entered the restaurant. It was quiet, the staff setting out breakfast cutlery and just one couple still dining. He halted beside them, smiling and yet solicitous.

'How is your meal?' he asked. 'Are you being well looked after?'

They nodded timidly, frightened of being asked to pass further judgement. Johnny wished them a pleasant evening and walked on. This was something that guests at Mount Conyngham would expect: the host to appear at their table and answer questions about the villa's history and the best local golf courses, or advise them on wine selection and immediately offer to take back any dish that didn't meet their expectations. Mount Conyngham would be far removed from the days when old Finbar once fawned his way back into the kitchens with a rejected steak from a Fine Gael TD and told the chef, 'Give that a rub with your balls for more flavour and wait five minutes before sending it out with our compliments to the Blueshirt at table six.'

Phoebe and he had planned their move carefully, waiting for the right property to come on the market. His wife spoke French and German fluently from her days as an au pair and had a good grasp of Spanish and Italian from when she worked as a translator in the European parliament. Although Johnny had left school at fourteen, he was skilled in the intricacies of bypassing language. Recently Phoebe wanted to come into the kitchens here to practice, but Johnny had warned that she would quickly unlearn every good habit acquired during courses at Darina Allen's Ballymaloe House Cookery School. He checked his watch. He had no one to answer to and could leave. What did it matter if he sensed that an incident might occur? But it wasn't in his nature to leave. He closed his eyes and thought carefully about the ponytailed guest. Any similarity in features could be coincidental. But an inner dread suggested that his instincts were correct.

Yet if he knew who the man was, he didn't know why he was back. Johnny returned to reception. Simon was on the telephone, filling in a docket for a room service order. Coffee and a double brandy. Johnny indicated to Simon that while the porter made coffee he would fetch the brandy. He entered the public bar. The office party was raucous. A blonde girl at the counter was ordering a huge round. Pete Spencer, the younger barman, had just finished serving her.

'Always check your change, miss,' Johnny warned quietly behind her. 'And check your handbag regularly. I'm afraid all hotels get pickpockets.'

The girl nodded and began to ferry her drinks down. Pete loaded up a tray with the remainder, sneaking a glance at Johnny. He had said just enough to plant suspicion in the barman's head that he was being watched, but not enough for his words to construe an accusation. Johnny guessed that Spencer was unsure if his employer knew that his brother had been arrested during a robbery in Malahide last year, when the stolen getaway car refused to start. It was a rule the Count had instilled in Johnny long ago: ignore newspaper headlines, they don't concern real people. Instead read the small court reports. Make the connections between names but never let people know how much you know. It was Simon who alerted him last year, saying nothing but tapping a small report lightly with his finger when handing Johnny the newspaper. Johnny needed Spencer for now, but it would be prudent to pay him off in full at the end of a shift a week before the hotel closed to lessen the possibility of a bogus accident and last-minute insurance claim. He got a large brandy and returned to Simon who was arranging coffee on a tray.

'What room?' Johnny asked.

'I'll look after it.'

'That's not what I asked.'

The old porter gave him a cautious look. 'Room 104. Go home, Johnny. I'll handle this.'

'Did his voice remind you of anyone when he rang down?'

'There's a lot of voices I choose to remember and a lot I choose to forget.'

'That sounds like you're saying you recognised his voice.'

'I'll make it my business not to recognise it when bringing this tray to his room.'

'I'll take that up for you.'

The porter studied him caustically, trying to twist this into a slur on his health. 'I'm still capable of carrying a tray.'

'I never said you weren't.'

'Then stop making a skivvy of yourself. Stay away from him. Get Marieke to say there was a double booking and turf him out.'

The offer was tempting but it left too much unresolved. When he walked out of here for the last time he wanted no ghosts to walk with him. 'I need to practice carrying a tray for when I start up in Enniscorthy,' he said gently. 'It's been a while, but I was trained by a master.'

Simon reluctantly yielded up the tray. Johnny walked to the lift, with no plan about how to handle this situation. The lift rose: the same blasted lift installed when Francis Xavier reopened this hotel. Again the memory came unbidden, bringing a sense of nausea. He took a deep breath as the lift opened on the first floor. Stopping outside Room 104 he knocked. A voice from inside told him to leave the tray outside as he was in the bathroom and would settle up later. Johnny used his skeleton key to enter. The guest was indeed in the bathroom. He obviously heard someone enter because he called out distractedly for whoever it was to take the money due from the cash on the bedside locker and add a ten percent tip.

'No tip required, sir,' Johnny replied. 'Just your signature on the docket.'

The man emerged, towelling his face and gave Johnny a wry glance. Face to face, Johnny knew that his instincts were right, though Alfie Flanagan had aged greatly in the past two decades. Even as a boy his hair was never this black. There was something pathetic in his attempts to still look young. The bags under his eyes belonged to a far older man, but his clothes looked like they came from the sort of second-hand charity shops where rich students browse when trying to dress down. Johnny placed the tray on the table and politely held out the docket. He decided to avoid further eye contact. Let the past lie. He didn't want to know why Alfie was here. The signature was a plausible scrawl that could pass for any name. Johnny had retreated into the corridor when Alfie summoned him back. His voice hadn't altered, still mildly condescending beneath its spuriously gregarious tone.

'I can't believe they still have you carrying trays. Don't pretend you didn't recognise me, Johnny. I've not changed that much and you haven't changed at all. As inscrutable as ever.'

'Alfie? Alfie Flanagan? I didn't recognise you with the ponytail.'

'I thought we buried the Count in that suit you're wearing.'

'My grandfather never wore grey.' He hated the unintentional defensiveness that crept into his voice. The corridor was empty. Johnny wanted to retreat to his office where he could bolt the door and think. Once he re-entered the bedroom he was in the paying guest's territory.

'Don't take it seriously,' Alfie said. 'I'm joking.'

'This suit is bespoke. It cost more than your grandfather paid the Count in a year.'

'The Count never needed a wage, with his gift for scavenging tips. There was no one better rewarded for turning a blind eye. He took his secrets to the grave. You look great. You've done well for yourself. It's amazing seeing you again. I remember you well as a boy here.'

When they were small Alfie only addressed Johnny if he needed someone to run a message. Otherwise he would ignore Johnny like the younger boy was invisible. Only on those four occasions before the reopening, when Alfie pressured Johnny to get into the lift with him alone, had there been any true interaction. For decades Johnny had deemed these to be unimportant before realising that, if he could remember them so clearly, they had clearly affected him. Johnny wondered what Alfie wanted now.

'Don't stand there like a servant,' Alfie ordered. 'Come in and relax. It's great seeing you. Join me for a drink. Take the coffee or the brandy if you prefer.'

His tone was friendly but insistent. If he had Phoebe beside him, Johnny would have told him to go to hell. But Phoebe wasn't here and his present status felt fraudulent as he reluctantly re-entered the room.

'I only have a minute,' he replied. 'It's a busy night.'

'It's good to make time for old friends,' Alfie said. 'Especially at the end of an era. You don't mind me returning for one last night, do you? I wanted no staff fawning over me. Just to take a last look around, for old time's sake. This was my home. I know we'd a house in Templeogue, but Daddy's mind was always focused on this place. My parents rowed a lot, Aisling creeping into my bed because she hated hearing their arguments downstairs. People are always happier on holidays – that's what I've found. Or if not happier, they maintain the pretence of harmony better. When Daddy moved us all into the best suite here, he said it was to let him keep an eye on business. But really it was to keep my parents on their best behaviour, because my mother thought it unseemly to argue with him in front of staff.'

'I don't remember arguments,' Johnny lied. 'I remember your mother dying far too young – a real lady. I remember how lost your father was afterwards, a ship with no anchor. A business was no substitute for a marriage.'

'There were arguments all right,' Alfie said. 'The Count and your father must have trained you well in the art of forgetting.'

'I've forgotten nothing.' Johnny closed the door. Alfie's unopened bag lay on the bed. A free night's accommodation in another hotel plus a hundred euro – no, two hundred – that was the maximum Johnny was willing to pay to get rid of him. Alfie held out the coffee. Johnny took it and watched Alfie sit on the bed and take a sip of brandy as he looked around.

'You gave me Rosie Lynch's room number. Even when we rebuilt the place we always laughed about putting anyone in Room 104.'

Johnny joined in cagily with his laughter. Rosie Lynch had been a call-girl in 1967 when an elderly priest suffered a heart attack while being entertained by her. It took all of Finbar's experience, plus favours called in through the Fianna Fáil Young Turks, to ensure that his cause of death remained a rumour,

laughed at by those in the know. 'Frighten me,' the priest report-
edly urged the girl after she bound his wrists to the bedposts
and blindfolded him. Brushing her breasts against his face, she
had whispered 'Somebody is watching in the doorway: John
Charles McQuaid.' Alfie chuckled, remembering how the fear
once instilled by Dublin's autocratic archbishop could induce a
cardiac arrest. He looked at Johnny. 'I didn't book in under my
real name. I wanted to be anonymous. This place has a lot of
memories. You kept Daddy's portrait in the lobby.'

'It was agreed in the contract.'

Alfie laughed. 'I'm not checking up on you. Nobody would
have sued if you threw it on a skip years ago.'

'Guests like it,' Johnny said. 'They often ask about him.'

'What do you tell them?'

There seemed no malice in the question but Johnny was cautious, like when dealing with a drunk standing on his dignity in the
public bar. God knows, Francis Xavier stood on his dignity there
often enough, returning most nights after he'd had to sell the hotel,
like a young King Lear, unrecognisable from his portrait, as his former staff ensured that he didn't bother guests. Johnny's father always
arranged for him to be coaxed into a taxi, paid for by the hotel, at
the end of each night, using the same driver who would help him
inside to collapse fully clothed on the bed, and leave a Baby Power
within reach for when he woke at dawn with delirium tremens.

'We tell guests it's a portrait of the original owner's son,
the man who rebuilt the hotel after the original building burnt
down,' Johnny said.

'Daddy talked about being terrified that the firemen trying
to be heroes might have actually saved the old kip.'

'He would have got planning permission to knock it down,'
Johnny said. 'It was just a few Trinity eggheads protesting about
architectural heritage.'

'What are you insinuating?' Alfie asked. 'I never said he started the fire deliberately. I'm saying it was so far gone when the firemen arrived that it would have been a disaster if they'd saved half the building.'

'He rebuilt it well,' Johnny said carefully.

'Here's to Daddy.' Alfie raised his glass in a toast. 'He was unlucky. This place could have worked. Your da and the others showed that.'

Johnny said nothing. Francis Xavier was unlucky alright in that, with the reopening so delayed by his extravagant plans, the Young Turks had been forced to find other drinking quarters. No expense was spared, with the hotel's labyrinthine lay-out designed to accommodate clandestine tête-à-têtes or other late-night political activities. The problem was that the Young Turks never came back, having settled into new watering holes and higher political roles. Then the North erupted and the Arms Trial came. The Young Turks were divided and scattered. Jack Lynch's sole vice when Taoiseach was pipe-smoking. This hardly encouraged a culture of late-night debauchery, while Francis Xavier always complained that the Cosgrave coalition government that followed 'wouldn't spend the steam off their piss'.

Vatican II hadn't helped business either, with curates able to play guitars and visit local pubs. Francis Xavier was also unlucky in that, with Finbar gone, the hotel started being raided for late-night drinking. On the third occasion the Young Turks didn't even bother intervening and Francis Xavier almost lost his licence. This was when Johnny's father organised the consortium to step in and save their jobs. This meant that while the after-hours drinking didn't stop, it was largely confined to Francis Xavier himself.

Johnny could see traces of Francis Xavier's features in Alfie, as he sipped his brandy. The fingers shook slightly although not with the tell-tale signs of an alcoholic. This wasn't how life was meant to work out. It should be Alfie wearing this expensive suit, with his sister Aisling married into a family as well connected at the Conynghams.

'I was sorry to hear about your brother,' Alfie said. 'I looked up to Charles.'

Johnny nodded. The consortium's secret hope was always that Charles would return as their saviour. Maybe if their father had died sooner, Charles might have been lured home to buy out the others. Johnny would never know. His brother was always a stranger to him, the six years between them too big to bridge until they both grew up. But by the time Johnny reached adulthood, Charles was already settled into a new life in Canada, leaving behind a reputation Johnny could never fill. Assistant manager of the Lord Nelson in Nova Scotia at twenty-three, then manager of the Montreal Hilton before his thirtieth birthday. Brothers rarely communicate when they share nothing in common. On his rare visits home Johnny had treated his brother with circumspection, like a potential future boss. When their mother died Johnny's father cried for days. Yet he took the telephone call informing him of Charles's death quite differently, retreating into a silence from which he never fully emerged during his final two years of life. Johnny had watched him grieve, knowing his own death would not have affected his father in this way. He had known which son his father would cry out for, sinking into a final morphine-induced coma in the hospice. Similarly he had known – before even opening the will his father never bothered rewriting – that his father had left Charles his stake in this hotel, with Johnny only inheriting it because Charles predeceased him.

'I see Simon still going strong,' Alfie said, anxious to break the silence Johnny was lost within. 'Still hoarding tips to stash with his Communion money.'

'Simon will live forever,' Johnny lied.

The people who die are those whom you least expect to. Johnny had given little thought to his brother while Charles was alive, knowing that no matter what minor success he enjoyed in Dublin he would always be seen as a failure in comparison to Charles's international stature. When forced to fly to Canada to sort out his brother's affairs, as his legal next-of-kin, it had felt at first like intruding on a stranger's apartment. Before Johnny's arrival an unknown confidant had removed any clues to romantic indiscretions or long-term relationships in what their father used to blithely call 'Charles's bachelor lifestyle'. Yet enough clues remained in the apartment's stylish ambience, its exquisite David Hockney photo collages and the set of original prints from the Doc and Raider Canadian comic strip, that broke barriers by being about two gay men, for Johnny to grasp why Charles had exercised his right to build a new life abroad. He had kept that life private from everyone in Ireland, including the younger brother he barely knew. It had seemed too late to get to know him now, especially when Johnny was unable to find a single personal letter in that apartment. The only remaining clues to this stranger – who had kept his illness secret from his family – were the rows of books on his shelves and his large vinyl record collection.

It seemed as if Charles – like Johnny himself – had remained faithful to vinyl records, preferring their more nuanced sound. But Johnny's real shock during his first night in his brother's apartment was not discovering that Charles was gay – which he always half-suspected – but discovering, with a deepening devastation, just how much they had in common. It was unsettling to recognise obscure titles on those bookshelves that mirrored the books Johnny possessed at home. He had thought that he alone inherited the Count's fascination with travel books by Irishmen.

But Charles's first edition of Denis Johnston's *Nine Rivers from Jordan* matched the copy Johnny had purchased from the Maggs Bros. rare bookshop in London. Here was Conroy's *History of Railways in Ireland* published in 1928 in London and Calcutta – a copy of which Johnny had inherited from the Count. Here was every travel book written by Dervla Murphy and a first edition of *In Patagonia* by Bruce Chatwin, identical to the one that was among Johnny's most treasured possessions.

Wandering through that Montreal apartment he had found novels by Ian McEwan, Paul Auster and Joan Lindsay that he frequently reread, alongside biographies of Irish sports stars. They would have had so much to discuss as brothers, in excited phone calls whenever the Irish soccer team qualified for a tournament or an Irish boxer won an Olympic medal; so much support they could have given each other if they had taken the time to know one another. Even their record collections shared great similarities. On that first night he had flicked through Charles's extensive collection of Blue Note recordings, instinctively knowing that he would find his favourite record if he searched long enough. Sitting in his brother's apartment, he had listened to jazz and cried like he hadn't allowed himself to cry since childhood, mourning a soulmate whom he had never actually known.

Johnny looked up now, unsure of how long Alfie had been watching him, lost in thought. Alfie's fingers toyed with his empty glass. 'Fuck it,' he said. 'Let's order a bottle of brandy for old times' sake. My treat. I'll tip Simon handsomely for bringing it up.'

'I'd love to,' Johnny lied. 'But I'm snowed under with paperwork. Have one drink with me in the bar. Honestly, that's all I've time for.'

'You work too hard,' Alfie said. 'You look harassed. We'll toast our fathers and grandfathers. Take one night off, for God's sake.'

'Any other night but this ...' Johnny began, but Alfie cut across him.

'Forget your precious hotel for five minutes. Just sit down, will you? I could use the company!' Alfie was agitated. 'It doesn't matter if you like old friends or not, they're still old friends.'

Here it comes, Johnny thought, the sting. For years he had waited for someone to dredge up how he deserved none of this. He inherited everything by fluke, by simply being the last in the line, the dull workhorse trudging away until fortune fell into his lap. Not just his share of the hotel but several hundred thousand Canadian dollars left intestate in Charles's estate. In Montreal there were rumours that the businessman who nursed Charles to his death allegedly tore up Charles's will, wanting to take nothing from their relationship except memories of love. Johnny didn't know how many people he would need to buy off before feeling comfortable with this wealth that was meant for someone else. Reluctantly he sat back.

'I know you're busy being a wheeler-dealer,' Alfie was saying. 'But could you not find time for even one visit to Aisling? You're the only person she ever talks about.'

Johnny was thrown by this approach.

'Aisling wouldn't know me. I haven't seen her in decades.'

'Time doesn't exist for her,' Alfie said. 'Her life stopped, aged seventeen. I wanted to bring her to London, but her doctors advised against it. There's a chemical cocktail holding her together. She needs medical supervision for her own sake. But it's years since she's been in a psychiatric hospital, do you know that?'

'When I last heard, she was in St Ita's in Portrane.' Johnny decided that he'd pay four hundred euro to be rid of him.

'These days she's in sheltered care,' Alfie explained. 'It's as close to independent living as she'll ever get. From the outside you'd swear it was an ordinary house. The staff are good to her, but I'm her only regular visitor.'

'You've lived in London for years.'

'She's my only sister, for God's sake,' Alfie replied fiercely. 'Six times a year I fly home and every month she writes to me. The nurses got her writing letters as a therapy. There's nothing in them about her life now. They're all about growing up here, so incredibly detailed you could rebuild this hotel from scratch just from reading them. She still calls this place home. I have her letters in my bag if you want to read them.'

'No,' Johnny said firmly. 'Her letters are a private family matter.'

'If you're not family to her, who the hell is, Johnny?' Alfie's finger circled the rim of his empty glass. It might be possible to ask Simon to bring up one round of drinks, but a bottle meant being trapped all night, like he had often been trapped with Alfie's father. Not long after the consortium took over, Alfie started to flit back and forth to London, bluffing his way into doing sound for young Irish bands touring there and claiming to manage singers always on the verge of a record deal. On visits home he'd treated the hotel bar as his private office, talking about film projects he was setting up. The last time Johnny saw him was on the day of Francis Xavier's funeral, when he booked a suite and ran up a vindictively excessive bill for his London guests, while the consortium gathered to shake his hand, knowing that his cheque was certain to bounce. It was a bad debt they didn't mind, knowing the unpaid bill would rid them of the Flanagan family. Anything Johnny heard about him in the years since was hearsay: tales of him being seen selling encyclopaedias in London or working as a short-order cook in fast-food restaurants. The truth was always mercurial with Alfie but Johnny felt convinced that he was telling the truth about regularly returning to visit Aisling. He could stop Alfie from opening Aisling's letters but couldn't prevent him from describing them.

'Even after she moved into sheltered housing she never mentions the other residents,' Alfie was saying. 'For her, unless something happened before her seventeenth birthday, it didn't happen. She constantly talks about how close you two were. Do you know what I'm trying to say?'

Johnny couldn't be sure. He let Alfie ramble on, finding the conversation unnerving. Half the memories that Alfie claimed Aisling talked about were so distant they might not have happened to him. Trivial events he had no reason to remember. But he found it shocking to be so perfectly preserved in her imagination, that she seemed to own his past more than he did. He didn't know how much Aisling had told Alfie. The Flanagans had trusted Johnny, to the point of overlooking his presence during blazing rows between Aisling's parents.

While his devotion to Aisling was taken for granted, it was implicitly understood that Johnny knew his place. From an early age they might have been inseparable playmates, but socially their parents were miles apart. Not even the advent of puberty caused the Flanagans to worry about Aisling and Johnny going away together on hostelling weekends. He was seen more as a chaperone than a suitor, a counterweight to Aisling's natural wildness, ensuring she remained untainted until it came time for her to marry into Dublin's social elite.

'Do you remember that night you pair got stranded on a Wicklow bog after losing your way hitchhiking?' Alfie was saying. 'She talks about that night so much you'd swear it was only yesterday.'

Johnny tried to calm a knot of fear. A memory returned of them shivering, watching headlights approach, bobbing in and out of sight along the bends of that isolated road and their fear that the motorist might not stop, and that, even if he did, the youth hostel might refuse them admission at that late hour.

The elderly farmer had been shocked to find anyone in such a remote spot. He went out of his way to drive them to the hostel, waking the warden to have a quiet word, while Johnny and Aisling sat, cold and mute after hours lost in the dark.

But it wasn't the cold and hunger he remembered most vividly from that night: it was Aisling, aged fourteen, standing naked on an expanse of twilit bog. Aisling had suggested they explore what was simply a dirt track, overriding his warnings and seemingly convinced that it was a shortcut which would bring them to their hostel. He had told himself that if the track grew too narrow he would make her turn back, but as the evening turned towards dusk it proved impossible to make her do anything. He had been scared when the track reached a dead end but Aisling seemed delighted, bouncing across the springy turf and calling him a scaredy cat who couldn't catch her as she kept running to hide behind sods of cut turf piled into high ricks to dry.

Her gaiety was so infectious that he had allowed himself to get caught up in it, laughing each time she evaded his grip to hide behind another turf-rick. Johnny kept his eyes closed now, as if afraid that Alfie might read his thoughts and see the image that vividly came back of Aisling suddenly stepping forth from one turf-rick, having removed her jumper, blouse and bra. Dusk was setting in, making the turf look chocolate-brown and her skin seem darker than he could ever have imagined. Even her small nipples looked brown in that light as she taunted him to follow suit, unzipping her jeans and becoming fully naked. Johnny had undressed too, conscious of her staring at his unavoidable erection as he trembled, not knowing what was about to occur. In some ways nothing occurred. There was no cuddling or lovemaking and they did not even kiss. Instead they had laughed insanely and danced around, enjoying a sense of freedom in that twilit place where nobody could find them, their bodies never touching as they spun around until it grew so dark they could hardly find their clothes again.

'I don't remember that night.' Johnny opened his eyes again. 'I know we went hiking a few times but it was decades ago.'

Alfie was watching him closely, as if commanding him to continue talking.

'Maybe I was too close to her to notice the signs of her illness,' Johnny said. 'All I remember about Wicklow was overhearing girls in one hostel complain that Aisling kept them awake in their dormitory by talking aloud, while pretending to be so deeply asleep that nobody could wake her.'

'We all missed the signs,' Alfie replied. 'None of us wanted to see them.'

Alfie was right. People claimed that Francis Xavier having to sell the hotel caused Aisling's nervous breakdown, but she was ill before then, her family unwilling to face the shame of her needing help. Even before she stripped naked on that bog, Johnny had begun to feel uncomfortable with her. The closeness between them was different after she entered secondary school in Loreto College, St Stephen's Green, and started to acquire new affluent friends. These classmates often visited the hotel; a boisterous cluster of legs and school uniforms crowding into the lift to be treated like royalty in the Flanagan suite. Aisling always ignored him on those occasions and he kept his head down, focusing on his work as a trainee porter. But such visits stopped once whispers started in Loreto about Francis Xavier's finances and his drinking. Aisling would come home alone, troubled and desperate to escape back into the fantasy play-acting which Johnny had willingly taken part in on that bog when so overwhelmed by seeing her naked that he almost lost control. The problem was that, although his sexual instincts had been strong and he was in love with her, the overriding instinct inbred into him was to ensure the survival of his family. His father and grandfather would have lost their jobs if Aisling told anyone about their games or if anyone walked in when they were naked. As Francis Xavier's empire collapsed Johnny always shook his head when people asked if he noticed anything odd about Aisling, but their closeness had been blighted by having danced naked on a Wicklow bog.

'It was only after she refused to leave her room for fear of being burnt by the sun that people grasped how disturbed she was,' Johnny said.

Alfie nodded. 'I remember the afternoon. She ranted so much about the sun making her blood too hot that Daddy snapped and slapped her.'

'I remember that too.'

Alfie stared at him. 'It's funny what you choose to remember.'

'I remember your father storming down to the public bar to down a brandy. His fists clenched like he wanted to hit someone. It was obvious that the person he wanted to hit was himself. Your father hadn't a violent bone in his body. He just couldn't cope with having to act as a mother and father to her. People didn't talk about schizophrenia or bi-polar disorder back then. A hotel was about showing your best face to the world. Anything else you locked away behind high walls and silences. Your father adored Aisling.'

'And I adored him.' Alfie looked away as if afraid to let Johnny see the pain on his face. 'Daddy was like a king to me. Do you know how it feels to see a king who is broken? He used to wake me at three a.m. The loneliest poor fucker. I was just a kid, but I'd get up and we'd sit talking. Such plans he had. If you can find anyone to listen to your plans for long enough, you wind up still believing in them yourself. I don't know if he was talking to me on those nights or talking to himself, but I felt like a knight at his side, the last faithful knight to a king whose kingdom was falling apart.'

It pained Johnny that he could never remember his father talking to him like that, even after Johnny's mother died. His father only spoke to him of practical matters, suppliers to be paid or sacked as unreliable. Maybe shoptalk was his father's way to hide grief, or maybe his father simply never felt close to him. There was no coldness in their relationship but it was like his father saw Johnny as an extension of himself, focused on practicalities, whereas Charles was the son who would soar beyond his horizons.

'I keep thinking back to those days,' Alfie was saying. 'Daddy was a sinking ship, so why did I focus my attention on him, when maybe I could have saved Aisling by forcing Daddy to face up to her condition sooner? The question has haunted me for years, Johnny. Don't pretend that what happened to her didn't also affect you. You're not totally heartless behind that suit. I was so caught up in Daddy's lousy battles that I didn't want to bring more grief down on him. It was obvious Aisling had acute psychosis and was deluded and hallucinating. Yet all Daddy cared about was ensuring there was no talk of hospitals, as if any ambitious young man was going to marry the schizophrenic daughter of a bankrupt drunk.'

Alfie lowered his face into his hands and went silent. Johnny studied his bent head, fighting the urge to pity him. Alfie Flanagan. Johnny remembered his mother fretting nervously over his clothes before he was forced to attend Alfie's birthday parties: Alfie casually ripping the expensive wrapping paper his mother had bought, barely bothering to glance at the gift before running off to play with his friends. The pity was gone. Instead he fretted about how much Aisling had told Alfie about the final months before her admission to a psychiatric hospital. During those months the childlike naked dance she first initiated on a Wicklow bog was repeated a dozen times, whenever Aisling orchestrated for her and Johnny to be alone in the Flanagan suite. On one occasion Alfie unexpectedly returned and Johnny needed to hide behind Aisling's bed while Aisling scolded her brother for walking in on her, claiming that she was getting undressed to take a shower. At their age such games should have been sexual, but somehow they weren't for Aisling. For her they seemed more about regaining the sense of innocent abandonment they had shared in Wicklow. Or maybe they were her way to make herself feel desired, desperate to cling onto his affection when everything else in her life was falling apart. Maybe she offered him glimpses of her body because it was the last currency she felt she possessed. Previously in their games Aisling was always the leader and risk-taker but he sensed the balance of power change on those afternoons, knowing that Aisling would have meekly complied with a request for any sexual act, although in truth Johnny was so naive back then as to know almost nothing about sex. Her nakedness was her way of clinging to him like a frightened child, trying to hold back time. Every time he saw her body he had needed to struggle against his desire to touch her breasts, aware of the nightmare if they were caught. It was this fear that made him stop going up to the suite. He never abandoned Aisling, like her father had sometimes claimed afterwards. His termination of their friendship had been about the financial survival of his father and his brother Charles, already building a career in hotel management abroad, thanks to the Flanagan family connections, a career that could have been halted by one angry phone call from Francis Xavier in Dublin.

Johnny was so caught up in memories that he only now became aware that Alfie had started talking again, like Johnny was the first person in months to bother listening to him. Johnny cursed him for turning up just when he was finally relinquishing control of a hotel he had always secretly hated.

'I must get back to work, Alfie,' he said, interrupting the flow of words. 'But we can go down to the bar and have a last drink together.'

'We'll have it up here.' Alfie picked up the phone and dialled reception. 'Is that you, Simon? Bring up two double brandies. In fact, just bring a bottle.'

Johnny reached across to take the phone from him. 'Simon, we're fine for drink.'

He replaced the receiver and Alfie stared at him, insulted.

'What's your problem? I was going to pay. I've not come here looking for favours.'

'I don't owe you favours.' Johnny's reply was sharper than intended. 'My father's consortium paid a fair price for this hotel.'

'They could easily afford to,' Alfie snapped back. 'Seeing as they robbed Daddy blind when he was trying to cope with a sick daughter.'

Johnny stood up, angry now. Alfie rose also, hands outstretched in apology.

'I'm sorry.' He sounded like his father on many occasions when Francis Xavier was on the verge of being barred. 'I shouldn't have said that. You owe me nothing, but what about Aisling?'

'I haven't seen your sister in decades.'

'At one time you saw all you wanted of her,' Alfie retorted.

'What exactly are you're saying?'

'You took advantage of her illness. Didn't I catch you myself one afternoon in the suite? You stripped her naked and then hid behind her bed, making her lie about being about to take a bath.'

'That's not what I remember.'

'You only remember what you want to.'

'I remember you and the Count.'

'What?' Alfie looked puzzled.

'The day after my grandfather was finally persuaded to retire he went back into the kitchens to say goodbye. You happened to be there and said, "This area is staff only. If you want to speak to someone wait out in the public bar".'

'If I did say that I was just a kid.'

'What you do and see as a kid matters. Your father would never have addressed the Count like that. He'd worked here all his life but to you he was just another hired hand.'

'I came to talk about Aisling,' Alfie protested. 'I barely remember the Count.'

'Then maybe your memory is selective too. I remember what occurred between us, though for years I trained myself not to remember.'

'What about you talking about now?'

'You and I playing in the lift before the hotel reopened.'

Alfie laughed. 'I hung around with Charles occasionally, but you were Aisling's friend. I can't imagine you ever playing with me.'

'I never played with you. You played with me.'

Alfie looked so bewildered that Johnny realised he genuinely didn't remember. Why should he? Johnny had just been another toy for Alfie to use until he got bored. Maybe what happened between them wasn't important? Maybe Phoebe was wrong to suggest that some of his reticent character traits were formed by being left confused and burdened by what happened in that lift. Phoebe was the only person he'd ever spoken to about this, surprising himself one night by blurting out the details, after they had discussed Luuk de Vries's bid and Johnny suddenly wanted rid not just of the bricks and mortar of this hotel but every secret held within these walls.

'"One for sorrow, two for joy,"' Johnny recited. 'What is seven for in that nursery rhyme?'

'I don't bloody remember.' Alfie sounded agitated now.

'It's for a secret never to be told. Maybe I was nine, but I was so innocent I might as well have been seven. You were thirteen. You understood what was going on.'

'Nothing went on. Nothing I remember.' Alfie strained his memory. '"Eight for a wish, nine for a kiss, ten for a bird you must not miss." That's your relationship with my sister. You obviously don't miss Aisling.'

'I'm discussing the lift.'

'What gives you the right to say what we discuss?'

'The fact that it's my name on the deeds of this building. On four occasions in the week before the reopening you called me away from playing with Aisling, saying your father wanted you to ensure that the new lift could hold the maximum capacity of eight people. You ordered me to squeeze tight into one corner so you could judge how many others would fit. You pushed up against me, something hard protruding in your pants. You kept ordering me to squeeze in and out of the space you had me confined to, pushing tight so I had to brush against you and could feel your hard thing twitching. Then you said "Hold tight, we're going up", and I felt your hand go down inside my short pants as you pressed the button for the lift to rise, rubbing yourself so hard against me I could barely breathe. I don't know how often we rode up and down from the top floor to the basement until you gasped and stepped back, telling me I could go, that you had passed the lift as being safe for eight people.'

'I remember none of this.' Alfie was wary now. 'Even if some larking around happened, we were just two kids messing.'

'You were four years older. You never even bothered to warn me to keep it secret after each occasion. You knew my family regarded your family as royalty and I'd be too scared to utter a word.'

'Royalty?' Alfie said. 'Let me get this straight. Your father's consortium screwed my dad out of his hotel. You screwed the consortium and now you're claiming victimhood while walking away from my family's hotel with millions in profit. If there's any victim here, it's me.' He paused. 'Okay, maybe not me because I'll admit to having fucked up my life. The real victim is Aisling whose life essentially ended after you rejected her.'

'Aisling wasn't mine to reject. She was out of my league and your parents made sure I knew it.'

'Out of your league?' Alfie laughed with sudden bitterness. 'Look at your suit. You married a South Dublin Fine Gael horse Protestant; the sort who always looked down their noses at my family.'

'You know nothing about my wife or who I am now!'

'You're still the same man,' Alfie taunted.

'So are you.' Johnny reined in his temper to a whisper. 'Alfie with an E.'

The quietude in his voice unsettled Alfie.

'What does that mean?' he asked.

'This room is double-booked.' Johnny looked down at his expensive shoes he always carefully shone. They reminded him of who he had become. The rule in such situations was to never let arguments get personal. 'There's been a mistake. Marieke at reception should never have given you the key.'

'I don't see anyone else booked in here.'

'The fault is ours. We'll ensure you're taken by taxi to alternative accommodation as our guest.'

'For fuck's sake, Johnny, will you even look at me? Don't do the Darcy trick of hiding behind a mask. Staring at you right now all I see is your father.'

'Can you not see that nine-year-old boy in the lift?'

'I don't remember him. But I do remember a fifteen-year-old playing with my naked, mentally unstable sister, so don't get sanctimonious.'

'I never touched her or asked her to ever remove her clothes. She kept doing it as if somebody had taught her, somebody close to her whom she trusted.'

'What the fuck are you accusing me of now?'

'Maybe it wasn't you on those nights when you said you comforted her in your bed if your parents were having another drunken row. Maybe it was the brother of some Loreto girl whose house she used to visit before they turned their backs on her. Or your father, so drunk one night that he mistook her for her dead mother.'

Alfie squared at him, trembling with such rage that Johnny was convinced he was about to punch him.

'Daddy was a good man. Maybe he was deluded when it came to money and couldn't handle his drink, but deep down and fundamentally he was a good man, so don't you say otherwise.'

'How about you? Deep down and fundamentally?'

Alfie wearily sat on the bed. It took him several moments to look up. 'No,' he said. 'I've spent my life having to play catch up. You were lucky to be born with no expectations. Maybe it's hard to be born poor, but it's harder to be born with a silver spoon in your mouth and see it snatched away. I'm not proud of some things I've done to survive, and if what you say occurred in that lift did happen then I apologise. It was a fucked up time to be a kid. But I never touched Aisling in any way. If I had I'd remember it clearly because she meant something to me.'

'Whereas I didn't?'

'Stop turning the tables: it was you I found naked with her. If nothing happened between you, why does she mention you obsessively in her letters? Are you saying you never even once touched her?'

'Not because I didn't want to,' Johnny said. 'I was so aroused and so scared I was almost bursting out of my skin.

One afternoon she stood directly in front of me, inches away and because I wasn't sure I could maintain my self-control I turned my back. But maybe I was leading her on, letting her take control like she'd always done in our games. And she did. I felt her breasts press against my back and then her hand on my chest going lower and lower. And when she reached – you know what she reached, what I'd been hoping she'd touch – I froze. You see, until then I'd blocked out what you did to me in the lift. But her touch was enough for it all to come back and, with it, the fear and guilt and secrecy. Isn't it funny: the first time a girl touched me sexually and the person I thought of was you? Her touch should have been pleasurable but you'd skewed everything. You left me not knowing what was normal; you destroyed my innocence, humping yourself off against my back when I was young and bewildered. And because the memory was too much, I grabbed her hand and pushed her away, scrambling into my clothes as she stood in silent tears, feeling worthless and rejected. Maybe I wasn't man enough to do the acts she seemed to want done to make herself feel desired. Maybe the flashbacks were too strong because I experienced them for years afterwards whenever any woman touched me there. But I wasn't rejecting her. I was refusing to exploit her vulnerability because I knew what it felt like to be used. Even though she seemed to be taking the lead, she was in no fit state to initiate anything. I refused to exploit her like you exploited me. And when I was fully dressed, I helped her get dressed, needing to lift her arms like she was a child, doing up buttons and straps because she hadn't the strength to do anything except sit on her bed and cry. And I held her, for as long as I felt I could, begging her to stop crying, until finally she looked at me and said, "All I ever really wanted you to do for me was just turn off the radio." "Aisling," I said, "there's no radio playing." "There is," she said. "It's driving me demented, playing the same tunes night and day. I don't know if it's the Russians or Americans, but they're broadcasting from inside my brain." That was two days before she walked down to reception in her bathrobe and asked at the desk for a stamp. She stuck the stamp to her forehead, let her robe fall and walked naked out onto the street with my father running after her, asking where she was going. She smiled and said she was going to the post box to post herself back. My father brought her inside and phoned the ambulance. Then he phoned the bar in the Ormond Hotel, knowing your father would be drinking there. It was my father who used his connections to get her a private room in John of God's. Your father stayed drinking in the Ormond until he took a taxi out to the hospital, so drunk they wouldn't let him in to see her.'

'At least Daddy went in next morning when he sobered up and kept going in faithfully every week till he died.'

'I visited her more often at the start than you did,' Johnny replied. 'You were too busy swanning around UCD, pretending to be Ireland's answer to Roman Polanski simply because your cronies ran the student film society.'

'I thought it was a teenage phase Aisling was going through,' Alfie said. 'If I didn't visit her enough at the start I've made up for it since.'

'Four times a week I used to visit. Finishing school, waiting for buses there, buses back. On my first visit I brought out an enormous teddy bear, getting slagged by every schoolgirl on the bus. I remember her clinging to it, sky-high with exhilaration one day, inconsolable in tears the next. I visited so often that a young doctor stopped me in the corridor to ask if I was her boyfriend. I didn't really know what I was, so I just said I wasn't the right person for him to talk to about her. "I'm not talking about her," he said, "I want to talk about you. You seem a lovely kid and probably think you can save her but nobody can. She'll never recover. I shouldn't say this, but whatever future you might think you'll have with her won't happen. You'll only get drawn in deeper. It's time to think about yourself because you're the only person you can save here. If I were you I'd walk out that door and not come back."'

'I thought the doctors were meant to be on her side?' Alfie said.

'Whose side were you on, vamoosing to London, sick of finding your father collapsed on the floor? You did the same. You saved yourself.'

The door opening caught them off guard. Simon entered with a tray. It held two glasses containing brandy. The third glass was a tumbler of clear liquid.

'One of you ordered double brandies,' he said. 'The other one cancelled the order. I made a Jesuitical call and brought single measures.'

'Put them on the dressing table,' Alfie said. 'Take the money from the cash there and a tip for yourself.'

'The drinks aren't on you.' Simon quietly put them down. 'Or on the house either because Mr Darcy owes you and your family fuck all. They're on me.'

Alfie laughed. 'Are you finally breaking open your Communion money?'

'I'm buying you a drink, Alfie Flanagan, for the pleasure of knowing I'll never have to buy you another. I'd advise you to drink it quickly: I took the liberty of ordering you a taxi that won't wait all night.'

'I'll drink at any pace I want. And cancel the taxi. Free taxis were the ruse you always used to get rid of my dad after fleecing him. I like this room just fine. You can go.'

'I'll go when Mr Darcy tells me. Mr Darcy gives the orders here.'

'Join us, Simon.' Johnny felt his self-assurance return with the old porter there. He could never recall Simon calling him Mr Darcy before. Simon raised the glass of clear liquid, the one he was nursing all evening.

'As you wish, Mr Darcy, but I'll stick to water.'

'This is a private conversation,' Alfie protested. 'It's none of your business, Simon. You're only an employee.'

'You've never changed, Alfie,' the porter said. 'That's the tone you used when you ordered the Count out of the kitchens after he retired.'

'Jesus!' Alfie reached for his brandy. 'Does everyone intend dredging up my past to use against me?'

'I'm only telling you what you told the Count: you've no business being here anymore.'

'There's unfinished business. Not to do with me, but with my sister. A fraction of the profit Johnny is making from selling this hotel would allow Aisling to leave the sheltered housing she hates. It would set her up to be financially secure and lead an independent life. She's more stable than she used to be, the drugs have improved over time. She could go home, but she has no home to go to. I can't afford to give her a home, Johnny. I'm asking nothing for myself, but you owe her something. The price of a one bedroom apartment so that, for the first time since walking out of here with a stamp stuck to her forehead, she would have her own front door. You blocked her out of your life. I'm asking you to just once show you're not an entirely cold-blooded creature.' He turned to Simon. 'Help me, Simon. You remember Aisling.'

'I remember her well.'

'What's Johnny giving you from his windfall? Let me guess? Statutory redundancy and not a penny more.'

'That's what I'm entitled to.'

'Johnny won't be your boss soon. Nobody else left here knows what we're talking about. So speak your mind for once, Simon. This was Aisling's home. What redress did she receive for having it taken away from her? What's she entitled to?'

'Why don't you ask her?' Simon suggested.

'Aisling is too timid to ask for anything.' He turned to Johnny. 'You're making a fortune from my grandfather's business. Aisling was his favourite. Surely you don't intend leaving her out in the cold?'

'Money is no use to Aisling,' Simon interrupted quietly. 'It might have been once, but not now when she's dying.'

'What are you saying?' Alfie asked angrily.

'You heard. You write often enough to say that you're coming and I read Aisling those letters aloud, although I doubt if she takes in their meaning. How could she, when she barely knows me anymore, and didn't even know who you were, last time you kept your promise and flew over. Early onset Alzheimer's and cancer. I talk to her a lot on my visits because she's a good listener and good at keeping secrets. These days she's like a child again, adrift on a boat at sea, recoiling in fear if anyone even touches the special mattress they have her lying on. At one time she used to grip my hand tight but she has no real sense of who anyone is now. It's a race against time as to which of us dies first. I hope it's her so I can at least be there for her funeral. My niece in Cork gets any few bob I own. Aisling has nothing for her next of kin to inherit, unless Johnny can be duped into signing over money to her.'

'Who gave you permission to visit my sister?' Alfie said angrily. 'Stay away from her.'

'It wasn't me who first went near her. I remember her playing behind my desk as an innocent child and one day her innocence was gone. I'm saying no more.'

'You've said enough.' Alfie rose to his feet angrily. 'How come Aisling never told me about you visiting her?'

'She was always scared of you,' the porter said. 'Ingrained from an early age.'

'Stick to carrying trays,' Alfie said angrily. 'It's what you were born for.'

'That's true,' Simon replied. 'I'm the same man I ever was, and so are you. I had time for your father, even when I needed to pick him up off the floor, but you were always a cheap hustler and never even good at it.'

The porter's words gave Johnny enough mettle to pick up Alfie's bag.

'Put that down,' Alfie said angrily. 'It's private.'

'Why did you really come here tonight?' Johnny asked.

'Hoping to talk to you, man to man. With Aisling so ill it's all the more reason why someone needs to take responsibility for her. I'm trying to make amends for having been a bad brother. Are you too mean to even set aside a small sum just to cover the cost of her burial?'

'If you wanted to talk to me, why use an assumed name?'

'I wasn't sure I'd get in the door,' Alfie retorted. 'You were always such a tight-arsed bookkeeper that I knew you wouldn't have forgotten any bad debts run up during my father's funeral. And can you blame me for wanting a look at my old home? All this was meant to be mine.'

'It's a totally different hotel,' Simon cut in. 'Only the name is the same.'

'It looks the same to me.'

'There have been changes,' Johnny said. 'The nightclub in the basement, for example.'

'What about it?' Alfie said.

'Marieke said you were thinking of paying it a visit?'

'Maybe. Or are you going to deny me even that simple pleasure?'

'I want you gone.' Johnny took a deep breath, recalling old Finbar's adage about never letting guests see you rattled. He opened the door and stepped out into the corridor, placing Alfie's bag down on the carpet.

'And forget the offer of a free bed elsewhere. I want you the hell out of my hotel.'

'My father built this hotel,' Alfie shouted. 'My money is as good as anyone else's.'

'Our grandfathers built up this business between them,' Johnny retorted. 'All your father did was burn down the original building and erect a house of cards in its place. It fell to my father to keep it from tumbling down. You've been barred from this hotel since your father's funeral and you're barred from Upstarts Nightclub as of now.'

'Who'll bar me?' Alfie mocked. 'You and your geriatric manservant?'

'Me and the police.'

'What will you charge me with?'

It was Simon who replied. 'What you were charged with in a nightclub in Luton.'

Alfie stopped, all mockery gone from his features. What replaced it was anguish. Finbar had always stressed how, if running a hotel, the important news stories were buried away on the inside pages. Minor court cases that most readers missed, barring orders, disputes over wills. Few people in Dublin would have noticed a tiny report in the *Irish Post* last autumn about an Irishman charged with selling ecstasy tablets in a shabby Luton nightclub. Johnny should have known that Simon would also spot the name during his microscopic perusal of every newspaper delivered to the hotel. Simon had been trained by the Count to miss nothing and silently store away all information for use only when necessary.

'You bastards,' Alfie said softly. 'Anyone can make one mistake. That has nothing to do with me wanting to spend one final night here.'

'I don't want to know what's in your bag.' Johnny touched it with his feet. 'Because if I have to open it I might find my suspicions confirmed.'

'Aisling's letters are in there, about being abandoned by you. Throw all the accusations you like, but there's things about you in those letters that maybe you don't want to know about.'

Johnny glanced down at the scuffed leather. 'Will I open the bag so?'

Alfie glared at him. Johnny stared back, keeping his gaze steady in this game of bluff. He didn't know what he was most afraid of finding if forced to open the bag.

'There's personal items of mine as well,' Alfie said, backing down. 'Everything I have left in the world. I'm moving home to Dublin. This is my first night of a fresh start. That bag is private, so hand it back in here.'

'Come out and get it,' Johnny replied. It was easier to control situations if you lured an unwelcome guest out from their room. Johnny's hands were sweating. He had the absurd notion that there were old Polaroid photos of Aisling in the bag: her fourteen-year-old nipples brown on a twilit bog, her face captured at a quizzical, bewildered angle. Some tribes believed their souls could be stolen by a photograph. If these letters really existed, then the soul of the child he had once been lived on only in Aisling's fossilised memories, memories of how close they once were before their innocence was severed. He didn't want to think back to being that child, to every childhood humiliation he had blocked out when reinventing himself as the man in this bespoke suit. His hands trembled as he knelt to undo the zip. The movement provoked Alfie out into the corridor like Johnny knew it would. He pushed Johnny away and picked up the bag.

'This bag is private,' he said, almost hugging it. 'If I made one mistake then I served my time for it. My grandfather started with nothing, so you just watch me do the same. I've plans you couldn't conceive of because you never had a spark of imagination. You were only ever Charles's idiot brother, cut out to be nothing more than a skivvy before a fortune fell into your lap.'

A bedroom door opened further down the corridor. Alfie turned and Johnny caught his look of recognition and then genuine terror. It was obvious that he recognized who the guest was in Room 107. The stocky man observed the scene in the corridor. He didn't even raise his hand as a signal but Johnny knew that both young women in the room behind him instantly stood still. From the brief glimpses that Johnny caught of the women who engaged in illicit rendezvous with this man, he had noticed how their faces changed every few months. But they were never prostitutes. Some weeks their faces were so similar that they had to be sisters. Johnny didn't know what drew such women to this man. For years he had made it his business not to know, just like he tried to make it his business that the corridor was quiet at this hour when the man always left to get home before his wife returned from her pottery class. Normally Johnny would usher any troublesome guest back into their room and close the door. But he didn't do so now, because the child buried away inside him relished seeing the fear in Alfie's eyes.

'Stay away from my nightclub,' Johnny said loudly. 'This is a respectable hotel, without a stain on our licence since some drunk briefly owned it decades ago. You are a known drug pusher and I believe this bag contains ecstasy tablets. We've seen off enough two-bit hustlers trying to sell drugs in that night-club. You've two minutes to be off the premises before I call the police.' He looked at the stocky man who remained motionless and addressed him for the first time in all the years he had been using Room 107.

'This will just take a moment, sir. I'm sorry to inconvenience you.'

'You're not the one inconveniencing me.' The man's voice so low it could barely be heard. 'Anyone who does rarely gets to inconvenience me twice.'

Alfie had already snatched up his bag and made for the lift, too scared to even retrieve his leather jacket from the room. Simon and Johnny followed. Alfie kept his back to them, squeezed tightly into a corner as though scared of what might happen if someone entered the lift behind him. Johnny would recognise the slouch of his shoulders anywhere. The slouch belonged to Francis Xavier on all the nights when Johnny's father coaxed him into a paid taxi, back to the shabby flat at Islandbridge where he was found dead after hotel staff spotted how he hadn't turned up to cadge his morning cure. Johnny wanted to feel hatred, remembering his own fear as a child in that lift, but could only feel pity. It was curiously liberating.

'The offer of a room somewhere else still stands.'

'Fuck your charity.' Alfie muttered, afraid to look around. 'My family never needed handouts.'

The doors closed and that was Johnny's last glimpse of him, his shoulders trembling. Simon silently opened the door to the service stairs and Johnny followed him down uncarpeted steps leading to parts of the hotel the public never saw. The laundry room with stacks of sheets to be washed, the back lane entrance that supply trucks used and where kitchen staff smoked during breaks. A door led out into the lobby. Alfie was gone. Johnny knew that he hadn't even stopped at reception to ask for a refund of his money. Simon glanced at the remnants of the coach party seated in the lobby.

'A fiver says that before the night is out one of them will ask me for an Irish coffee without the whiskey.'

'Will you miss working here?' Johnny asked.

The porter shrugged. 'I was always only passing through. That's why I turned down your father's offer to join the consortium, even though he offered me a loan. He was a decent man, your father.'

'Do you regret not taking up his offer?'

'Just because I never left doesn't meant I ever stopped feeling I was only passing through. The strain of running this hotel crushed your father and for years I watched it almost crush you.'

'Do you think Alfie had ecstasy tablets in his bag?'

Simon nodded. 'Alfie was always a moocher, quick on the make. I don't know if he came here to talk about Aisling or simply tried to shake you down for a few bob when the chance arose. But not only am I sure he had drugs on him, but I know he planned to call the cops, so they'd raid the club, even if it meant him getting caught if he didn't manage to slip away in time. He'd do another stretch in jail, just to see the Darcy name dragged through the paper like his father's name was. This was his last chance for revenge on behalf of his family, even though he hasn't really any family left.'

'How long have you been visiting Aisling?'

'Since her father died. Somebody had to and it was right that it wasn't you. The poor girl was frozen in time. She and Finbar were the only Flanagans I ever respected. Your family always had more class.'

'Should I go and see her? I always felt guilty for running away.'

'How do you picture her?'

'Young, vulnerable, beautiful. Troubled but radiant when she smiled.'

'Do her a favour. Remember her that way.'

They watched one girl from Room 107 step from the lift and slip unnoticed out the front door. In three minutes' time the second girl would follow, the stout man leaving shortly afterwards.

'I don't fancy Alfie's chances of making a career selling drugs in Dublin nightclubs,' Simon said. 'His first night home and he has already inconvenienced a man who hates being inconvenienced.'

'What about your career, Simon? Marieke would take you back in a flash when this hotel re-opens.'

'She'd need to take me back in an urn. Eighteen months was all the doctors gave me.'

'Doctors can be wrong.'

'The pain in my gut isn't.'

'Then let me prise you away from Dublin. Phoebe is almost finished overseeing the refurbishments in Enniscorthy. Eight bedrooms, exclusive end of the market. Come and be our first guest, our guinea pig. It will cost you nothing. I'd love you to cast your eye over the place.'

Simon smiled wryly. 'Fifty years working here and you want me take a busman's holiday by visiting another hotel? If I'm honest I never liked hotels and I'm not sure you ever liked this one either.'

'For me it was never about liking this place.'

'Then make sure you like Enniscorthy and believe in yourself as the true owner down there.'

'I'm the owner here.'

Simon gripped his shoulder with surprising strength. 'My bollix. I've known you since you were a wee scut whose ears

I had to occasionally box. You fooled the staff but you never fooled me. You never felt the true owner here. You were a keeper, a custodian, a caretaker for the ghosts in your head. Your real life will only start when you leave here. So when you walk out this door, don't look back. Take no ghosts to your hotel in Wexford and that includes me.'

'I promised my father to look after this place. It's all I've ever known. I don't know who I'll be without it.'

'A rich fucker serving over-priced cognac.'

'Go home, Simon.' He knew this porter was the only person here he'd miss.

'I've nothing waiting at home except an empty bed and painkillers. I've never asked you a favour, but I'll ask one now. Before you move to Wexford make a bonfire of every memento of this place.'

'There would be a lot of memories in that bonfire.'

'A lot of old guff. A hotel is an empty shell. The guests who come and go are too busy to remember any of us.' Simon pointed as the lift opened. 'Here's our guest's second lady friend. You'd be wise to give Marieke a break and position yourself at reception to be the one who doesn't notice him sliding back the key. He'll leave cash in the room as usual.'

'Is there brandy in your alcove?'

'For emergencies on my special shelf.'

'Will you join me in one?'

The old porter shook his head. 'There's no satisfaction in drinking brandy. I can't pretend to pull the wool over your eyes. Let me top up my water from the bottle marked Smirnoff in the bar.'

Simon walked away. Left alone, Johnny found himself shaking. He entered Simon's alcove and poured a large brandy. Marieke looked across, surprised because he had a rule about never drinking in front of staff. He had seen people's respect for Francis Xavier diminish with every drink. But Johnny didn't care how out of character he was behaving. He poured another brandy. Pete Spencer could fiddle the entire clientele for all he cared just now. The stupid carpet with its woven FFs could self-combust. The walls of this hotel could tumble down and still Johnny knew it wouldn't rid him of this cocktail of anger and guilt. He remembered how, when dying in the hospice, his father would fly into unexpected rages; the nurses bewildered by how he summoned the strength. An elderly priest sneaking a cigarette in the makeshift smoking area told Johnny how, when people feel death approaching, they often need to find a way to expel any buried pain locked away inside them.

Maybe for Johnny it was the same with leaving this build-ing that had been central to his life: every dark moment had to be relived, its consequences finally understood. For years Johnny had sworn to batter Alfie Flanagan if they ever met, because of what the older boy stole from him as a child. Had he been too cowardly to do so, still cowed by the Flanagan name? Would it have felt more of an exorcism if his abuser had been carried out of here bleeding? No: Johnny knew that violence was not in his nature and if he stopped being true to his nature, Alfie would have robbed him of everything.

Simon returned and looked at the glass in Johnny's hand.

'That's your second drink,' he said. 'Go easy or you'll be siphoning off vodka next.'

'I'll light that bonfire in my garden, Simon. But until then I've a hotel to run. I owe it to my father.'

'You owe nobody nothing.'

'Maybe I owe it to myself. It's in my nature.'

The guest from 107 hadn't yet come down. He told Marieke to take her break and stood at the reception desk. The office party was in full swing. He'd need to ensure that the bar was cleared soon after closing time; younger customers steered towards the nightclub, older ones nudged out into the night. There was a balance to be struck between profit and caution in deciding when to stop serving. Two ladies approached the counter. Decades of training took over as he leaned towards them and smiled, as smoothly as old Finbar would have done; his mind focused purely on this hotel that still needed to be run.

What Then?

My sister warned me about what older workers might do during my first days working in the factory, the usual rites of initiation. Not that anything too serious would happen to me because I wasn't what the factory hands would call a lifer; a man destined to spend his working life engaged in manual labour, unless he got promoted to the position of chargehand, a poacher turned gamekeeper, stranded in the limbo of being neither one of the bosses or one of the lads anymore.

I would never be one of the lads. My job was a temporary one, arranged by my sister – the most glamorous and efficient secretary in that industrial complex. Her boss had pulled strings to ensure that, aged fifteen, I would pass my summer holidays clocking in at the Wire and Cable factory. Here I could draw a wage and learn something about life instead of being stuck at home, alone in a house where my father's absence was due to him being at sea and my late mother's absence resonated everywhere.

I was only passing through this factory. Therefore while men might have some fun by sending me in search of 'the long wait' or to fetch them a glass hammer, their pranks and wind-ups were harmless compared to what they would do to one of their own. I had heard of young men being strapped to the mechanical hoist that lifted the heavy coils of copper wire high above the factory floor and left suspended in mid-air during lunch break, when the bosses' backs were turned. Such a young lad – good at soccer and at chatting up girls – would curse them angrily, but later on would laugh with them in the pub after work on the first Friday he received a pay packet. He would have gained sufficient status to be able to slag the other men back, proud to have passed their test by not having complained to any boss about his rite of passage. In reward he would receive the silent nod which conveyed that he now belonged among them.

By comparison I was merely a civilian in the territorial war zone of the shop-floor, where two crews manning conveyor belts competed to see who could earn the most bonus money. Here cocksure young dudes strutted their strength to impress while old codgers learnt the knack of how to pace themselves as they drew closer to the bell for the final round. This rang on their sixty-fifth birthday when retirement, a pension and daily walks to the bookies replaced this hubbub of quick-witted slagging in which they had passed their working lives.

Sixty-five seems like an impossibly old age when you are fifteen, an age when twenty-one sounds old and twenty-seven sounds positively ancient. My temporary workmates were kind to me, partly because half of them fancied my sister and wanted no bad reports filtering back to the offices and partly because many possessed sons my own age and knew that I had been touched by loss only a short time before.

Because I was shy it was probably no harm that Jack McCann – the fifty-year-old man I was supposed to be helping – was quiet-spoken and not prone to unnecessary chat. Our factory produced heavy duty electrical cable that needed to be carefully wound onto huge wooden spools. As a former carpenter, McCann's job was to then hammer wooden slats around the circumference of each eight-foot-high spool to seal in the cable.

In theory I was meant to hammer in nails as well but it took me so long to drive one six inch nail into the wooden spool that McCann devised a routine where I simply handed him each slat, before helping him roll the sealed spools out into the yard where a forklift waited to load them onto trucks. I liked how McCann never asked patronising questions about school. Mostly we worked in companionable silence, McCann benignly tolerating my ineptitude in this adult world where I was out of my depth.

It was because he probed so rarely and our silences grew so long that one afternoon I shyly confessed that I possessed the seemingly unrealisable ambition to become a writer. After seeming to acknowledge this revelation with a stoic nod, he focused for so long on driving six-inch nails into the wood that I presumed my words hadn't even registered. Then, after slotting home the final nail with just four hammer blows, he stepped back to observe me.

'I never met a writer before,' he said.

'I never said I was one,' I replied, hastily.

'Well then, what's the story? Either you write or you don't.'

'I enjoy writing bits of poems,' I said. 'But I don't even rightly know if they're proper poems or what the hell they are.'

He shrugged, matter-of-factly. 'Time will tell: it has a knack of sorting out most things.'

'But don't go telling the men in here that I claim to be a poet,' I added, terrified about what slagging might ensue.

He shrugged again. 'Nobody has a clue who they are at fifteen. I thought I was going to be a priest.'

I couldn't tell if McCann was being serious.

'What happened?'

He leaned his shoulder against the spool, indicating for me to do likewise so that we could begin to roll it out into the yard. 'I got waylaid by fast women and slow horses. And I couldn't read the small print spec for the job because it was written in Latin.' He looked at me. 'So do you want to be a poet or not?'

I glanced at the forklift driver manoeuvring his machine into position as we rolled the huge drum out through the open doors into the sunlit yard.

'I do. It's just that I don't want anyone in here thinking me a proper eejit.'

'You'd only be a proper eejit if you cared what anyone thinks of you,' McCann replied. 'Don't wind up like some fellows in here who have spent their entire lives doing shag all beyond anxiously looking over their shoulder in case someone might accuse them of ever having had an original thought in their heads.'

'I've never even met a poet,' I said. 'I couldn't even tell you what a poet looks like.'

McCann gave the sealed drum one last rap with his knuckles as if to test his handiwork and then tipped the wink to the forklift driver to hoist it up with the other spools on the lorry.

'If you've never met a poet, then at least you've two weeks left to meet a man who once did. Have you ever bothered to chat with Charlie?'

'Who's Charlie?'

'If you didn't know the score you might call him the biggest eejit in here. Yet there's nobody that the other men have more respect for than Charlie because he's never given a toss what anyone thinks of him. He has worked at just about every labouring job a man can do. They say he even briefly played for Shamrock Rovers in the 1940s. There's so much stored inside Charlie's head it must be like a galaxy in there. You know the two long bays where the copper coils are kept? Walk down between them and you'll find Charlie's office at the very end next to the wall.'

'Charlie has an actual office?'

McCann laughed. 'That's what we nicknamed it. Or the Machine Gun Post, because it's so well fortified, with stacks of broken pallets and oil drums, that it's a wonder he can climb into it most mornings.'

'What does he do there?'

'Mainly he's staying out of sight and marking off time before he turns sixty-five. His health isn't great so we cover up for him if bosses start getting shirty about him not being well enough to pull his weight. Officially he's meant to be weeding out defective cables or untangling wire. When Charlie turns sixty-five on August 3rd the bosses will go through the motions of making a speech before turfing him out the door. But they know that if they try to get shut of him even one day earlier every worker here will down tools and strike. Charlie hasn't been the same since he buried his missus two years back. It left him fierce shook. He has a daughter in Australia but I can't see Charlie boarding a plane to visit her. Go down and talk to him. You share an interest in common.'

'Why? Does he write poems?'

McCann shook his head. 'Not that I'm aware, but his house is packed with books and he loves reciting poems. Yeats is his favourite and another geezer called Pound. Charlie isn't a man to draw attention to himself but every Christmas Eve, when lads smuggle in a few bottles of whiskey and a singsong breaks out in the canteen, Charlie recites a Yeats poem. He never gives a toss if lads are listening or not; he ploughs to the final line.' McCann led the way back inside to where the next spool of wire waited to be sealed up with slats. 'I do my best to pop down for a chat but it's hard to find time now when we're working against the clock to send this consignment down to the docks. So, to be blunt, you're about as useful to me right now as an ashtray on a Honda 50 and you'd be of more use if you went down to have a chat with Charlie because

I know he gets lonely. Say I sent you. He'll welcome the company and you'll always be able to say that you once talked to a man who once talked to Willie Butler Yeats.'

I regularly passed those long bays, stacked to the ceiling with every kind of electric cable, and had never seen a man down there. I wondered if McCann was winding me up and, as he nodded at me to go, I half hoped it was a wind-up because I was shy and unsure of what to say to a man who was about to turn sixty-five. I had spent my first pay packet buying a *Selected Poems* by Yeats, but while mesmerised by the early poems that brimmed with an unearthly mysticism, the older poems had left me perplexed, like a strong whiskey that I wasn't yet mature enough to handle. I had always imagined that if I ever encountered some echo of this poet it would be in the form of an apparition glimpsed on a deserted lake isle in Sligo and not from an old factory hand in this rust-pit of high-voltage cables. But because McCann was watching I walked on and squeezed through a stack of old boxes to discover a tiny old man with round glasses sitting on a stool, methodically inspecting tangled cables. After a moment he looked up.

'If those piss artists have sent you for "a long wait" then just play along for a while and take your ease, son. There's tea in that flask if you're thirsty.'

'Jack McCann sent me.'

The old man observed me more carefully. 'McCann is no messer. Does Jack want something?'

'He asked me to ask if you ever met William Butler Yeats.'

'And why would he ask you to ask that?'

'Because I confessed to him that I write poems myself.'

The old man nodded. 'That's a gift I never had, even though I've always loved reading and rereading poems. They become like old friends who never die; you just understand them differently the older you get.'

He closed his eyes and began to recite a poem I didn't know. The images were complex and I couldn't fully understand them, but they opened up in me a desire to want to grasp their meaning because they felt like a glimpse into another world.

'That's Yeats in old age,' he said when he finished. 'A tad cantankerous and discontented but still trying to make sense of it all.'

'And what do the lines mean?'

Charlie shrugged. 'That's the magic of a good poem; it can mean one thing to you and something totally different to me.'

'Do the other men not think you're odd, reciting poems?'

He shrugged. 'I never asked them. I can't say I particularly care.'

'But, be honest, did you really know Yeats?'

The factory hand shook his head. 'I never claimed to have known him, I just told Jack that I met him once.'

'And did you know that he was a great poet when you saw him first?'

Charlie laughed. 'I hadn't a snowballs who he was. In fact the first few times I saw him I thought he was astray in the head. I got my first job at thirteen years of age as a messenger boy trying to manoeuvre a big black delivery bicycle that felt as heavy as a tank. I'd see him around Merrion Square: a big shock of white hair, his head thrown back, and his hands flailing in all directions as he walked along, muttering aloud and gazing skywards. "What madhouse are they after letting that eejit loose from?" I asked a policeman outside Dáil Éireann. "He's no eejit," the copper replied, "that's Willie Yeats: a great man for scribbling the auld poems".'

Charlie put down the cable he had been trying to untangle. 'I spent months on that delivery bike, bouncing over cobbles and avoiding tram tracks before my boss dispatched me with a massive parcel out to the back of beyond, a house in Rathfarnham called Riversdale. The hills would break your heart on that bike. Anyways I knock and who opens the door only the old fellow with the white hair, so distracted looking that he barely even took in my presence as he bent down to sign the docket until I says to him, "I believe you're a great man for the old poems?" Yeats took a step back and asked who had told me this. I told him it was a copper and that, when you're only my size, you don't argue with coppers. This made him laugh and he looked at me properly and then at the size of my bike and asked if I ever fell off.'

The old man seemed lost in memory, staring out across the bustling factory.

'I told Yeats my boss had told me I'd grow into the saddle and I asked him what was it to write poems, because I'd never met a writer before, although I'd probably already met every other class of blaggard. He asked if I'd read any of his poems and I said, where in the name of Jaysus would I have read them, but that my teacher had taught us the first act of Julius Caesar before I needed to leave school and I could still recite chunks of it. I remember Yeats glancing back into his hallway like there were a million urgent tasks awaiting him there and then he asked if I was thirsty. I said I'd murder a glass of water, but it was a poor choice of words because he shook his head and said we'd already had too much murder in Ireland. But if I could recite the opening of Julius Caesar he'd find me lemonade and maybe even some of his wife's biscuits.'

'Are you saying Yeats asked you in?' I said to Charlie.

The old man nodded, keeping an experienced weather eye out for any sign of a white-coated chargehand or foreman who might accuse me of slacking. 'Maybe he took a shine to me or felt sorry for me after the long cycle, but either way he stood me up on a chair in his study and listened as I launched into Shakespeare, giving each character a different Dublin accent so that Brutus sounded like a North Wall gurrier while Mark Anthony was a toffee-nosed Rathgar butcher. Yeats laughed, but not at me, he was laughing because he was amused and I suppose he was happy. He was in his early seventies, but for those few moments you'd swear we were two kids mitching from school.'

'And so what was he like?' I asked.

Charlie shrugged and straightened the glasses that seemed too big for the bridge of his nose. 'He was himself. His desk was covered in sheets of paper. I could see they were all drafts of the same poem he couldn't seem to get right. Lines repeated and lines crossed out but always the same title: 'What Then?''

Charlie closed his eyes and spoke softly, his voice different, as if remembering the way in which Yeats once spoke:

All his happier dreams came true —
A small old house, wife, daughter, son,
Grounds where plum and cabbage grew,
Poets and Wits about him drew;
'What then?' sang Plato's ghost, 'What then?'

The old factory hand looked up. 'Isn't it funny? That poor gee-zer had achieved universal acclaim and written so much, but yet he still didn't know if that was enough. Whatever class of struggle he was engaged in, it would never be over; there'd always be one last poem to write or some verse that wouldn't come right. He was someone who would never have to face my fate next month. Poets never retire: I mean, they don't even have a steady job, do they? Inanyway when he went off to fetch lemonade and came back in and saw me looking at all those spidery handwritten drafts of his poem, his manner changed.

He read a few lines aloud, uncertainly, and says to me: "What do you think of that?"'

'He asked you what you thought?' I said.

Charlie nodded, reaching for his flask and pouring some lukewarm tea into a chipped mug, which he handed to me. 'He did and he didn't. He might have addressed the question to me but even at thirteen I knew that he was really questioning himself, not just about what he thought of this particular poem but about all the poems he'd written in rooms like that. I was so unimportant – a scruffy little messenger boy – that maybe he could think aloud by talking to me, knowing we'd never meet again. But I think I actually really saw him in that moment of uncertainty … not as some public figure but just an old geezer who was still not convinced that he had done enough. I'm not far off his age now and I think back to who he was – a famous man with reams of unfinished poems and letters littering his desk and I often ask myself, why did he bother to invite in a messenger boy? Do you know why?'

Charlie studied me from behind those round glasses, with one corner of the frame held in place with Sellotape.

'No. I don't know,' I replied.

'Me neither, but I'm getting close to knowing. I think that, just for once, he enjoyed not being treated as a genius. I hadn't come to him in pursuit of enlightenment or endorsements. All I wanted was a glass of water and I was more thrilled that he gave me lemonade than if he'd given me his collected works. Because back then I just saw some old lad who happened to write poems. He recited those opening lines again and, despite his fame, I sensed his insecurity; he didn't know if the lines were enough to justify his life. I was a slum kid, yet he looked at me like I was his judge and jury, like the ghosts of his uncles and aunts had sent me out on that bicycle as a test, because if his poem didn't move me then maybe all he'd done was in vain.'

'I write poems,' I said, 'but I never had the courage to show them to anyone.'

'Why not?'

'I don't know if they're good enough. I don't want folk making a laugh of me.'

'That's the risk,' Charlie said, picking up a strand of wire to start untangling it. 'I once stood in a dance hall in Camden Street trying to find the courage to ask a beautiful girl up to dance, convinced that she'd say no in front of everyone. It turned out that she'd been watching me all evening. Forty-eight years we were together and I still think she's watching over me at times, though more often I feel what I think Yeats felt on the afternoon when he invited me in.'

'What's that?' I asked.

'It's what all old men feel: loneliness. This factory is a kip, but it has men shouting and laughing. Sometimes they've time to poke their head in here to chat to me and sometimes they don't. Or maybe Jack McCann sends a young lad down to talk because even in here I get lonely. But it's nothing compared to the loneliness of empty rooms at home. Yeats had a wife, a daughter and son. But they were out that afternoon and lone-liness can ambush an old man at any time: the loneliness of knowing how infirmity lies ahead, that you simply have to accept what's to come. What you achieved in the past makes no difference to how you feel now. You start every new day with the same questions bothering you: did I do enough, and at the end of it all what happens then?'

Charlie stared down at the twisted cable. 'I know you can't imagine ever being my age. I couldn't imagine being sixty-five when I cycled back from Rathfarnham, glad to escape in the end, because Yeats was an old man and, for young lads like you, life is about living in the here and now.' He looked up. 'They turf me out on August 3rd but if you want to read me a few lines of one of your poems before then, you'll be only the second poet to ever do so.'

'McCann says you played for Shamrock Rovers,' I said.

He shrugged. 'I made the first team twice and only then because of a flu outbreak among the stronger players. I wasn't good enough for league football but I gave it a shot because there's nothing worse than having regrets.'

'Have you regrets?'

'I wish I'd told my wife more often that I loved her. That's all. Maybe I'll get the chance in the next life; I don't know. I haven't a clue about what comes next. Yeats gave me a gift when I was leaving: a book.'

'His poems?'

Charlie shook his head. 'Are you joking? A cowboy book he'd just finished reading. He said that Zane Grey was his guilty secret. I'm still waiting for a poet to present me with a poem. If you decide to do so you know where to find me.'

'I don't know if my poems are any good,' I said.

'If you're never satisfied with what you've written, then maybe you're on the right path because you sound like the only other poet I met,' Charlie said.

I nodded and walked back towards where McCann was still hammering in nails. He'd need my help to wheel his drum out into the yard. I felt different, more grown up. I had met the man who met Yeats. He took me seriously, like Yeats took him seriously as a child. I didn't know what would come next for Charlie after he left that factory. Nor did I have any clue about what would happen to me in later years. But I felt ready to embrace the future, suddenly aware that, no matter what hand fate dealt me, it would never be enough to quench the doubts and questions in my head. I would always be plagued by a yearning to know more. This unease would remain just as intense if I ever reached the age that Yeats was on the day when he indulged a messenger boy with lemonade: renowned and yet still plagued by uncertainly, still striving to make sense of what then, of what comes next.

Coming Home

His cousin Anto saw him first on his return, just after dawn.
But Shane knew that nothing would prise Anto away from his
post, leaning against the open doorway of the corrugated iron
workman's hut, gazing out at the light drizzle that had halted his
work. Although only in his second year as a Corporation workman, Anto had already acquired the ingrained mannerisms of
the older men among the squad of road maintenance men with
whom he worked. Though Shane thought that 'work' was perhaps too big a word for what Anto was now securely employed
to do for life, which seemed to mainly consist of tentatively
poking at potholes as if they were unexploded landmines and
scurrying back to wherever his hut was parked to drink tea and
play cards at the least drop of rain.

During his first few months working for the Corporation
Anto used to joke about the farce of officially starting work at
this hut at eight o'clock and then lounging around inside it for
an hour until a truck arrived to transport them a few hundred
yards to whatever patch of road they were meant to repair. But
more recently Anto grew defensive and annoyed if anyone in
the family slagged his job. Shane used to tease him more than
most, but at least Anto had a job, unlike Shane who was now
suddenly having to play catch up with his own life.

Anto had never got on with Shane, ever since Shane nut-
megged him twice on the green in front of all his mates when
Shane was thirteen and he was nineteen. Anto once fancied

himself as a footballer, but Shane could now tell that, at twenty-four, Anto was beyond caring. It showed in the flab on his stomach, the fag on his lips, the slouch that came from perpetually leaning on a shovel or a bar counter.

Anto shouted something, but Shane couldn't tell if the remark was directed at him or at one of Anto's workmates filling a kettle for tea at a fire hydrant opened up on the pavement. Shane kept his head down and cut across the huge green where horses were always tethered. The horses shied away, like he was a stranger, though he – of all the lads who lived on the Crescent – had always possessed a gift with animals.

Maybe at one time horses hadn't grazed on this sodden green, being ridden by boys in and out of Finglas to be bought and sold at the Smithfield horse fair. But Shane's earliest memories were of waking to the noise of whinnying, and knowing that, at any time of night, he could pad across his bedroom lino to stare from the window at these patient animals standing like sentinels on the moonlit grass.

The horses were what he especially missed during the last three years of living in digs with the Allen family in England. Of course he had also missed his family and the pals he grew up with, but everybody who signed schoolboy forms at the football club missed their family and friends. His affinity with these horses was different and he had never been able to talk about them – not even to other Irish boys training at the club – until Ray O'Farrell was signed. Shane had known instinctively that the British lads could not understand and would have simply cracked jokes about him coming from the Wild West.

But during his early months away he had often taken a bus into Manchester city centre, in the free hours that the club allowed lads like him to themselves, in between training and their half-hearted attempts to make them study. Not to buy anything in the shops – this wasn't likely on the £15 a week pocket money that the club supplied – but just on the off-chance of seeing a mounted policeman on horseback. Sometimes he would follow the horse through the crowds until the policeman noticed and got suspicious. Homesickness was a symptom the club understood. They even had pep talks about it from the Under 17s coach, a former Scottish international who had broken his leg playing for the reserves while trying to make yet another comeback from a series of cartilage operations. But wanting to wrap your arms around a horse's neck – especially a police horse – would have been seen as taking homesickness a step too far. Not that he had even been likely to approach a policeman on horseback during his first year in Manchester when shop-owners were still trying to reopen their city centre businesses after an IRA bomb attack destroyed the Arndale Shopping Centre. The youth coach had even advised him to be cautious about betraying his accent when using public transport.

Shane put his bag down on the wet grass now and tried to approach an old black horse, which he recognised, tethered to a rope. The horse shied away at first, then let Shane run his fingers through its tangled mane. But Shane couldn't be sure if this was because the horse still remembered him or if it was just so broken down in health as to be beyond caring who touched him.

The green sloped slightly towards the church and then fell away down a steep incline. On a thousand occasions he had chased a football down that slope, deftly bringing it under control with a flick or a back heel to prevent the ball bouncing into the path of oncoming traffic. He had always been the youngest player on any team back then, dismissively ordered to fetch the ball when it went out of play, but he had still always been the first to be picked. By the age of nine he was sick of playing with kids his own size. He sought out games with lads three or four or five years older, never caring about how big they were because the larger they came the easier they were to nutmeg. Such older lads used to shy away from kicking him at first, but ten minutes into any game, they would either forget about his age or become fixated by it, kicking out angrily.

These disorganised games, played from dawn to dusk on this waterlogged green, had prepared him for any rough treatment he later received when togging out for Tolka Rovers, and at least in league games the presence of a referee made it less likely that he would be seriously injured. By the age of eleven, he was aware of arguments within the club about what age group he should play for. The Under 12s would win the league that year without him. The Under 14s desperately needed a striker. But Eddie, the Under 12s manager, was never going to give way. Shane became his star and Eddie became his protector. Shane trusted him with implicit devotion, even though Eddie was never slow to give Shane as much of a bollocking as any other player who stepped out of line.

All the scouts came out to watch Eddie's team that year when the Under 12s went unbeaten in the league and in two cups: scouts from Arsenal, Liverpool, Spurs and Celtic, and from clubs like Brighton and Tranmere, whom you would not even suspect of having scouts in Ireland. 'You can look but you cannot touch,' Eddie would mutter to them, and they certainly did look. Not just at Shane, but at Derek Brown in midfield who had been convinced he was about to get a trial when a scout from Wolverhampton Wanderers turned up, with Eddie needing to break the news that the man had come to check out a scut of a lad called Robbie Keane, playing against them for Crumlin United.

Eddie made sure that no scout could tap up Shane on the football pitch or outside the rusty shipping container that served as their makeshift dressing room. But Eddie was not around in the evenings. The polite knocks on the front door always came at the same time – two minutes past eight approximately. Perhaps the clubs presumed that all mothers watched Coronation Street and there were strict rules about scouts making a poor impression by interrupting their favourite soap opera. After having spent the past three years at the club, nothing would surprise him about the tricks and strategies that scouts engaged in.

These scouts always arrived quietly; friendly middle-aged men with weatherworn faces who wanted nothing stronger than a cup of tea and a quiet word. Back then Shane hadn't wanted them to be quiet. He had longed to open his bedroom window and shout out to the whole of the Crescent that a representative from some Premiership team was sitting in his kitchen. Always there were certain parts of the conversations that he was allowed sit in on, but for other parts he was sent upstairs. Initially his age was the big stumbling block; he was too young to sign for anyone until his fifteenth birthday. But Shane had felt that everything would change once he celebrated that birthday, if only his parents would stop listening to Eddie's cautious warnings and simply give him his chance to go.

Although there were other days back then when he had not always been sure if he wanted to go. Eddie had spent two years as a teenager on the books of Liverpool back in the 1970s – though Eddie didn't talk much about his time there. It had been hard for Shane to imagine how this man, who now sold cylinders of gas for Superser heaters door-to-door from an open-backed truck, was once photographed by the *Evening Herald* about to board an aeroplane, with the back-page headline hailing him as the future of Irish football. Shane had known from the start that his da didn't want him to go, but he had also known that his da would not stand in the way of letting him make his own decision.

Throughout his life, until he left home at fifteen, Shane's da had been like a shadow on the touchline at every match, never interfering or shouting advice but being a quiet supportive presence: not allowing him to get too excited about scoring a hat-trick, or too downhearted on the rare occasion when he played poorly.

His ma had been the stumbling block back then. The closer his fifteenth birthday came, the more the pressure had got to her. Was she standing in his way and holding him back because he was her first born? But why did the clubs want him to leave home so young, she would ask; why couldn't he finish his education and have something to fall back on? Once or twice when Da was at work and the younger kids, Marie and Sam, were playing upstairs, his ma would look at him and start crying and he would cry too, both of them at the kitchen table overwhelmed by the enormity of this decision that would irrevocably alter their lives.

But then the most famous club of all had come knocking, like a summons that nobody could ignore. His dream had never been to play for this club – because he never dared to believe that he was good enough – but just to simply travel to see a match in their ground one day. His bedroom wall was covered in posters of that team. When their scout arrived, Shane had sat in the kitchen, knowing that this was the moment, and when he looked across at his mother he saw in her eyes that she knew it too. Her resistance was broken by the sheer glamour of the name. When Eddie called in later that evening, not even his arguments about the wisdom of Shane possibly starting out at a smaller club – where he might have more chance of making a break-through – had worked. Instead Shane had grown furious with him, feeling that he was now only one step away from paradise and this gas cylinder salesman was trying to keep him a little boy forever. 'Just because you were a total failure over there doesn't mean that I'll be one too,' he had shouted at the man, regretting his words even as he spoke them because there was no way to take them back. Eddie had left the house soon afterwards, standing with Shane's father for a moment in the front garden to light up a cigarette, neither man speaking as if they both implicitly understood that there was nothing more to be said. Shane always planned to make it up to Eddie, by emphasising in press interviews just how much Eddie had done to help his career. However, the opportunity for those press interviews never came.

Turning away now, after stroking the horse, Shane knew that he should not have boarded that cheap coach by himself last night to get the boat back to Ireland. At the very least he should have told his family that he was coming home, but that would have made this homecoming worse. They would have insisted that he fly home and would have been waiting for him at the airport when his plane touched down, nobody knowing what to say. He remembered his ma once describing how her older sister entered a convent in the 1950s to become a nun, but arrived home with her tail between her legs, after a mere eighteen months. It took weeks before his grandmother would even address her and then all she finally said was, 'You would have brought far less shame on this family if you'd simply had the decency to come home from that convent in a wooden box.'

Nobody became nuns or priests anymore, and no one in his family would ever say such spiteful words against him, but Shane knew that he had failed himself and failed them too. This failure would seep out in whispers, with his kid brother Sam being taunted about it at school. If Shane ever bothered to play football on this green again, vicious tackles would rain in from lads who only a year ago had been in awe of him when he came home with Ray O'Farrell, still a success story to be reckoned with.

He remembered that weekend just before his seventeenth birthday: Ray and himself sitting on the garden wall like kings with girls gathered around and Sam shyly sitting between them, basking in his big brother's fame. Ray wasn't somebody he would have palled around with in Ireland. They might probably never have met, except as rival fans at Shelbourne and Cork City matches. Ray was built like a hardman and acted like one too, whereas Shane was slight and swift and always being ordered to stay behind in the gym and work on the weights to bulk out. But because they were both Irish, the club had paired them off when Ray arrived from Cork, switching their digs so that they shared a room in Mrs Allen's house where they could sink or swim together.

No one in England knew the difference between Cork and Dublin anyway. Ray and he had needed to endure the same jibes and sly digs. Yet generally people liked the fact that they were Irish. It made them seem novel, as if expected to be the life and soul of every party, to sing and tell jokes at the drop of a hat. And Ray could do all that. Not sing pop songs, but ancient come-all-ye songs from Cork, the like of which nobody in the club had ever heard of, about The Boys of Fairhill or a lethal cider nicknamed Johnny Jump Up. Even the jaundiced driver on the team bus would stop talking to listen to Ray sing:

> *For rambling, for roving, for football or courting*
> *For drinking black porter as fast as you'd fill*
> *In all your days roving you'd find none so jovial*
> *As the Muskerry sportsman, the bould Thady Quill.*

In fact even the senior pros tolerated Ray, especially the continental ones who loved it when he stood on the side-line of the training ground to give a loud running commentary on some seven aside game, mispronouncing all their names in a ludicrous posh mock-BBC accent, before one of the coaching staff chased him away. Nobody else would dare to do it, but nobody else could have got away with it. It was the Cork charm, laid on in thick doses whenever necessary. Ray could have roguishly talked his way out of any situation, except the sliding tackle that came, two minutes into injury time, during a meaningless match in a deserted stadium in France nine months ago.

That pre-season tour was just a perk to kick-start their final season together as a youth side, before apprentice contracts were offered to a chosen few at the year's end. The tour consisted of a succession of easy games against soft French kids who might as well have been playing in snowshoes for all the talent they possessed. When Ray got the ball that afternoon he didn't even look around. The team were seven goals up. God knows why the referee bothered to play injury time. Ray should have laid the ball off first time but delayed too long, drawing out the moment for effect like he sometimes stretched out the punch line of a comic song. He never even saw the tackle come from behind; not that it was really a tackle, though, more of an assault.

There had been no television cameras or photographers, but Shane didn't need reminders. Every night for the following month he had relived the images slowly in his head, the studs thudding in against Ray's knee bone, the leg contorting out of shape and then that snap – a sound like no other – before the blood came and the bone protruded. Ray had started screaming but Shane didn't really hear him. It was as if that snap had silenced everything else and kept reverberating inside his skull. The fight that followed became a free-for-all, with even the coaches involved. The kid who crippled Ray was a puny nobody who had just been told by his club that he was being let go. His French teammates had defended him with the mob mentality of all footballers, although Shane could see that they were disgusted with him too. Then suddenly the pitch was cleared, the players bustled back onto the bus and told their clothes would be brought by car to the hotel, while Ray still lay screaming on the grass, being attended to by anxious medics.

The doctors had needed to operate twice. 'Shag it,' Ray joked when Shane later visited him in hospital. 'I went to France hoping for a quick screw, I didn't expect to come back with three of them permanently in my leg.'

Nobody could say that the club didn't do enough for Ray. He had the best of doctors and physiotherapists and then they flew him back to Cork first class. Any player can break their leg at any time, but Shane had always imagined it happening at Anfield or Highbury, with the crowd rising to salute your courage in a blaze of cameras and lights. Yet a career-ending tackle could come at any moment, even during a meaningless training session of a wet Tuesday afternoon. It had affected all the youth players so much in the first few weeks that the coach kept screaming at them, 'Are you men or Nancy-boys?' Nancy-boys was his favourite term of homophobic abuse, making him seem like a Brylcreemed fossil from another era. He had obviously been proving that he was no 'Nancy-boy' when he broke his own leg, subsequently losing his house and his model wife in a fog of alcohol, before the club gave him a lifeline back into coaching the minnows in their food chain. Gradually the other lads forgot their fear. But they weren't going back to digs with an empty bed across the room and to Mrs Allen who broke down in tears on the night when Ray left for Cork, summoning Shane down to the front parlour, which she and her husband ordinarily kept private, so that he wouldn't be alone.

'He was the loveliest lad,' she said, 'but I knew he was wasting his time. I've almost stopped taking in your type.'

'What type?' Shane had asked.

Mrs Allen looked at him and stopped speaking, as if realising what she had just said.

'You Irish boys,' her husband replied quietly for her. 'I know the club has a long history of Irish pros playing for it, but they've always been seasoned pros who cut their teeth elsewhere before being bought in. I've seen dozens of young Irish lads like you come up and down the stairs here or hang around at the club, but it has been forty years since any Irish lad made it all the way from being an apprentice to playing for the first team. Sure, with all the money involved now, who is going to take a chance on you at this club anyway, unless you are God almighty? The stakes are too high. If any gap appears in the first team they just go across to Europe with a cheque book and buy experience.'

Shane remembered Mr Allen's words again as he patted the old horse one last time and stepped off the sodden green now to cross the road and reach the first terrace of houses on the Crescent. Nobody was up and about yet, but a kid in his pyjamas appeared in the window of McCormack's house to stare down at him. It must be Joey's kid brother who had only been a baby when Shane left. From the age of four Shane used to call for Joey McCormack so they could walk to school together. Throughout childhood they were inseparable, kicking football for hours against the wall in their gardens. Every time that Shane had come home during his first year with the club, Joey would run over to his house, wanting to hear about the dressing rooms, the grounds and training schedules. But more recently Joey had become distant, often looking slightly puzzled as to why Shane kept calling in to see him on visits home. At first Shane put this down to jealousy, but now he realised that it was simple indifference. Life had moved on: Joey had new friends, new interests, a new life. All his old pals were the same. Eddie's famous team had broken up, the better ones playing for Cherry Orchard and Home Farm. Eddie had started from scratch again and was now coaching a bunch of snot-nosed eight-year-olds, giving them his heart and soul.

With Eddie, Shane had always known where he stood. But in England you learned to mull over every remark. Anything of importance was always said out of earshot, behind your back. During these past months, when senior management started coming to look at him again, it felt utterly different from being thirteen years old and under Eddie's wing. Now faces from higher up in the club's hierarchy would appear unannounced on the touchline to watch the second half of youth games. Every lad on the youth team knew that this was for real – management weren't making a selection, they were plotting a cull. There was nowhere to hide from those merciless, calculating eyes. The mood among the lads was different now: everyone watching everyone else, aware that not even a handful would survive the cut.

Before their pre-season trip to France, Shane never doubted that he would be offered a contract. Maybe one or two other youth players had more skill but they were headless chickens, not so much without discipline as without brains. Over the past three years he had overcome homesickness, which was so bad during his first months away that, on several nights, he had packed his bags to catch a cheap coach back to Ireland, sitting shaking on his bed, alone in that small bedroom but somehow finding the inner courage not to give in. He had bulked up with enough weight and shown enough strength of character and leadership to be awarded the captain's armband. But now, when it really mattered, he found himself chickening out of challenges. Not so blatantly that any ordinary spectator might notice, but holding back just enough for those experienced ruthless eyes on the touchline to notice and for other players to sense his fear and exploit it.

Nobody ever questioned his courage before. He had needed to get twelve stitches above his eye and had broken three ribs in his first year. But every night he woke in a sweat, still hearing the snap of bone and the sickening silence before Ray's scream. If no Irish player had made it in the club in forty years, why the hell did their scouts keep calling to parents with their promises? He could be sitting his Leaving Certificate exams in Dublin now, still walking to school with Joey, eyeing up the girls and maybe playing for the B-side of a League of Ireland club, with his da quietly watching each match from the empty stand.

Instead at this stage he was out of sight and out of mind. On one occasion last year he had been named in the panel for an Irish Under 18 team. His mother had excitedly phoned to say that a neighbour had just seen it on the teletext. The FAI put in a call to the club, but then some kid whom he'd never heard of, playing on the books of lowly Huddersfield Town, had recovered from injury and regained his place in the squad. Huddersfield Town? That Irish team had gone on to win the Under 18 European Championship: the final shown live on Irish television. They came home as heroes, like Jack Charlton's teams, a big crowd at the airport, an open-topped bus parade and everything. Half of them were only signed to Mickey Mouse teams, down in the lower divisions or back in Ireland. For some reason his ma had sent him the press cuttings about their homecoming. Da would have known never to do that.

This morning was his homecoming parade. He knew that he would never go back to that stadium, even as a spectator. It was more a meat factory than a football club; a mincing machine for dreams. For a few illusory years you were officially a player, with your own swipe card and all. You walked along the plush carpets, ate the best of food in the canteen, had doctors attend to your every ailment and bruise and yet, in reality, you were nobody. Just another face in the corridor down to the dressing rooms, a face whose absence would go unnoticed when you got the call to visit the manager's office. Shane had seen it too often already; lads of seventeen and eighteen sitting alone in the empty stand, crying their eyes out. The way that people passing by averted their eyes until a groundsman was sent up through the deserted rows of seats to quietly tell them it was time to move because some starry-eyed fourteen-year-old was due to get shown around the stadium with his parents.

During the last four games of the season Shane had bottled it totally. It felt as if his body was filled with lead. He would wear himself out during the opening ten minutes, so frantic to make up for lost time that he didn't properly pace himself. Early in the second half of each match he was substituted, sitting apart from the others on the bench, noticing how the coach stopped offering him encouragement or advice. The other lads on the bench said nothing to him either; they knew that, if Shane dropped out of the reckoning, there might be an unexpected chance of a contract for another one of them.

Shane wasn't just coming home this morning, he was running away. He told himself that at least he was leaving on his own terms, saving himself from the indignity of being called into the manager's office. Almost the entire youth team would endure this fate over the coming days, with only two at most being retained for another season. All his ex-teammates still wanted to believe that it was going to be them; they were terrified of the emptiness facing them once they walked out of that office, with their swipe cards cancelled, their names already discreetly wiped from the system.

Shane didn't know if he ever would bother playing football again. Because even if one day he got signed by Shelbourne in the League of Ireland — where Eddie had suggested years ago that he learn his trade — he would never be known as the kid who was good enough to play for Shelbourne. He would always be the kid who came home from England, the kid who was only good enough to play for Shelbourne, the boy with the golden touch and the glistening future already behind him.

Shane stopped at the gate to his family's house. There seemed to be nobody up yet or at least no light on in the hall. His da's old Nissan Sunny was parked in the narrow driveway he had built in the front garden. A burst football lay there that Sam must have been kicking around. A wooden gate blocked off the side passageway, but Shane knew that if you reached your hand over it you could open the bolt on the far side.

The dog came down by the side passageway to greet him, not bounding but moving slowly, his leg stiffened by arthritis. At least he didn't bark as if at an intruder. Shane dropped his bag and knelt to put his arms around the animal. The old dog panted after the effort of just taking those few steps, but his eyes retained the same familiar look as always, as if mildly perplexed by life.

Once Shane stood up after embracing the dog he knew that he would have to face them all: Da, Ma, Sam and Marie. To face the cramped kitchen that seemed to get smaller with every visit home; the small bedroom that he would now share with a younger brother who didn't really know him, after three years away. He patted the dog one last time and rose. There was a light on in the kitchen. He knew that his da would be up before any of the family, starting the breakfast, ready to call up the stairs. His da turned as Shane pushed open the kitchen door. He had a fish-slice in his hand, which he was using to fry rashers. He eyed his son's travel bag.

'It's yourself,' was all he said. 'Would you go one rasher or two?'

Only twice in his life had Shane ever seen his da lose his temper. That unflappable quality, the way you never quite knew what he was thinking, used to annoy Shane. Even when Shane signed youth forms for the club his da had refused to get over excited. But now Shane was thankful for the lack of questioning, for the way in which his da was buying him time to explain his presence in his own way.

'I wouldn't say no to a rasher,' Shane replied, 'and a sausage if it's going. I'm starving.'

Shane sat down at the table. Not even the mugs had changed in three years. He had missed this house so much. Yet just now it didn't seem like his home. How would he ever fit back in here? His father continued cooking, making as little noise as possible.

'I got sent home,' Shane explained. 'The club don't think I have the bottle. They're not going to offer me a contract.'

'They should have phoned,' his da said. 'It shouldn't be you having to tell us like this.'

'It's not official till Friday. I just didn't want to wait around, knowing that everybody would be looking at me with pity. It's hard enough failing without the whole world knowing that you failed.'

'Failed?' Shane saw that his da's hand was shaking as he put the rasher and some black pudding on a plate. The man turned. His eyes were clear and blue, staring directly at him. 'You're eighteen years old, son, so stop talking bollix. Is Eddie a failure, the way folk around here respect him? Am I a failure, the way I have raised the lot of you by working shifts up in Unidare? How could you be a failure, son? You haven't even started living your life yet.'

Supermarket Flowers

The memorial shrine began on the evening after the accident with just a single bouquet of yellow daffodils purchased from a local supermarket. They looked so inadequate and pathetic, as a tribute to the seven-year-old girl who had been knocked down while waiting at the bus stop beside the old stone wall of my front garden, that I was tempted to cut a dozen blossoms from my flower beds to bulk out this floral display. But adding my own flowers to the bouquet sellotaped to the buckled bus stop would have felt wrong and intrusive. That's the word I'm seeking. On that evening I felt trapped inside my own home, fearful that I might be trespassing on someone else's grief by even just walking down my driveway to the footpath where the accident had occurred during chaotic lunchtime traffic.

Thankfully at the time of the crash my two young granddaughters – whom I mind for three days every week – were in the conservatory, enjoying the hour of television that I try and ration them to. They didn't hear the collision that killed the child. Only the beeping of motorists caught in a sudden tailback lured them away from the television. But they couldn't properly grasp what was happening, because I only let them briefly peer out the front window before they drifted back to watching *Peppa Pig*. Once certain that my granddaughters were settled at the television I ran out to see what I could do, which in truth was nothing beyond trying to offer any comfort possible. One of the onlookers standing around for no reason except curiosity told me how a French tourist had accelerated too fast, trying to beat the traffic lights when exiting the shopping centre car park opposite my house. She lost control of her hired car while steering with one hand and checking directions on her mobile phone with the other.

The car struck the girl while miraculously leaving her mother unharmed, despite ploughing so hard into my wall that a section of the seventy-year-old brickwork collapsed. The distraught mother was in such shock that she barely seemed aware of my presence or of the voyeuristic bystanders who seemed disinclined to grant her any privacy. I ran back inside to fetch a blanket but it wasn't my place to cover the face of her dead child, so I placed it on the footpath beside the mother to use if she wished. The police arrived within moments, with the ambulance not far behind. I kept checking my front door to ensure that my granddaughters didn't innocently wander out to be confronted by the child's corpse.

The French tourist sat in her car, the driver's door opened. Something about her bewildered, exhausted look reminded me of my own daughter, Audrey, who is always running late, agitatedly trying to multitask while playing catch up with her busy life. When the police needed to question the French woman, I offered them the use of my front room. Whatever she had done – and she was not shirking responsibility – she also deserved privacy away from those prying eyes. I would have asked the young mother in, but I knew that she would not be separated from her daughter whom she kept trying to cradle. Eventually the child's body was stretchered onto the ambulance, but one policeman remained behind – cordoning off my stretch of pavement for forensic examination.

Audrey was curious about my collapsed wall and the policeman when she collected her girls at half-five, but she was so fussed that she had no time to ask, upset because they were already late for the dance class that I considered them far too young to attend. I was relieved that they had little real idea of what had occurred. 'Granny Minder' is what Amy, the oldest by three minutes, calls me – unaware that this takes my unpaid role for granted. I doubt if she calls her other grandmother 'Granny No-Minder'. My son-in-law's mother has always been too busy or posh or shrewd to have time to mind her grandchildren, spoiling them instead with treats on their brief fortnightly visits to her. I tell my friends that it's easier for Audrey to drop off the girls at my house rather than cross the city to reach their other gran. The real reason is because so many sparks fly between her and Audrey, who both possess such equally abrasive temperaments, that John used to joke about how our son-in-law had in essence married his own mother.

I'm more compliant; or maybe with John gone, Audrey feels I need an activity to keep my grief at bay. If so, nothing is more all-consuming than two pre-school children whose constant need for attention keeps me focused on the present. They exhaust me and I miss my morning ritual of finishing the crossword in under forty minutes while half-listening to the radio. But they add a great sense of purpose to my Mondays, Wednesdays and Fridays. What I miss most are my long afternoons spent gardening. I think the twins would enjoy digging and planting, but Audrey is obsessive about keeping them clean for the numerous classes they attend, so I never dare to let them help me tend to what John and I jokingly used to call 'Old Mrs Clarke's garden'.

This reference was our affectionate homage to the elderly lady who sold us the house forty years ago, much to her auctioneer's consternation after more affluent couples placed higher bids. But Mrs Clarke was impressed by how, when admiring her

garden, I complimented her on her white jasmine, before bend-
ing in my mini-shirt to sniff the plant and apologetically correct
myself, realising that it was potato vine which looks like jasmine
but lacks any fragrance. Convinced that the house was beyond
our reach, I had chatted away happily about the glorious heather
in her rockery, expressing delight that she was blessed with such
rich acidic soil in which heather thrives. The richer couples so
annoyed her by ignoring the garden and expressing disappointment at the lack of central heating, that Mrs Clarke stunned
everyone by accepting our bid, announcing that she wanted the
stewardship of her garden to pass into safe hands.

While our name for the garden was our private joke, it
reflected how I felt a certain sense of custodianship – not towards
the house which, when money allowed, we slowly gutted and
modernised – but towards the front and back gardens that she
loved and her front wall against which she had grown an array of
flowering shrubs, chosen so that some plant would always be in
bloom to reflect her love of contrasting seasonal colours.

I was wise not to cut any flowers on the night after the
crash: they would soon have been barely visible on the buckled
bus stop the French driver had ploughed into. A predominance
of yellow flowers accumulated in the following days, with the
footpath outside my house transformed into a site of pilgrimage
for grieving strangers. Maybe this sounds far-fetched but they
looked like pilgrims when they appeared, often in silent clusters.
Each visitor sellotaped more yellow flowers to the bus stop as
tokens of loss and remembrance. From my front window, the bus
stop resembled those brightly decorated trees that stand beside
rural holy wells, to which visitors traditionally attach rags when
making a wish.

On the Monday after the accident, my granddaughters
knew that a girl had died outside my house; their friends having

seen footage on the news over the weekend. They were fas-
cinated by the array of flowers, but oddly detached from the
event, not grasping how such a tragedy might occur to them.
The police tape was gone and it was a bus stop again, though
commuters were quiet and respectful at the sight of the flowers,
knowing that they were standing in what, for now, was still the
site of a public tragedy. That's what my footpath had become,
though in truth nobody owns a footpath. But I had always felt
responsible for the pavement directly outside my house. Until
they erected a bus stop there I had always cut the grass verge that
bordered the road, just like old Mrs Clarke had done, seeing it as
an extension of my lawn. When they built the shopping centre I
even placed a row of stones there, planting flowers around them
to stop motorists destroying the grass by parking on it. Not that
I minded strangers parking outside my house, but I felt protective of the grass verge, as if it was another duty of care passed
on by Mrs Clarke. Secretly I was relieved when the verge was
tarmacked to make room for the bus stop; it meant that my duty
of custodianship had ended.

But in the fortnight after the crash this sense of owner-
ship seemed to pass to the grieving mother, who returned every
evening to add more yellow flowers to the withered bouquets
still sellotaped to the bus stop. She never stood directly in front
of the rubble from my wall, but hovered close by for hours,
maintaining a vigil. One night I went out – not that it was my
business but I felt sorry for her grieving on her own.

'Would you like to come in?' I asked. 'I can make tea. You
really shouldn't be alone.'

'I'm not short of friends,' she replied. 'They never stop calling, talking nonstop. This is the only place I can be alone with
her.' Then she looked at me accusingly. 'You took the French
woman into your house.'

'Only to let the police take a statement.' I sounded defensive, as if caught taking sides. 'I had brought you out a blanket ... just in case ...'

'I remember,' she said. 'I don't know how we'll get through this. Tea would be nice, but I won't sit in the same room that French bitch sat in.'

We did sit in the front room. I thought that perhaps she wanted to talk, but she just stared out at the flowers on the bus stop, so self-absorbed in her grief that she barely seemed aware of me. Or maybe she just didn't know what appropriate words to say, like the people who only attend Mass once a year and say 'Thanks' instead of 'Amen' when receiving Communion. Maybe she needed to work out her grief for herself and her sole method of expression seemed to be these gaudy bouquets. When she finally rose, she thanked me for the tea but I knew I would never go out to her again. Her pain was private and there was nothing I could do.

By the end of the month the original flowers were so withered that the bus stop was a bizarre spectacle of fresh and faded blooms. When she arrived one night with a scissors and a large plastic sack I felt such a surge of sympathy that – if it had not felt intrusive – I might have gone out again to comfort her as she cut through twists of Sellotape and dumped every flower into her sack, leaving the bus stop bare at last. I felt her distress and empathised, while glad that she found the courage to move on. I also felt a guilty relief that the tawdry display was gone; it meant I would no longer be subjected to Audrey's thrice weekly harangues about the unfairness of her girls being confronted by reminders of that child's death.

My relief lasted half an hour before the mother returned with an identical batch of supermarket bouquets to sellotape onto the damaged bus stop. Her fresh start seemed to mean that only fresh flowers were to be displayed from now on. But because grief needs a focus and makes you do irrational things to survive, I tried not to blame her when she returned every second night to replace her bouquets – whether withered or not – with fresh flowers, tending to the bus stop with the same care as I tend to John's grave on my monthly visits to the cemetery. But a bus stop is a public space and not a grave. I was also perturbed by a new development. She purchased plastic candles that flickered on and off all night and arranged them on the parts of my wall still standing, as if the bus stop was no longer sufficient and she needed to colonise the stonework too.

I resented this sense of my space being violated, while trying not to condemn her. As I say, grief makes you do odd things. My mother would have called it attention seeking, however life had made my mother hard. I felt pity for this young mother, grieving alone. But I was also tired of listening to Audrey's complaints about why anyone should expect to be allowed to litter a public space with flowers. I was beginning to agree with Audrey because, in the end, a bus stop was not anyone's private shrine, no matter how deep their grief: it was where commuters gathered to crowd onto buses and schoolgirls gossiped on their way to class. Audrey kept complaining about the twins being perturbed by these constant reminders of tragedy. I knew that if Audrey wasn't complaining about this, she would complain about something else, because ever since she was a child Audrey had used litanies of complaints as the only way in which she seemed able to express love. But my heart told me that I wanted to take back my wall, my footpath and my privacy.

This was not to diminish the anguish the mother was experiencing. I knew the anatomy of grief. I nursed my husband through cancer until I could do no more for John at home. I held his hand in the hospice when he was not only in pain but petrified of death. I let John's nails dig into my palm with what last ounce of strength he could summon and, when the pressure of his fingers eased, something also died inside me. I cried in that hospice, with Audrey trying to comfort me while unable to stop crying herself. When I gained enough strength to try and comfort her in turn, I had sensed her clam up, retreating into herself as always in times of stress. My granddaughters were not there, because what good would it do them to witness death? You must prepare them for life but shield them also. Being too starkly aware of death can cloud a child's consciousness in ways they are not able to articulate, casting a shadow over the edge of their dreams.

That is why the twins never saw me cry two years ago at their grandfather's funeral, even though I had known they were too young back then to understand or remember what was happening. I made it my business to somehow find the strength to stand in the church and accept condolences from friends and neighbours, from workmates of John's in the insurance company and from women whom I had not seen in the forty years since I was officially forced to resign from the civil service on the day after I got married. I held my emotions in check for John's sake and Audrey's sake and the twins' sake, no matter how young they were, and when I cried – and, by God, how I cried – nobody was forced to witness it, because I made sure this front door was shut and I was alone with my grief.

My grief was private and yet my grief was everywhere. It spilled out of drawers where John's socks remained neatly folded. It ambushed me in the closet where his golf clubs were stored beside the hoover. It waited for me on the bend of the stairs where John always lightly brushed my hair whenever we passed on that spot – an unconscious habit left over from our courting days. In the plastic bags of his clothes that I forced myself to donate to charity shops on streets that I still avoid, in case I see anything belonging to him displayed in the window. In love letters that I kept and other love letters that I burnt, knowing that John would never want Audrey to read them. In the most ordinary of items that would seem precious to nobody else because I was the only one who understood their significance. The receipt John kept from a hotel where we spent what was regarded as an illicit weekend because we were not yet married. The bill from a restaurant where we could not afford to eat, but where we went anyway because it marked the first anniversary of the night we met and – even though we starved for days afterwards – that meal was a private declaration of our love. I came to understand the full weight of grief, because I nearly went crazy under that weight, here in the privacy of my house.

Privacy is not a dirty word. John and I lived out our joy and pain in private. Again I don't diminish that young mother's grief. But it was no greater than my mother's unspoken anguish after losing a six-year-old son to TB. Or the grief of my aunt who frantically ran to a frozen local quarry when she heard that her son was playing there with other boys, and arrived too late to do anything except watch his body being brought to the surface after the ice cracked. To lose a child is to watch the future die. Maybe this trumps my grief after John's death. But her grief was no greater than that endured by my mother and my aunt and neither turned their grief into an attention-seeking pantomime of public flowers. This sounds harsh and I wasn't trying to be cruel, but you can only sympathise with anyone for so long, because in the end you must move on with your own life.

This is what I was doing when I asked old Mr Andrews to repair my wall. He had retired as a handyman but still did jobs for his old neighbours who feel more like friends. I could have called out assessors from my insurance company and claimed for the cost of the repairs on my household policy. But I had never made a claim in forty years and I just wanted the job done. The wall was there when old Mrs Clarke moved in as a newly-wed and it was no one else's business when I decided that the time was right to restore it back to its original state. Mr Andrews had started work when the young mother called to my door one evening, with a panic-stricken look.

'You're fixing the wall,' she said.

'It needs to be done.'

'But can you wait another fortnight, please?'

'Two months have passed, love, though it probably only feels like yesterday to you,' I said kindly.

'But I need a fortnight,' she pleaded. 'You see it's been hard to raise the money.'

'I'm not asking you or anyone to pay for my wall,' I said. 'Please, put your mind at ease. If I was seeking money it would be from that motorist who skedaddled back to France, though she'll have to come back for any trial. I intend to restore the wall to its original condition.'

'But you can't fix it yet,' she said. 'It takes six weeks to get those oval memorial photographs done and I only sent Kim's photo away last month.'

'Do you mean you've ordered a photo for her grave?' I asked, confused, and she shook her head.

'I had Kim cremated. I couldn't bear to think of her lying in the ground. I scattered her ashes on her favourite playground.'

'Then where do you hope to put the memorial photo?'

'On the wall. When we are fixing it up. I don't want any-thing fancy: just a marble plaque with her name and photo and the date she was born and the date she was murdered.' She saw the shock on my face and lightly touched my arm. 'Don't think that I ever expected you to pay a penny of the cost. I've been waiting to save up enough money before talking to you. I'll pay to repair the entire wall with the plaque on a new stone in the middle. I've a friend, Jerry, who's good with stone. He does gardens, you see.'

'I've been using Mr Andrews for forty years,' I said.

'But Jerry is good and we want the wall done right.'

'It will be done right. By Mr Andrews.'

'Can you trust him to insert Kim's plaque properly?'

I kept my voice calm. 'I've no plans for a plaque on my wall.'

'But I'll pay,' she said. 'Enough for a whole new wall. We don't need to use those old stones: it could be something classier. Jerry has contacts in the trade.'

'I don't want a new wall.' I tried to be reasonable. 'That wall is as old as the house. It was another woman's wall before me and after I die it will become someone else's wall to do whatever they want with. But it isn't your wall.'

She looked away and I thought she was going to cry. If she had, I might possibly have even relented and let her erect her plaque, though I knew that Audrey would have paroxysms of outrage. But when she looked back her eyes were dry and perplexed.

'Then where exactly do you expect me to put Kim's memorial photo?'

'I don't know,' I said. 'If you weren't going to have a grave, perhaps you shouldn't have got one made.'

'Are you telling me how I'm meant to mourn my daughter?' she asked, infuriated.

'I'm telling you nothing of the kind,' I said. 'How could I when it's not my business? But can't you see? None of this is really my business. It must be unimaginable to lose your daughter, but it only happened here by chance. I never asked for a bus stop outside my house. Your daughter could have died at any bus stop anywhere, the way that French woman was driving. It's not your fault that you happened to be standing here and you shouldn't blame yourself. But it has nothing to do with me. I don't want a plaque on my wall and if I'm brutally honest I don't want more flowers on that bus stop because my granddaughters hate being constantly reminded. Lucy has nightmares and Amy has started to wet the bed. I know you're in grief but I need to think of my grandchildren. Maybe's its time you expressed your grief somewhere private. Have you discussed this with your own mother?'

'I don't talk to my mother. We fell out.'

'I'm sorry,' I said.

'And I'm sorry for Lucy and Amy.'

'They're young,' I explained. 'Reminders of death upset them, though I know that wasn't your intention.'

'You don't understand,' she said. 'I mean that I'm sorry they have to grow up with an unfeeling cow for a grandmother.'

She stalked away and I didn't reply: she was hurting and it was better for her to lash out at me than at someone close to her. I hoped that she had people to protect and comfort her. But what I really hoped was that I had brought this whole business to an end. Not that I expected her to remove her flowers, there and then with me watching. But I hoped that maybe, when she had time to reflect, she might return to clear them away or just let the ones presently there wither over the following days so that they would slowly fall asunder in the wind and rain.

The next morning proved me wrong. She must have spent hours driving to all-night garages to buy flowers: the entire bus stop was bedecked in them. My granddaughters arrived and where they had once marvelled at the colourful array, they looked genuinely scared by this wild abundance. Audrey raised her eyes to heaven, flustered and running late as ever.

'For the love of God, Mummy, can't you just go out with a scissors and cut the damn things down before I have to do it myself?'

I said nothing to her about my conversation the previous evening. I said nothing until, after she left, Amy anxiously touched my fingers. I bent down to hear her nervously whisper, 'Granny Minder, why does the dead girl's ghost keep coming back with more flowers?' That made me phone the bus company, complaining that two months had passed without the buckled bus stop being replaced, with passengers finding it impossible to read the timetables on it as they were obscured by flowers. Two days later their maintenance men erected a new pole and, as promised, added a sign stating that it was their property, not to be interfered with.

It made no difference. The following morning I found fresh bouquets of daffodils sellotaped to the new bus stop. There were also flowers on the windscreen of my car. But these came from no supermarket. They had been pulled up, roots and all, from my garden – her way of showing that she knew who I had contacted. I kept my temper. I lodged another complaint with the bus company who sent their maintenance men to remove the flowers. This had become a war of attrition. I thought I knew what to expect next morning, but when Amy clambered from Audrey's car she took one look at the bus stop and climbed back in, in tears. My daughter strode towards to the bus stop, her anger so fierce that commuters backed away. She tore at the Sellotape until every small bouquet lay scattered on the roadway.

'What are you doing?' I shouted from my doorway.

She stopped and held aloft two floral arrangements that had been left at the base of the pole. The sort of flowers you see in hearses: arranged in the shape of letters that spelt out the names, AMY and LUCY.

'Why must I take care of everything myself?' Audrey shouted. 'I only started bringing the twins here to keep you occupied, instead of moping for hours on your knees in that god-awful back garden that was always too big. But I'll take them away if you can't keep them safe.'

She strapped the girls into their booster seats and drove off. Later that morning she sent a long apologetic text, urging me not to mind her when she flew off the handle because of the stress she was under running her business as a life coach, saying that she appreciated everything I did for the girls. However I wasn't angry with Audrey, although I knew that something in our relationship was irrevocably altered. I was angry with this stranger who insisted on publicly parading her grief and inflicting it on my family.

I sat up awake all that night in the straight-backed chair at the unlit window of my front room, a sharp scissors in my hands. But the young mother did not come back. Next day I slept fitfully in an armchair, waking to survey my front garden, my half-finished wall, my bus stop. Audrey sent two texts, alarmed that I hadn't replied to her and worried that she might not be able to dump her girls here again. Ordinarily after our rows she arrived with flowers, but she would know that flowers were the last thing I wanted to see. I ignored her texts because I had a rendezvous to keep and business to sort out once and for all before I let her twins back under my roof.

I sat up again on the second night, this time at my bedroom window, with a sharp kitchen knife that would cut through however many layers of Sellotape she tried to use, because I knew the young mother would be unable to stay away. Her grief needed a target and that target was me. But I refused to be a target or a compliant doormat anymore, shaping my life around anyone's needs – be they my daughter or this stranger. I was beyond emotional blackmail and beyond tiredness, waiting for headlights that were bound to come. It was 3am before she parked at the bus stop, staying in her car for several minutes as if making sure that no lights appeared in my house. But I didn't need to turn on lights. I knew every creak on every stair in that home I had made with John. I felt that John was there as I descended the stairs or at least his absence was there – the grief of his loss brought back by this turmoil. I felt as raw as the night he died in the hospice.

She was attaching flowers to the bus stop when I opened my front door. This time there were only two small bouquets as if she was already losing heart in the battle. She surely sensed me coming but continued to work so that I was behind her by the time she had the second bunch sellotaped on. I raised the knife with such fury that for a moment I think we both half feared I would stab her. Instead I cut through every layer of Sellotape in one go.

'Take your blasted flowers and get the hell away,' I said as daffodils scattered everywhere.

'I'm mourning my daughter,' she said, near tears.

'Mourn her somewhere else because I've had enough of your grief. I've known grief too but I never inflicted it on strangers. Get off my footpath and go home to your bed.'

'To do what?' she asked. 'Lie awake, staring at the ceiling or swallow the horse tranquillisers the doctor prescribed to knock me out? Don't they realise that, when I do black out into sleep, I still dream about her and torture myself with the same questions? Why did I dawdle in that charity shop and make us miss the previous bus by seconds? Why was I deliberately cross with her at this bus stop, imagining the fun we'd have becoming the best of friends again the minute we got home and I produced the secret treat I had for her in my bag? Kim could be a little bitch at times and so can I, but we loved each other to bits. Now she's gone and all I have left is this spot where we last stood together and you're trying to rob me of that.'

'I'm robbing you of nothing,' I said. 'I'm protecting my family. How dare you spell out my granddaughters' names in funeral flowers?'

'That was wrong and I felt really sorry after, but like I said, I can be a bitch at times. I wasn't thinking right, I was trying to make you understand what it feels like to lose someone.'

'Do you think I don't know? I lost a brother to TB when I was small. I lost my husband. I lost two children to miscarriages that I've never even told my daughter about, because what right have I to burden her with my sorrows?'

'Well I never lost anyone before, because I've never loved anyone like I loved Kim. Oh, I thought I did for a time – the young fellow who was her so-called father – but only when Kim was born did I understand true love and now you're trying to take her from me.'

'I didn't crash that car,' I said. 'This has nothing to do with me.'

'The police know that woman's address in France but won't give it to me. When it goes to court it will be the State against her, like I'm simply a bystander. You took her into your house. You were serving her tea before Kim's body was even cold. I hate her, but she's not here to hate. You are.'

She grabbed the knife, leaving me too startled to move as she raised it. I knew what she was going to do and I couldn't feel angry with her. I was the one crazy enough to come out in the moonlight to a deranged woman. It was my own fault if she stabbed me. But she didn't. Instead she swept the knife in one swift movement across her wrist. The pain must have been excruciating but for several seconds she remained as motionless as I was.

Then she fell forward and I caught her before she could hit the footpath. I cradled her as best I could, aware of her blood soaking into her clothes. She looked up at me as if unable to believe what she had done, like a lost child desperate for me to tell her that everything that happened over the past two months had been a bad dream. I couldn't tell her this. I don't know what I said. I just kissed her forehead and spoke in the soft tone I used to use when Audrey was small and cried in bed because the girls at school didn't like her; the tone I used with John when his morphine intake was so high that I wasn't sure if he knew I was still there. A passing taxi driver stopped and dialled 999. I couldn't say how long it took the ambulance to arrive. When the paramedics prised her from my arms and put her onto a stretcher she was weak and disorientated from loss of blood.

'Are you a relation?' they asked. 'We can only let a relation ride with her in the ambulance.'

'I'm her mother,' I lied. 'Now are you going to stand there all night talking or are you going to get my daughter the help she needs?'

She was conscious and could easily have denied it. But she didn't and while the paramedics worked to stem the blood spurting from her wrist, she gripped my hand with her other hand, so tight that her nails dug into my palm. We kept up this silent pretence all the way to the hospital. As they wheeled her inside I took her phone from her pocket. Among her contacts was a number listed as 'Mum'. I dialled it. A voice answered, cross from being woken from sleep. When I said hello she asked who the hell I was and what was I doing with her daughter's phone.

I offered no explanations but just named the hospital where her daughter was. I waited in the corridor until a taxi arrived and a worried looking woman rushed in. Then I discreetly put down the admissions form I was meant to be filling in and walked out into the dawn light. A line of taxis waited outside the ugly modern building but I wanted to walk, despite my exhaustion. When had I last walked home at dawn? I needed to go back to the night I lost my virginity in John's small flat, although I didn't lose it; I gave it willingly to him. It was five months before our marriage, and I walked home, flooded with such exhilaration that I had felt I was striding forward to embrace everything to come, good and bad, in our shared future.

Now I felt no exhilaration: just a sense that while the future I once dreamt of with John was over, my life wasn't over because John would never have wanted that. I knew my own mind and what I had to do. When I reached home, I turned off my phone and slept deeper than I had slept since his death. It was six in the evening when I woke. There were four missed calls from Audrey on my phone, but I hadn't time to listen to her messages. The DIY store opened until eight and I knew that Mr Andrews wouldn't mind accompanying me. I liked how he asked no questions about why I wanted to buy such decorative tiles. There was nothing suitable in the garden section but we found what I wanted among those feature tiles that should be used sparingly to break the pattern of a tiled kitchen wall.

I asked him if he could cement two of them into my front wall when he finished rebuilding it and he nodded. He made the whole job so neat and flush that while those two tiles might seem incongruous there, you need to look very close before you even spot them. I doubt if old Mrs Clarke would approve, but this is not Mrs Clarke's wall: it's mine to do what I like with. Audrey didn't even notice them when she dropped off the twins, more respectful now, fearful I might cut down the two days I have agreed to take them to just one. But Amy noticed immediately and Amy loved them.

191

'There's one for me and one for Lucy,' she said and when I nodded she asked if the top one could belong to her. She now pats it goodbye every evening when running out to her mother's car, after I have tidied up the twins who love getting mucky from helping me in the garden.

No flowers have been placed on that bus stop since then. But I know enough about grief to know that one day the young woman will eventually be drawn back here to face her demons. She will never knock on my door, but I know that she will see these tiles and understand why they are there: our secret never to be told to anyone else. Two tiles, each with the motif of a yellow flower, built into the wall in remembrance of a young girl who loved daffodils, a girl with no thought of death before death so cruelly thought of her.

The Rivals

The taxi driver bringing Simon to the hospice maintained a respectful silence, as if suspecting that he was visiting a dying relation. But Simon felt half-tempted to initiate a conversation, on the off-chance that the driver might know something about the total stranger whom Simon was being press-ganged into visiting.

He possessed no recollection of having heard the name of James J. Hennessy before a three a.m. email this morning. The ping on his phone had woken him in the disconcerting famil-iarity of his childhood bedroom, unchanged since Simon last slept there four decades ago. He had suspected it to be another reminder from his publisher back home in Manhattan that this trip to Ireland could not delay the proofs of his latest novel, but felt compelled to check that it was not a family emergency. This protective impulse came from having raised three daughters. In the past their first impulse was always to contact him – whether at home or abroad – whenever any mishap occurred, as if he could somehow still magically make their problems disappear, like when they were teenage girls needing a lift home or emo-tional consolation if a high school romance unravelled.

Such free and easy communications from his daughters had ceased in the eight months since Simon divorced their mother – or, to be precise, Lisa divorced him. Neither he nor Lisa asked their daughters to take sides and their separation was amicable, or as amicable as their respective lawyers allowed it to be. There had been no great schism or furious argument, no adulterous secret exposed, just a gradual drifting apart during the years when they were so focused on being good parents to their daughters that they neglected tending to the spark of also being good lovers to each other. This emotional void had remained unaddressed until the night when Lisa announced that while she still loved Simon, she was no longer in love with him and couldn't cope with this absence of passion in her life.

Their daughters had already left home to embark on new lives before this rupture occurred. In some ways this realignment in their parents' relationship should not have affected them, but of course it did, deeply and traumatically: removing the bedrock of certainty that children cling to, whether they be fifteen or fifty. This divorce left his daughters conflicted, anxious to express equal love for both parents but unable to dash off emails with the same casual familiarity. Their anxiety to show no favouritism eerily mirrored how Lisa and he once tried to be even-handed with them, so that no child felt overlooked when the girls were younger and competing for attention.

Therefore, when reaching for his phone at three a.m., Simon had known that it would take a real family emergency for the email to come from one of his daughters. Ironically the email did indicate a family emergency, but one unconnected to him. He had wondered if it was sent to the wrong address because its message meant nothing to him:

James J. Hennessy is dying.

Perhaps Hennessy was an American writer with whom Simon had once shared a stage at a literary festival and the intern publicist at his publishers had given Simon's email address to a journalist cobbling together an obituary. But the message was too abrupt to come from someone trying to solicit a standard commiserative press quote. Simon was still so jet-lagged that he had decided against replying until the morning. But as he drifted back asleep his phone had pinged with a second email:

> My father knows you have returned to Dublin. He is convinced you wish to make your peace with him before he dies. Isn't it time to let bygones be bygones? Brendan Hennessy.

Simon glanced out of the taxi now as the driver pulled up outside the hospice, which looked more like an anonymous Midwest hotel than a medical establishment. As Simon emerged from the cab a young man outside the entrance nervously extinguished his cigarette and walked forward to offer a handshake.

'Brendan Hennessy?' Simon asked.

'Fair play to you for coming, Mr Curtis,' the young man replied. 'It means a lot to my family. I'm not sure Da would have bothered visiting you. He likes to nurse grievances like a slow whiskey, as you know better than most.'

It seemed wise to simply nod. Simon knew nothing about the cancer patient dying here. This was what he tried to discreetly explain in his reply to the young man's email:

> Dear Brendan, I am back from New York to visit my own father in a nursing home. You may be mixing me up with someone else. I'm not sure I know James J Hennessy. But my thoughts are with your family at this difficult time and I hope you manage to redirect your message to the right recipient. Sincere sympathy, Simon Curtis.

The young man's reply had arrived within minutes:

> Mr Curtis: all I seek is a smidgen of magnanimity and maturity on your part. I long ago abandoned hope of drumming sense into my

father's head and now I'm running out of time to do anything for him. What can you gain by prolonging a rivalry that only caused bitterness between you? Doctors can do nothing for my father but you can. It would mean a lot to his family if he didn't need to take your feud with him to the grave. I know how, in your youth, you and he locked antlers, staking out your territory in acrimonious arguments. Why prolong this row when it's clear, even to someone as stubborn as Da, that you won the war? It's you who achieved fame by fleeing Ireland to escape his shadow. I cannot tell you how hard it is to witness the pain he's enduring. If my father owes you an apology for harsh words that should have been left unsaid, I apologise on his behalf. I don't know you, Mr Curtis, though I feel I do, having grown up hearing so much about you and him as young poets spurring each other on to greater heights with your rivalry. My father never wavered from his belief in the advice he gave, that your work would never become radical if you ran away from the rigour of his criticism, because you were too scared to let him sharpen your vision in the same way that Ezra Pound recrafted Eliot's *The Waste Land*. But he always said his criticisms were about your work and not about you. He liked you personally and felt guilty about leaving you with no intellectual option but to leave. I apologise if I am rambling. I'm typing this email watching over him on the graveyard shift in this hospice, while morphine briefly allows him some respite. I don't know how long Da has left. But it feels like he's holding out for something. I think that something is you. I'm pleading. End this feud. Let him die in peace.

Such a perplexing email had proven impossible to ignore. It felt too cruel to tell a young man watching over a dying father that his message struck no memory and any feud existed inside his father's imagination. The only appropriate reply was to offer to visit this hospice. The deserted lobby was dotted with armchairs, festooned with soft toys. Brendan Hennessy followed his gaze.

'The medical staff make him as comfortable as possible and respect our privacy. I appreciate you coming, especially with your own father in the nursing home.'

Simon nodded. 'It's hard to believe he's still alive at ninety-four. I remember him trying to drink himself to death after my mother died. I'm only back in Ireland to let my sister take a holiday in Spain. I do what I can from America, but all the heavy lifting with his care falls on her.'

This was not the full truth. His fortnight in Dublin was also to allow his ex-wife the privacy to take one final sift through every bookshelf and cupboard in their New York apartment. Although he had retained the lease on the apartment, Lisa was welcome to any of their belongings accumulated during thirty years of marriage. He had assured her there was no necessity to leave any inventory of what she took away. This was partly to give her full rein to keep any possession that retained precious memories for her. But it was also because Simon sensed how hurt he would feel if confronted by the meagre list of items she would bother to box up to be transported to her childhood home in Johnston, Providence County, Rhode Island.

For Lisa a clean break meant a clean break. It amazed him how seamlessly she had settled back into the house left to her by her parents, rekindling old friendships in a town she left decades ago. She retained an affinity towards her native place whereas all that Simon remembered about the Dublin from which he had emigrated, aged twenty-two, was his perpetual sense of feeling like a disaffected outsider.

'I know your sister to say hello to,' Brendan remarked, leading the way across the lobby. 'Well, it's her son I know really. We both played football for Tolka Rovers. His mother is a good woman.'

Simon nodded. 'People in Ireland talk about the tragedy of emigrants needing to leave, but I couldn't wait to escape. It's just a pity that all the responsibility for Dad's care has ended up on my sister's shoulders, but I had a family to raise in New York and I honestly never thought he'd live this long.'

Brendan paused at the empty reception desk and hesitated. 'This probably sounds an odd question, but does part of you still feel like a child while your father is alive?'

Simon stopped also and nodded, already feeling an affinity towards this young man. 'Fathers have a quizzical way of staring at their children. My father's stare was a mixture of unspoken pride and unbridled scepticism. If I told him I'd won the Pulitzer Prize he'd be chuffed for me but his gaze would make me feel like I'd just told him the dog ate my homework. I used to think he didn't believe what I told him but then I realised he was pet-rified that life would go pear-shaped for me. His generation had conformity beaten into them at school. My novels baffled him, and my poems too, back when I published my sole collection of adolescent verse. But what truly perplexed him was how – after I left school with a good Leaving Cert, the first in my family to do the Leaving – I refused to settle for a pensionable civil service job that would have given me the financial security he never knew as a factory hand.'

'That's one thing you and my da had in common start-ing off,' Brendan said, 'a ferocious determination never to get trapped in the civil service.'

'What did your father do in the end?' Simon discreetly fished for clues to a jigsaw he needed to piece together before going upstairs to face a stranger.

The young man laughed ruefully and led the way towards the stairs up to the first floor. 'He served forty years hard labour in the Department of Agriculture – always just passing through on his way to Europe, as he kept promising himself. I doubt if he learnt to tell one end of a cow from another. But he built up an encyclopaedic knowledge of other odd professions that poets whom he admired undertook to survive, from Eliot's slaving in Lloyds Bank to William Carlos Williams working as a hospital doctor.' He paused. 'Are all relationships with fathers this complex?'

'You'd need to ask my three daughters.' Simon deflected the question.

'They wouldn't count. They grew up watching a father do a job where he felt fulfilled, instead of coming home so frustrated he couldn't stop himself verbally lashing out at those he loved.' Brendan glanced at Simon as they ascended the staircase, fearing he sounded disloyal. 'Sorry for talking so much. We're all beyond exhaustion, barely aware if it's day or night. I'm not saying that Da hasn't got good points, but we never saw eye to eye. I hoped that over time we'd grow close, but time is refusing to allow us that chance. Is your father content in his nursing home?'

'He's as happy or unhappy there as anywhere else, because he no longer knows where he is.'

'It's how we discovered you were home. A neighbour visiting her mother there recognised you.'

Simon nodded, happy to solve one piece of the puzzle. 'I'm doing what my sister calls the whiskey run. Nurses turn a blind eye when she brings in a small whiskey every afternoon.'

'Does he know who you are?'

Simon shrugged. 'Not really at first. He knew we were somehow connected but wasn't sure if I was his son, his dead brother or a workmate. He thinks he's back in the factory where he worked. He curses the shop steward for calling a work-to-rule, which explains why everyone is sitting around. I thought he'd fret over my sister's whereabouts but his sole concern was about whether he'll get paid his wages. I soon realised there was no point discussing his grandchildren in New York. I needed to keep going back in time until I hit a bedrock of memory where he suddenly sensed who I was, though in his mind I'm still a teenager. But I came into focus for him and he said my name. He could even remember things from my childhood that I've forgotten, because the son whom he remembers isn't really me anymore, or at least the person I am now. But memory is fickle; what people choose to remember or what they inadvertently get mixed up about.'

Simon paused at the top of the long stairs and stared at the young man, hoping he would decode this last sentence as a plea for information. Initially he thought the tactic worked because Brendan acknowledged his stare with a slow nod.

'I know why you're looking at me like that. You're not the first to think it. People say I look the spit of my father back when you knew him. It used to bother me because we have such different personalities.'

'In what way?'

'Da hasn't changed: still dogmatic and entrenched in his views. There isn't much Da hasn't a strong opinion on.'

'And you?'

'If you grow up with a father permanently at war with everyone, and mainly with himself, you become a peacemaker. I feel I've spent my life trying to hold my family together. It's what I'm trying to do now, making the peace between you.'

'There's something I must tell you,' Simon began. 'I genuinely have no quarrel with your father.' He wanted to add that he actually had no recollection of him, but lost his nerve. The taxi was gone and he was stranded in the midst of someone else's false memory.

'It's good of you to say that,' Brendan Hennessy replied. 'I suspected you were probably not still as caught up in the feud. Let's face it: more happened in your career, it's easier for you to let go. But it still bothers him and right now it's about his needs. When you're ready we'll go in. My mother is waiting. All my siblings too. Word gets around, you know.'

'I'm not being good in saying it.' Simon felt panicked, conscious of the sensitivities of this situation. 'I'm trying to talk truthfully. I never had a quarrel with your father. There's no feud to patch up.'

The young man nodded. 'I appreciate your generosity in being so forgiving. But isn't that a bit too easy to say, if you're honest with yourself?'

'How do you mean?'

'The quarrel was important enough to make you leave Dublin to find your own space, as Da says, or your own limbo, as he sometimes puts it when reading another of your novels set somewhere odd like Tahiti. I'm just saying that maybe you felt you could leave your rivalry behind by emigrating but quarrels don't go away just because you do. Watching Da dying I've realised that everything in our past must eventually be confronted. Rows between writers are like family arguments: hard to resolve because they're like having a row with yourself. Maybe this doesn't feel important to you now but I see Da's anguish, running out of time when tormented by so much unfinished business. I think he can't give up battling cancer until he deals with his buried pain and feels he can let go. Maybe Da doesn't grasp this behind his stubbornness or maybe I'm talking horseshit and only dragged you here because I need to feel I'm doing something for him. Since Da got ill I feel twice my age. It's only a month since the doctors opened him up, took one look and closed him again. That's an uncanny echo of what editors did for decades with his submissions, apart from a few experimental magazines run from bedrooms in places like Arkansas. You were wise to switch to novels.'

'It wasn't wisdom,' Simon replied. 'It was economics. I needed to make a living.'

Brendan produced a faded Polaroid photograph from his pocket.

'This was taken the last night you met, when you quarrelled over who had the right to consider himself to be Joyce's heir-in-waiting. No disrespect, but I think you both had excessively long hair and unrealistic expectations.'

Simon studied the photograph. The scruffy hair and ill-fitting clothes dated it back to the late 1970s. Before fading with age, the colours must have been lurid and unstable. Written in biro in the white space beneath the washed-out image were the names of Simon and Hennessy and a caption: 'The final show-down, May 1978'. The photo showed two unsmiling young men in a dreary suburban lounge, seated at a table with two pints of Harp lager and some typed manuscripts. The figure on the left, looking trapped and ill at ease, was undeniably Simon's younger self. The other figure radiated a confident air of superiority. A drinker must have been prevailed on to snap this Polaroid, as if James J. Hennessy deemed it necessary to document their encounter.

Simon felt oddly discommoded because both figures in the photo felt equally like strangers. His father had dementia as an excuse for being unable to recall aspects of his life, but Simon suddenly wondered if he had spent decades mentally blocking out his past. Critics often commented on how untypical he was as an Irish writer in that nothing autobiographical leaked into his novels. Joyce had loved and hated Dublin in equal obsessive measure: these contradictory impulses affording him a lifetime of imaginative engagement with his native city. In contrast Simon's emotional disengagement from Dublin had propelled him on forays into contrasting locations; each novel forging its own space by being set in seventeenth-century Brazil or modern day Haiti. Such societies felt no less unreal than the suburban lounge bar he vaguely recognised in this photograph.

But the fact was inescapable that this anxious-looking teenager was somebody whom Simon had once been and who – despite the distance constructed around his new life – still existed somewhere deep in his psyche. He thought of Yeats's lines, 'O chestnut tree, great rooted blossomer, Are you the leaf, the blossom or the bole?' If he could not deny having been this youth, then he could also not deny having once known, even if only in passing, the patient dying in this hospice.

'Are you okay?' Brendan observed him with concern.

'It feels like a long time ago.'

'Da tried to set you straight about some terrible piece of juvenilia, after an editor had patronised you by offering to publish it. You stormed out, feeling threatened by his home truths about your work just not being good enough to be printed yet. At least that's how Da remembers it. Maybe you remember differently. He was always circumspect about how often you two circled each other like tiger cubs, avoiding this final confrontation until you had no choice but to go for each other, no holds barred. Do you want to sit down, Mr Curtis, you look shaken?'

Simon felt shocked not at some revelation but by the banality of memories only now trickling back. He had not blocked them out for any particular reason: they were so inconsequential he had forgotten them until now. At eighteen he had formed a local poetry circle. The gatherings were poorly attended: a factory hand who wrote hard-laced doggerel, a nervous young woman who never found enough courage to read, a civil servant writing pastiches of Keats and a few other locals whose poems made Simon's adolescent verses shine by comparison. Not that the reading sessions were competitive; Simon recalled a relaxed, supportive atmosphere. This changed when a condescending newcomer arrived, remaining silent while the others read their poems but then placing a copy of Ezra Pound's impenetrable *Cantos* on the table and – as if setting a test – demanded to hear everyone's opinion of *The Pisan Cantos LXXIV–LXXXIV*, written while Pound was held captive in the late 1940s. Simon remembered the older youth's incredulous shake of his head when people confessed to not having read Pound. He could not recall his name after so many years but his instincts told him it must have been James J. Hennessy.

He remembered how others in the poetry circle looked intimidated at the prospect of needing to express opinions about the poems they expected this newcomer to read. But Hennessy proffered no poems, declaring his work as so superior to Simon's juvenilia – and Simon's work so superior to everyone else's – that it would be unfair to read aloud. Instead he had pontificated about modernist literature, dissipating any camaraderie until people left early and only Simon and he remained. Hennessy had grown less confrontational then, declaring that Simon's poems contained a raw promise. He urged Simon not to saddle himself with a no-hopers workshop but to keep pace with his betters by meeting Hennessy instead to get proper criticism of his work. He even gave Simon an address for David Marcus who edited the *New Irish Writing* page in a national newspaper, explaining that while Simon's work wasn't good enough to be accepted, submitting poems would make Marcus familiar with his name.

The memories being summoned felt so distant they might have occurred to someone else. Simon recalled a second encounter: the atmosphere friendly as Hennessy pontificated about literature, with Simon nervously feeling out of his depth. Perhaps there were other meetings, casting Simon in the role of apprentice learning from a master, but he only recalled the final encounter, immortalised in this faded Polaroid. Simon had naïvely expected Hennessy to be pleased by the news of David Marcus's acceptance of a poem that Hennessy had suggested he submit to *New Irish Writing*. Instead the older youth flew into a fury, savaging Simon's poem as derivative and hackneyed, and raging about Marcus rejecting numerous more superior poems by him.

This was something he could definitely recollect: the youth's anger at Marcus's seeming inability to recognise the originality of Hennessy's poems. Hennessy kept belittling Simon's poem with such vehemence that he made it sound as if Marcus had faced a straight choice between the two of them, with none of the hundreds of other hopefuls who submitted poems entering the reckoning. He then boasted again about his encyclopaedic knowledge of *The Cantos*, as if Simon's ignorance about Pound settled any dispute between them. But Simon could not recollect any previous dispute: he just remembered the sour taste of the unwanted lager, his discomfiture and desire to escape from that bar. Maybe this was the moment when they became rivals in Hennessy's mind, but Simon only recalled his relief that their encounters were over because Hennessy's fury allowed for no possibility of them ever meeting again.

Had he been hurt by Hennessy's words? Possibly. But after he managed to move to America and began writing fiction, his career took off so quickly that he banished memories of adolescent rivalries, just like he banished memories of everything else he was fleeing from: childhood poverty and his father's drinking following his mother's early death. For decades Simon's life was too rushed to allow for reflection, although the way in which his daughters had now started new lives gave him an insight into his father's loneliness at being widowed so young.

What if Hennessy's life had not been equally busy? Had the realisation that someone as seemingly gauche as Simon could get published before him, marked the moment when his brilliant future stalled, an anticipation of fame giving way to a reality of endless rejection? Simon had only thought about him once in all these decades. During an episode of *The Sopranos*, Simon had experienced a wry flashback when watching Tony Soprano warn a young punk off his territory. This is what their last meeting had been: a turf war settlement. Two young poets imagining that their nondescript suburb only had room for one Caesar. Had he ever looked back, Simon might have laughed at their inflated egos, their inability to see how those same streets would produce successful rock bands, film directors and other writers who enjoyed more commercial success than Simon. Simon never resented such people their success. Why should he? They were not rivals. They shared nothing in common beyond an accidental birthplace; briefly playing in the same housing estates before they left behind childish things to enter the wider world. But perhaps James J. Hennessy remained trapped in an arrested adolescence?

A door opening disturbed his thoughts. A woman emerged. This must be Hennessy's wife. Stress was etched into her face, as if she hadn't slept properly in weeks, passing beyond exhaustion so that she was only still propelled forward by fretful nervous energy as she allowed her husband's suffering to outweigh her need for food or rest. Simon did not believe in any spiritual hocus-pocus that might allow Hennessy to enter heaven or hell, but he knew enough about bereavement to sense how this woman would face a purgatory of grief with every familiar space transformed into a site of emotional ambush. He understood her anguish in a way that, as a boy, he was unable to comprehend the depth of his father's grief. He rose to console her and also try to dampen her expectations by tactfully explaining how fleeting his meetings had been with her husband. But once she began thanking him for coming, he realised that she was in too frantic a state for his words to register. He suspected she talked about her husband to strangers in the hospice canteen with this urgent intimacy, knowing that her words served no purpose but unable to stop because talking gave her a sense of doing something for him.

Simon put out his hand, as if this gesture might cause her to pause long enough for him to speak. Instead, gripping his fingers for support, she drew him into the hushed, crowded room where a man lay dying, the skin so taut over his bones that he resembled a wizened octogenarian. Simon would have passed him a thousand times without knowing they had once met. But, after viewing the faded Polaroid, he felt a disconcerting sense of familiarity; Hennessy's intense stare remained the same all these decades later. It honed in on him so fiercely that Simon felt unable to turn and greet anyone else present. The man nodded towards his son.

'Brendan felt you wouldn't come, but I knew you would.' The gaunt figure swallowed, trying to disguise the effort it took to talk. 'I tried to keep my illness quiet but word gets around. At such times you find out who your real friends are.'

'That's true,' Simon replied cautiously. The panic he felt replicated his terror when starting a new novel with no idea of the plot. He had learned the importance of trying to stay calm and let whatever was meant to unfold reveal itself.

'The older I get the more I realise that your real friends are your oldest ones. Old friends stay friends whether we like one another or not.'

'We never had a falling out.' Simon was relieved to be able to make one true statement. His words pleased the patient who nodded with what vigour he could muster, casting his eyes around the room to ensure that everyone present had heard. This brief respite from his fearsome stare allowed Simon to realise that, in addition to Brendan and his mother, there were six other silent witnesses, presumably Hennessy's extended family sharing this vigil. No introductions were proffered. The patient's disconcerting gaze fixed on him again.

'You're right.' His voice barely above a whisper. 'Deep down you and I never really fell out. We respected each other too much. We had a rivalry but that's different; it's how we spurred each other on. But we let it get out of hand. It's been a silly waste of so much of our lives, hasn't it?'

'What can I say?' Simon replied cautiously, feeling very alone in that room.

'There's nothing to say or apologise for. We met when we were both too immature. From then on we were like two Olympic front runners, so busy watching for each other's next move that we didn't realise how quickly we'd get overtaken at the bell. That rivalry cost us dear and for what?'

Simon wasn't sure how to answer. He sensed how James J. Hennessy had spent decades scanning newspapers for references to Simon. The dying man nodded as if convinced he was reading Simon's thoughts and that the obsession had been equal on both sides.

'Do something for me,' he whispered. 'When you return to New York open the filing cabinet where you keep my work. I don't wish to know what comments you wrote on the margins of poems cut from magazines, just like you don't want to read my commentary on your novels. I won't deny that some of my early commentary was unworthy. But that's part of being young. Ambition burns so bright it obscures what really matters. Only the written word matters. Posterity shall judge our work – not you or I. We writers are pawns in the hands of posterity, isn't that true?'

'That's true.' Simon nodded but simple agreement would not be enough here. Two more strangers entered the room. Word had spread about this showdown and everyone close to Hennessy felt obliged to be a witness.

'I visited New York once,' Hennessy said. 'I checked but you're not in the phone book.'

'People who want to get in touch generally send letters care of my publisher. Not many bother. An odd invitation to do a reading or conduct a workshop. You need a dozen things to keep the wolf from the door. My publishers are loyal, though my novels barely wash their own faces, sales-wise. But some get optioned for film and my publishers are like casino gamblers, afraid to stop feeding the one-armed bandit in case they miss the jackpot. They've been so thoroughly decent that I hope one film gets made, just to repay their faith.'

Simon stopped, cognisant of talking too much about himself. It was Hennessy's work he was meant to praise but he knew nothing about what, if anything, had been published.

'I visited your publisher's office when over there,' Hennessy said. 'Not to leave you a letter; I knew we needed to meet face to face. I'm not vain enough to imagine your publishers would know my name – although my reputation is strong among modernist small presses in America. But I knew that if they phoned you, you'd have come to their offices so we might talk.'

'Did you ask them to phone me? I'm genuinely sorry but they never passed on any message.'

Hennessy shrugged, embarrassed; his veneer of self-assurance slipping for once. 'I changed my mind and left. Having them call you felt too much like a summons and I made a mess of the last time I summoned you. Back then I was only trying to give you advice, but you were so defensive it scarred our friendship. In New York I wanted no repeat. I wanted to wish you well and to say let bygones be bygones. A publisher's office wasn't the right place. For our encounter to work we needed to meet by accident, with defences down. A magazine profile mentioned what street you live on. I spent a lot of time at a sidewalk table outside the café on the corner but the stars didn't align because I never caught sight of you.'

'They knew me in that café,' Simon said. 'If you'd asked they could have shown you what door to knock on.'

'Only beggars knock at doors.' Hennessy's tone contained wounded arrogance but also genuine pain. Simon had been told that any visit must be brief. Maybe he had already overstayed his welcome, but he sensed that whatever unfinished business that Hennessy imagined as existing between them was not resolved to his satisfaction. It was impossible to know what to say, but everything depended on his words. Hennessy's family scrutinised him so expectantly that it felt as if the dying man's sense of validation and their perception of his life hinged on whatever Simon said next. But he could not recall reading a single poem by Hennessy that he could praise. Had he known in advance what purpose this act of reconciliation was meant to serve, he could have spent the afternoon in the National Library, scanning small Irish magazines in the hope of finding Hennessy's name somewhere in the distant past.

Looking back, it shocked him how little he remembered about his own past in Dublin. Only random memories survived. The mixture of expectation and fear when he ran downstairs if he heard the postman deliver a letter, convinced this would be his first magical acceptance and unable to contain his devastation when the envelope contained another rejection slip. His loneliness some nights, walking home from town to save money after he left school and had no job and nothing to sustain him except an uncertain self-belief. There were short-lived romances but he could no more remember the names of those girls than he could recall his former schoolmates. Ireland felt like a different world and after his father died he would never return. So was it possible that Hennessy's memory was not at fault but his own? Maybe he was once equally obsessed by a petty local rivalry. For all of Hennessy's talk back then of Louis Zukofsky and poems needing to burst inside the reader's consciousness like shrapnel painted by Jackson Pollock, they had been two adolescents knowing nothing of life. The weight of the watching eyes made Simon unsure about his own past. Nothing had prepared him for this hospice and once he started to speak no second draft would be allowed. All he had to guide him were Hennessy's eyes staring with fierce determination, as if beseeching Simon to make sense of – and atonement for – the decades when Hennessy laboured over poems that may never have been published.

This expectant silence allowed no escape. Simon was acutely aware of Hennessy's family waiting for him to take control and summon up appropriate words of judgement. Hennessy's stare felt like a writer's worst nightmare, like confronting a blank page he had no idea how to fill. Feeling like a character in a novel Simon leaned close to the bed, anxious for his voice to convey intimacy but carry to every corner of the room.

'It was you.' He desperately tried to summon inspiration. 'Always it was you.'

The patient nodded weakly, anxious for Simon to continue. Simon had no idea what to say but had to reinvent himself as whoever Hennessy imagined him to be.

'You were the one who …' He was about to call Hennessy his inspiration but stopped. This might allow Hennessy to ask which of his works most inspired him. Simon searched for another lie, but maybe this time it was no lie because he allotted this forgotten figure from his youth a role never granted to anyone before.

'You were the one always in my mind serving as my ideal reader.'

Something change in Hennessy's gaze. It grew less fierce. His honour was appeased – not his vanity because illness had robbed him of vanity, like it was robbing him of life. But Simon sensed that, by accident, he had conjured up a role which gave purpose to this man's life. The undercurrent of tension diluted in the room, like he often sensed the mood change in an auditorium during a play: the audience suspending disbelief, letting nervous actors relax into their roles.

'You know the loneliness of sitting alone at a desk,' Simon continued. 'The doubts that enter a writer's head, imaginary mocking voices that can trample the fragile phantoms we try to conjure. Only when a first draft is finished can you show it to editors for their opinion. But I'm talking about the start of the process, when the work is too raw to talk about, let alone show anyone, when it's so tentative you're afraid to think too far ahead. That's when we writers are at our most vulnerable and alone. We were never really friends, were we?'

The man seemed too absorbed in Simon's words to nod, but a flicker of his eyes registered agreement.

'Sometimes you need the judgement of people closer than friends because friends can do damage trying to be kind. You don't need kindness when alone at a desk, not knowing if what you've written is good because sometimes, as you know, the words turn to muck in your mind. You need advice but you can't allow anyone enter the room. That's why during my darkest moments of self-doubt, when I've no other instinct to go on, I ask myself, "what would James J. Hennessy think of this?" Of course I never knew because you weren't there. But you became my imaginary litmus test: the young rival I was once scared of but always respected for your uncompromising integrity. I can't tell you how many opening chapters I tore up and was glad I did so. But on other occasions I persevered, even though I'd no sense of where I was going, because a voice in my head – and maybe these instincts were wrong because I don't want to put words in your mouth – said that you just might respect this book for being different, feel the task was worthwhile. No writer is ever truly alone; we have one imaginary reader we long to satisfy. I hope you don't mind me appropriating you for this role, but you've been my ideal reader, a crucial part of my journey, not all the time, but at the vital times. I hope that occasionally I second-guessed your thoughts and if you read my books you found some merit there.'

Hennessy was silent, absorbing these words: the whole room awaiting his reaction. Simon knew he had played an emotional three-card-trick, switching the dynamic so that instead of him having to pass judgement on Hennessy's work he had empowered Hennessy to serve as Simon's judge and jury.

'The best of your books are good,' the man pronounced at last. 'You went through troughs. But you needed to churn out prose for a living, which is why you abandoned poetry where you might have made your mark. I had you at an advantage. I only wrote when I needed to. That's why my oeuvre is small, distilled to perfection.'

'That's how it should be.' Simon sensed how important it was to let the man in this bed sound magnanimous. 'Even the best of us, if we get lucky, will only be remembered for one poem or one line of verse. Everything else gets swept away. Only time decides what deserves to be remembered after our journeys are over.'

'You're right,' James J. Hennessy agreed. 'Time will decide, not us. We took different routes. But I want you to know that when your novels didn't lose their way they surprised me for being better than I ever expected.'

'Maybe those were the books when I listened to you in my head.'

The man closed his eyes as if unable not to succumb to sleep. Simon again became aware of the pain he was in. His fingers closed over the morphine pump, his gaze more diluted when he reopened his eyes. 'My advice is a luxury you won't have for much longer. The staff in this hospice are letting me die with what dignity I can muster. But my goose is cooked. I'm not afraid of where I'm going. I'm entering oblivion.'

'You'll always be alive in the memory of those who love you,' Simon said. 'And you'll always exist in my mind in moments of self-doubt. You never needed to be physically present for me to sense you at my shoulder.'

The man released his grip on the morphine pump to reach for Simon's hand, grasping it with what strength he could muster.

'Let bygones be bygones,' Hennessy said. 'Keep writing. I promise that one day you'll get there.'

The man's grip was so weak it felt like shaking hands with a ghost. His wife touched Simon's shoulder.

'I know you'd like to stay longer,' she said. 'But he's worn out. The nurses didn't want visitors except family but he always talked so much about you that you feel like family. I'll have Brendan show you out.'

Simon went to say some final words to Hennessy but the man was already in an uneasy sleep. Simon looked around at the family members watching in silence. Words seemed super-fluous so he just nodded as Hennessy's children came forward to shake his hand. Hennessy's wife kissed his check and he knew that subconsciously she was auditioning for her public role in the coming days when she would need to summon the strength to greet mourners at his funeral. Brendan silently led him downstairs and across the eerily deserted reception area. They stepped through the tall glass doors, outside into the late evening sunlight.

'I've hailed a taxi on the app on my phone,' Brendan said. 'It will be here shortly.'

'You go back inside,' Simon replied. 'At times like this you want to be with your family.'

'Trust me, I want to be anywhere but up there. At the best of times Da and I didn't get on and this isn't the best of times.'

'You've done your best for him.'

'So have you. I suppose I should probably thank you.'

'There's no need. I was glad of the chance to come and say goodbye.'

'I don't mean for coming; I should thank you for thinking on your feet. My family are so wrapped up in Da's suffering that they swallowed your charade, but they always allowed themselves to believe in whatever myth Da spun and wound up believing himself. I can't believe I wasted your time, dragging you here for nothing.'

'I came willingly,' Simon said.

'You came bewildered,' Brendan replied. 'I only realised it when I showed you the photo. Before that I thought you were apprehensive at meeting an old adversary, but then I realised that you hadn't the foggiest notion who Da is. It would have been nice if he had been your ideal reader because he was never my ideal father.'

'I wouldn't know what type of father he is,' Simon said.

'How could you when – after all his talk – you know nothing about him?'

The intensity of the young man's stare was a replica of his father's. It contained such anger that Simon felt unnerved.

'I wasn't sure until I saw the photo, but I remembered us meeting then.'

'Not like he remembers it. There was no great literary feud, was there? You never left Ireland to get away from him. You never gave him a thought in years.'

'Just because we remember things differently doesn't make them untrue.' Simon watched a taxi turn in through the gates and ascend the winding avenue. 'Truth is like a shoelace; it splits into different strands when it gets frayed.'

'I'm glad I never read your novels if your metaphors are that stretched,' the young man said bitterly. 'Why can't you speak the truth, plain and simple?'

Simon turned. 'If the truth was ever simple, writers would be out of a job. Your father and I had an argument years ago. Because I don't remember it as a feud doesn't mean it didn't happen. Maybe your father has an inability to forget slights, but maybe I've an inability to remember things I don't want to remember; about being so poor I could barely afford a typewriter ribbon and so insecure I had to go abroad to reinvent myself. This afternoon after I smuggled whiskey into my own father and he gradually realised that I was his son I became eighteen again in his mind. He was suddenly remembering events from the year I left school and haunted local factories and offices for any class of job. Things I'd forgotten about, but as he talked I realised why I had blocked them out. If journalists in the States ask me if I feel Irish, I say no. If they ask if I was shaped by Dublin, I deny it. But maybe I was so busy running away and feuding with myself that I had no time to remember feuding with anyone else.'

The taxi had pulled up, the driver waiting for one of them to open the passenger door.

'I spoke a bit sharply just now,' Brendan said apologetically. 'I suppose I'm angry that his life doesn't match up to his myths and I can't take that anger out on him. I'm scared because I'm losing him and I still don't know exactly who I'm losing. I always defined him as being your opposite. When I was young I used to imagine tracking you down and punching you for having stolen his ideas and his success.'

'Has he published much?'

'The odd poem here and there, but they dried up.'

'That's probably more than Gerard Manley Hopkins published before he died unknown in this city and was buried in an unmarked grave. I don't know if posterity will remember him but it certainly won't remember me. I just know there's a lot of people up in that room who love him.'

'We've all been orbiting his ego since we were small.'

'Even if you love him with infuriated exasperation, that's still love. I've three daughters in America. Since divorcing their mother I feel a separation growing between me and them. It's not that they don't love me but their sense of love is diluting as they get caught up in their own lives. I never rowed with my father like you rowed with yours, but that's because we were never close. I sent home money to my sister when he got ill and I offered to fly him to New York to meet his grandchildren. But I knew he'd never get on a plane and I never brought my daughters to see him because I never wanted them to see where I came from. If that's the example I gave them, why should my daughters feel particularly close to me?'

Simon knew that his father was probably sitting now in baffled silence in the nursing home, awaiting a siren to announce the end of another long shift in the factory where he imagined himself to be on a work-to-rule. Maybe Simon had succeeded as a writer in ways that James J. Hennessy never possessed enough talent or courage to emulate. Yet compared to this young man beside him, Simon had failed as a son, despite this trip home to appease his sister and assuage his own guilt.

'I wish I was getting in this taxi,' Brendan said. 'I wish I was anywhere but here.'

'But you'll stay to the bitter end,' Simon told him. 'Infuriated exasperation is a stronger emotion than diluted love. I tell you one thing. If I ever find myself lying in a hospice, I would trade whatever tiny success I've eked out for the thought that one of my daughters would care enough about me to track down the person they honestly believed to be my rival.' He raised his chin slightly. 'If it helps, feel free to unleash that punch you once wanted to deliver on your father's behalf.'

'Da would kill me if I did that,' Brendan replied. 'He always called you a good man. At least that's something he and I can agree on. Goodbye, Mr Curtis.'

They shook hands. Simon climbed into the taxi which moved off. He didn't look back because he knew the young man was standing there, waiting to find the strength to return to the room where his father lay dying. The taxi driver glanced across.

'A tough visit?' the man asked. 'Is it a close relation?'

'We were sort of like brothers.'

The driver nodded. 'It can't be easy so.'

Simon stared out at the unfamiliar streets that were once his home. He had planned to spend the evening correcting the proofs of his novel but they would have to wait. Instead he would sit in companionable silence with his father in the nursing home until nightfall, two strangers who left it too late to ever truly know one another.

The Unremembered

Ieper was where she would find him, Catherine was certain. That is, if her father was still alive. Why should she care after all these years? But she did care. Every night at eight o'clock in this town, at the Last Post Ceremony at the Menin Gate, just after buglers from the local volunteer fire service had played 'The Last Post', and as the assembled crowd were about to bow their heads for a minute's silence, a visitor would recite 'The Exhortation for the Fallen':

> *They shall grow not old, as we that are left grow old:*
> *Age shall not weary them, nor the years condemn.*
> *At the going down of the sun and in the morning,*
> *We will remember them.*

With one voice, the crowd always quietly replied, 'We will remember them' before the 'Réveille' was played. Catherine remembered everything about the past. Her father presumably also remembered the same events. But she suspected that their competing accounts of love and betrayal – and of a family torn apart by his disappearance forty-six years ago – were so different that they had little chance of agreeing on anything, even if their paths somehow did manage to cross again by chance in this Flemish town that looked to be frozen in the past.

But Ieper wasn't frozen in time. Catherine had realised this over the past three days while searching its streets for him. She had watched how the Market Square accommodated the elaborate staging for a British television extravaganza, broadcast to commemorate the Battle of Passchendaele in 1917. Now two days later the same space was accommodating a funfair: a garish cacophony of flashing lights and inane music where children clambered onto fairground rides, oblivious to the elderly British visitors wandering towards the Menin Gate for this evening's ceremony.

This town was no museum; it just masqueraded as one when wheelchair-bound Second World War veterans visited, or when museum staff tried to provide details for the grandchildren of fallen Great War soldiers of the exact location where their ancestors died. Catherine decided that *masquerade* was the wrong word, because Ieper possessed a subtle duality. It made a large part of its livelihood by paying constant homage to the past while always also remaining immersed in the present: staging open-air rock concerts beside the Cathédrale Saint-Martin or dumping sand on the Market Square cobbles when ladies' beach volleyball tournaments were held there. While coping with the incessant war pilgrims, its inhabitants got on with their real lives, working in small factories and mushroom farms that were discreetly located among the numerous Commonwealth, French and German war cemeteries that formed a necklace around the town.

It would have been different if Churchill got his way. After the Armistice, Churchill wanted the ruined town preserved as a monument to the British Empire's dead in the battles for the Ypres Salient. He might have succeeded had Ieper formed part of the British Empire he was in thrall to. But Flemish people had no interest in living amid a mausoleum of twisted wreckage. They wanted the remnants of their old streets cleansed of severed limbs and unexploded bombs. For them Ieper was no monument: it was their home. Slowly they recreated their old town, brick by yellow brick. Perhaps it was a forgery because every building, by necessity, had to be a pastiche of what originally stood there, but this forgery replicated their previous way of life.

Of course you cannot recapture the past. This made Catherine even more puzzled by her need to return here, forty-five years after last visiting Ieper with her father. Her feet ached now, after hours spent circling the same streets and ramparts. Her eyes felt jaded from constantly scanning the crowds enjoying coffee and beer on the seats outside each bar and café. Why was she still bothering to search for him? Surely at some stage a daughter's duty ended. She had expected age to bring certainty to her life. Yet here she was at sixty-one, as incapable of understanding the past as when her father brought her here from Dublin, as a sixteen-year-old in 1972.

It had been her father's second trip to Ieper. Two years before that, in 1970, he had confided to Catherine and her mother that a previously never-mentioned uncle had become the black sheep of the family by dying in a British uniform during the Second Battle of Ypres. Her father deemed it wise to never mention this connection to the British Army in the working-class Dublin docklands where they lived, especially after the outbreak of the Northern Troubles in 1969 escalated a volatile political situation. Therefore they were sworn to secrecy about this uncle, a corporal in the Royal Inniskilling Fusiliers, killed by a stray shell while laying down a makeshift track in teeming rain. His limbs had been so widely scattered as to be unidentifiable and therefore, like so many others, he was denied even the dignity of a grave. But Catherine's father had announced his determination to quietly visit Ieper on his own in 1970 to pay homage to this family outcast on the fiftieth-fifth anniversary of his death, while warning them not to mention this politically sensitive trip to anyone. If anybody asked about his absence, they were told to say that he was gone to London to support a friend who had a greyhound running at the White City dog track.

Two years later in 1972, Catherine had been surprised when he not only announced his intention to return to Ieper to again to mark the anniversary of his uncle's death, but this time he wanted to also bring his only daughter with him. Catherine's mother was initially reluctant but eventually agreed to let her go; the first time Catherine was ever abroad. At sixteen everything changes: your body, desires and thoughts. In the emotional tumult of adolescence, she had been mesmerised by Ieper's charm, too self-absorbed to realise how each street had been rebuilt from scratch, when the only thing left standing, after the pounding shells ceased in 1918, was the blackened stump of one corner of the enormous Cloth Hall. On their first evening here she had needed to be comforted in his arms when overcome by sadness during the Last Post ceremony. Her tears came when she gazed up at the columns on the Menin Gate where the names of fifty-five thousand men were listed whose bodies had never been found. Men like her great uncle, whose name was engraved so indistinguishably high up on one panel that she needed to take her father's word when he pointed towards it. She had felt overwhelmed at the enormity of all those deaths; by how so many lives were irrevocably altered – children growing up, knowing nothing of their fathers except that faded War Office telegrams were stored in drawers: their mothers unable to reread them or throw them away.

It had taken Catherine a few days to grasp that nothing in Ieper was quite as it seemed: the town having made a conscious decision to reinvent itself as a replica of its former self, with just for once all the King's horses and men managing to put Humpty Dumpty back together again. But once something is broken it can never truly be made whole again; it only looks the same to outsiders.

This was how Catherine came to feel about herself during that visit, on the surface seemingly so carefree and pretty that the hotel manager wouldn't stop flirting with her. But prettiness can be a prison for a shy sixteen-year-old, acutely aware of how men kept stripping her naked in their minds with sneakily invasive stares. During their visit her father told her about the many attempts by British and German soldiers to capture Ieper. In school she had studied Oscar Wilde's *Ballad of Reading Gaol*, with its line that 'all men kill the things they love.' The Germans and British must have surely loved Ieper, she had thought, because they did everything possible to kill the town until nothing remained except the memory of how it had once been.

That was how she had felt about herself on the long train and ferry journey home to Dublin, so defiled by her father's odd behaviour that she was irreparably altered behind the facade of her demure smile. Not that her father ever tried to sexually touch her at an age when she was so keyed up with hormones that her body felt like it was spilling out of itself. Instead her loss of innocence was caused by witnessing the behaviour of a man whom she realised she didn't properly know.

The father whom Catherine thought she knew vanished; an unremarkable man with a minor clerical job supervising the unloading of ships in Dublin port. That father was no saint – she had grasped this from the worry on her mother's face if he arrived home, hours late, for his dinner. But his sporadic drinking binges and occasional gambling sprees seemed like venial sins compared to the cardinal sins committed by some violently unpredictable dockers, and a young daughter will forgive her father anything when desperate to believe in him.

Her problem at sixteen was that she could no longer believe in her father. During their visit to Ieper she saw him inhabit multiple split personas, tailoring stories to elicit the sympathy of whatever solitary woman he chatted up and then discarding each will-o'-the-wisp fabrication when he latched onto some-one else. Such womanising presumably also occurred on his first trip here alone, when he could conveniently forget about his wife and daughter at home. In 1972 her existence could less easily be ignored, but her father had seemed so caught up in make-believe as to be barely aware of Catherine's presence during those interminable evenings when he parked her on a crowded open air bar terrace. His sole concession to parental responsibility had been to occasionally replenish for her the gin and tonic that her mother would have been horrified by, before he slipped away, just wanting a word with some woman he claimed to remember from his first visit.

Often these women rejected his overtures, but he could hone in on others who listened with fascination to any story he spun about the relative he claimed to be honouring on this pil-grimage. Perhaps he imagined that Catherine was too far away to eavesdrop. In truth she hadn't wanted to listen, as she realised that her mother had only agreed to let her accompany him to force Catherine to unwittingly act as her father's chaperone.

This realisation made Catherine angrier with her mother than with her father, back when she was still too much a daddy's girl to direct her fury at him. But every evening she simmered with resentment, hearing him reinvent different reasons for his visit to suit whatever woman he chatted up. Mostly he still claimed to be honouring an uncle whose remains were never found. But in other yarns she overheard him spinning, nobody related to him actually died amid the quagmire of mud and barbed wire, but he was paying homage to his grandfather who returned from Flanders to live for another forty years, remaining so shell-shocked that he sporadically collapsed in involuntary seizures: one spasm causing his death when he struck his skull against the fireplace. This fictitious grandfather had refused to ever discuss Flanders but endured a paroxysm of coughing after he lit his first woodbine each morning, caused by nerve gas lodged in his lungs from a chlorine gas attack near Langemark.

When using this chat-up line, her father always said that his grandfather's silence about the trenches was exacerbated by finding himself on the wrong side of Irish history. When his comrades marched off to war, cheering girls had run along the Dublin quays to shower them with kisses, cigarettes and rosary beads. But Dublin was transformed by an uprising against British rule in 1916. When his imaginary grandfather returned, no cheering crowds lined the quays, just Republican shrews shouting 'traitor' at each survivor who walked or was stretchered down the gangplank.

This often led English tourists to ask about the Northern Ireland Troubles; about paratroopers opening fire on Civil Rights protesters in Derry on Bloody Sunday or three teenage Scottish soldiers lured to their deaths by girls in a Belfast pub; about internment and loyalist murder gangs hunting innocent Catholics on the streets or why the IRA had murdered inoffensive female cleaners when planting a bomb in Aldershot. Her father always expressed bewilderment at such atrocities, telling them to take his word that – for him as a Dubliner – Northern Ireland was a foreign country. Taking her father's word for anything was unwise. Her mother discovered this, four months after that second Ieper trip, when he left a Dublin bookies and was never again seen, though a neighbour who worked on the B&I passenger line claimed to have glimpsed him drunkenly disembarking in Liverpool the next morning.

In the decades since, there were other sightings in English cities; old workmates from Dublin who approached him in pubs, only for him to ignore them and walk away. Occasionally, in the early years, a registered delivery arrived with no return address: just a pile of English banknotes – the result, Catherine suspected, of a rare win on the horses. But even these stopped. The final communication was a postcard that arrived on her mother's birthday, with a Coventry postmark and the words: 'You would forgive me if I could explain.' No signature or X for a kiss, just eight enigmatic words that left her mother in tears and Catherine confused by her father's eloquence, until, months later, she opened an old copy of *The Irish Press* and discovered that her father must have stolen the words from an Anthony Cronin poem printed there.

White lies had been her father's speciality. When Catherine moved to London to train as a social worker, she painstakingly went through the records of the Commonwealth Graves Commission to confirm what she already knew. While two hundred thousand Irishmen enlisted during the First World War – many of them trade unionists from the Dublin docks, desperate to feed their families after being blacklisted by employers following the 1913 Lockout – nobody with the name her father invented for his fictitious uncle ever enlisted, let alone died in Flanders.

Everything he told them was a fabrication. So why did she care, decades later? All that her father had bequeathed Catherine and her mother were unspecified debts. For months after his disappearance men called to their door, until they decided that her mother didn't know his whereabouts and was too impoverished to pursue for money. Lung cancer took her mother in 1979, a cancer exacerbated by forty cigarettes a day, but in Catherine's mind her cancer was caused by the stress of those menacing callers, by her mother's sense of abandonment and by rumours swirling around the docks.

Forty-five years later, Catherine was just left with a sense of incompleteness and the ache of an unknowable secret. Her legs felt weary now after these three days traipsing through Ieper in search of him. As she paused in the Market Square to gaze across at the restored Cloth Hall, she felt envious of the visitors from Australia and New Zealand and India who could visit the In Flanders Fields Museum located there to seek information about relations who went missing amid the mud of no man's land. A century later the dead still left tiny records of deployment that an archivist could uncover; whereas her father had left no trace for decades, until he showed up, by fluke, in the backdrop of various photographs posted on a Facebook page.

Catherine had long abandoned hope of ever finding him, when six months ago, out of idle curiosity, she clicked on a Facebook page devoted to the Menin Gate Last Post ceremony. Numerous visitors had posted photographs here. In one photo, dated August 2nd last year, a group of Second World War veterans who had laid a wreath, posed on the steps after the ceremony ended. Four figures in the front row were wheelchair-bound. But it was the figure at the end of the last row who caught Catherine's attention. He stood to attention like the others, his blazer identical in colour to their uniforms, although bereft of medals or military decorations. He blended in so well that the only disconcerting aspect of the photograph was the expression of the elderly ex-soldier beside him, puzzled as to the identity of the extraneous stranger who must have blithely gatecrashed their photograph.

This man was undoubtedly a gatecrasher because, when Catherine had scrolled through photos, she found him photo-bombing three other veteran groups at the Menin Gate on

August 3rd and 4th 2016. She laboriously scrolled back to the same dates in the previous year and found him again popping up in early August, 2015, always the last figure in the back row of groups of ex-servicemen. He must have mastered the art of unobtrusive stepping into the frame at the last minute and stepping away so quickly that most veterans were unaware of his presence until afterwards. His expression never changed. The only difference was that he possessed two different blazers, choosing whichever one blended in with the uniformed veterans he spied on any chosen day.

Age had withered him but Catherine still recognised her father's features. On the night she discovered these photographs she hadn't known what to think. She had felt a weary tightness in her chest: a weight of responsibility suddenly lodging there. It was he who had neglected any duty of care for her, so why should she take on the burden of being a daughter again? Her initial temptation was to walk away from a man she had presumed was dead and get on with her life without being encumbered by having to make sense of the past. But Catherine needed to understand her family's history, even if she had nobody to pass it on to.

When emailing the ex-servicemen associations who posted the photos she discovered that they had no clue as to the identity of this extraneous figure. The only way to possibly find him was to come here during this week when he seemed to visit and hunt down an invisible man. Of course her father wasn't invisible – merely anonymous, as men his age often were.

Catherine was increasingly noticing how solitary women of her own age were equally anonymous. Therefore, as the Cloth Hall clock struck seven and she turned to trudge back to her hotel, it was perhaps unsurprising that – when she unexpectedly found herself face-to-face with her father, approaching among the throngs of people corralled onto the Market Square pavement – the man looked straight through her as if she wasn't there. He was striding, as purposefully as was possible for a man in his eighties, towards Menenstraat and the Last Post service due to commence at eight. Behind him the Cloth Hall roof stood out against the garish lights of the fun fair. He would have strode right past if she hadn't put out a hand to touch his immaculately ironed blazer. He glanced at her face, his gaze puzzled and then imbued with the shock of gradual recognition.

'Catherine?'

Catherine felt barely able to breathe. Having tracked him down, she realised that secretly she had longed not to find him, so she could claim to have at least tried before laying his ghost to rest.

'What are you doing here?' His tone reminded her of when she would creep downstairs for a glass of water if unable to sleep as a child. She was shocked by the residue of anger it awoke, although she kept her voice quiet.

'What are you doing, still pretending to be someone you're not?'

The serenity he possessed as he approached was replaced by a look of panic.

'Stay out of my life,' he replied quietly. 'You've no business being here.'

'And have you? In some ways I feel I lost my father here, the beginning of the end. You lost nobody, you simply ditched your wife and child. Do you even know that Ma is dead?'

'Of course I know. I bought Irish papers for years in corner shops in Coventry until I saw her death notice.' He looked around, desperate to escape.

'And reading her death notice absolved you of all responsibility?'

'It would have been worse if I stayed.'

'For who?'

'Everyone.' Flustered, he tried to slip past. 'Leave me alone, please. There's somewhere I need to be.'

Catherine blocked his path. 'Edging your way into photographs, still playing at being a fraud?'

Guiltily he stopped, aware that he was trapped. 'I don't know why you're here, Catherine, but let me be. I haven't time for games.'

'That's not how I remember Ieper. You chatting up women within earshot of your daughter. I've known men desperate for sex, but how pathetic was that?'

'You remember wrong,' he replied defensively. 'That's the problem with wars: everyone remembers them wrong.'

'The war ended a half century before we set foot in this town.'

'It depends on what war you're talking about.' He looked around. 'Did I ever tell you that Churchill wanted Ieper preserved as a ruin? The Belgians told him to go to hell or, should I say, the Flemish did. Belgium is like Ireland: an unhappy marriage – two peoples glued together in one nation, united only by simmering tensions. The Flemish wanted to shape their own future. That's a chance we never had.'

'Because you ran away.'

He shook his head. 'I'm not discussing our family. I loved your mother but our marriage was a mistake. I only realised this after you were born and I needed to look after you both as best I could. I accept I was useless at it. The family who might have guided me died here a century ago.'

The crowd pushed past, most of them oblivious to their confrontation. But some people glanced back, noticing her look of resentment at his remark: a resentment carried over from being a teenager marooned at a bar terrace on this square.

'Keep your lies,' she said. 'I'm not some lonely widow to chat up while your daughter was seated here. I used to feel sickened in my stomach from those unwanted gin and tonics until you'd dispatch me back to our hotel bedroom, where I'd hear you creep in at dawn: the Don Juan of the Dublin docks.'

'I never wanted to bring you. You were foisted on me by someone and I'm not referring to your mother, although she had all kinds of mad suspicions.'

'I wonder why,' Catherine said. 'Years ago I combed the records for the uncle you claimed you lost here. No such soldier existed. It was a sham: our pilgrimage that you claimed we needed to keep secret because any Irishman who ever donned a British uniform was regarded in Dublin as a traitor.'

'They were considered traitors,' he said defensively. 'Nobody had time to bother with the nuances of history, especially after the Northern Troubles kicked off. Riots in Belfast. The B-Specials beating up Catholic protesters looking for civil rights. If you had family connections to Flanders you kept them quiet back then.'

'But the thing is that you didn't,' she said. 'And even if you had lost somebody here, you never cared about anyone but yourself.'

He looked away, at the flashing fairground lights. Then he shook his head wearily. 'You know nothing about those times in the early 1970s. Do you not think I've spent years berating myself about how I screwed up? I longed to find you but I don't even know your married name. Even if I could track you down I didn't want to show up like a beggar on your doorstep. You know nothing about my life. Still, I never expected you to rage at me like a Ringsend fishwife.'

This wasn't how Catherine had envisaged their encounter either. She had imagined spying him through a crowd and gathering her emotions as she picked a quiet moment to approach.

She had never anticipated them suddenly being face to face, both equally rattled.

'What's there to know?' she asked. 'Everything you ever told me was a lie.'

'My grief isn't. Do you think I'd return to this town if my grief wasn't real?'

'Your grief at what? All you ever lost was me and Mum, through your own selfishness.'

A gap emerged in the crowd and he managed to dart past her. A family blocked the footpath in front of him. Catherine thought he was planning to dodge around them, but then realised that he was not fleeing, he was waiting for her to catch up. When she drew level he glanced across.

'Let's find somewhere quiet,' he said. 'Give me a chance to catch my breath. You can't just stomp in on someone's life.'

'That's right.' She hated how she felt unable to resist a barb. 'You can only stomp off and disappear.'

They didn't speak on the crowded Menenstraat until they neared the Menin Gate where police blocked off the traffic as the crowd grew. He turned right at the old city ramparts and strode along Bollingstraat towards a brasserie with glass doors located in a cellar built underneath the ramparts. She could imagine walkers above them, staring down at the moat on the other side. It was calm inside the brasserie: the furnishings stylish and minimal. He sat at a table and ordered two glasses of a beer called Wipers Times.

'You obviously think I've moved on from gin and tonic,' she said.

'Beer wasn't ladylike back then. You were always a lady, even as a girl. Classy. More intelligent than me. I was proud of you. I probably never showed it.'

'I'm more a Chardonnay woman,' Catherine admitted. 'A half bottle in front of the television at night. When they put my generation into nursing homes with dementia, they'll keep us quiet by force-feeding us Chardonnay on intravenous drips.'

He smiled. 'You're a young woman still.'

'I don't feel young.'

They went quiet as the waiter brought their beers. The man returned to the counter, leaving them alone.

'I hope I didn't force-feed you too many gin and tonics,' he said.

'They made me feel grown up and drunk. Watching you chat up women.'

'I never chatted up women.'

'God knows why you felt that having a teenage daughter would help your chances as a ladies man.'

Her father smiled ruefully. 'You were camouflage.'

'For what?'

He looked at his drink. 'It's a long time ago.'

'I'll remind you. You chatting up English women and then local women and then, later some evenings, those local women seemed to summon men with whom you would discreetly slip off to commit God knows what acts down some narrow lane off Rijselstraat. I didn't know what to think, nursing my drink, which by then was just melted ice cubes. I'd need to ward off middle-aged Romeos chancing their luck with me, but I always felt I had a duty to stay sitting there, even though I had no idea what you were doing with the men in those lanes or if maybe they were pimps bringing you to other women. I kept wondering what I'd tell Mum when she'd interrogate me after we got home.'

'What did you tell her?' he asked.

'What could I say, except that we visited graveyards? I didn't mind the Commonwealth ones: open spaces, neat white crosses. I felt safe in them. But I couldn't tell her about the times we visited the German cemetery at Langemark. A hidden place, hard to see into. I remember how creepy it felt, the gravestones laid out flat, each grave containing dozens of German bodies. And the bones of thousands of nameless other Germans heaped together in some vast plot.'

'Kameraden Grab,' he said. 'The Comrades' Grave.'

'I remember my feeling of dread, imagining thousands of corpses squeezed in there. But my dread was really because I sensed you had some ulterior motive for being there. And, sure enough, local men would appear from nowhere: you telling me to stay put while you slipped off to share cigarettes with them and disappeared behind the wall.' She looked at him. 'What were you doing with them, Dad? Were you gay? I mean, are you gay?'

Her father's gaze turned to bewilderment.

'Why would you think that?'

'The fact that you kept furtively disappearing with men. I've looked up the term on the internet. Cottaging. But at sixteen I could hardly walk into Charleville Mall Library and ask the fusty librarian there for a book on gay sex. Early in the trip I thought you were chasing women, but the longer it went on the more scared I got about what to tell Ma. Are you bisexual?'

'Mother of God, where do you get these terms?' He laughed in incredulity at her question. 'Let's just say that whatever I was buying, it wasn't sex.' He grew sombre. 'Let's just say I was naïve and scared. I needed to mind you on that trip here, but I had other responsibilities too.'

'To whom?'

He anxiously checked his watch. She was unsure if he was worried about missing the Last Post Ceremony or seeking an excuse to get rid of her. 'It was a long time ago,' he replied quietly.

Catherine studied the war memorabilia lining the walls. 'Nothing is a long time ago in Ieper. The past has been frozen here since that war ended.'

'Maybe that war never ended.'

'What do you mean?'

He was momentarily silent, searching for the right words. 'Maybe the survivors thought the war had ended when they went home, carting off their maimed and gassed and disfigured. And politicians tried to make the war seem over by building monuments to the missing. But the malevolence unleashed by war, the murderous evil still lurks underground here, like a crocodile waiting to bite. A war ends when the casualties end. In Ieper the casualties never stop. Oh, it's rare enough now when anyone dies, but it still happens: a builder digging foundations for a house or a farmer burning stubble in his fields. Unexploded shells keep working their way up towards the surface, inch by inch, decade by decade, itching to complete their task.' He paused. 'Those shells brought me here.'

'Shells?' Catherine asked, puzzled.

He nodded. 'You've checked the records. Officially I possessed no uncle lost on the Ypres salient. I possess no relatives, full stop. Except you and any children you have, but I never felt any right to intrude on your life. I lost your mother through my own fault. Drink, stupidity, gambling debts: the weakness of a flawed man. I look old, Catherine, and inside I feel older still. I've no life except my annual visit here. Sometimes I step into other people's photographs just to leave some record that I did exist. I spend my days in a Council flat in Coventry. Visiting food banks to survive and spending hours in the local library to stay warm in winter. I shuffle about in tattered cardigans. The only colour in my life are two blazers, waiting to be worn here if I can skimp and save a few shillings a week to pay for my trip. Knowing that every year may be my last chance to pay my respects to the dead.' He paused. 'No, that's a lie. To pay my respects to the unborn.'

He looked so vulnerable that Catherine reached across to touch his fingers.

'Don't upset yourself,' she said, distraught at his pain.

'I deserve to be upset.' He gripped her fingers for a brief second, then made himself let go. 'I deserve no pity from you. I wrecked your mother's life and yours. I condemn myself. Life would be easy if we got a second chance to live it, after we understand what it's about. But it doesn't work that way. I've no right to complain, compared to the young men herded to their deaths here, never even given a chance to make mistakes in life. I can't walk far but on every visit I sit in the small Ramparts Cemetery next to the Lille Gate. Studying the ages of the tombstones I see that many were only boys who probably never learnt to shave. Maybe it's no harm they never held a cut-throat razor: their hands would have shook so much with unadulterated fear. The older I get the more I think about the young men on both sides. Yet in 1970 I felt they had nothing to do with me. They were British or German or French or Belgian. Oh, I knew thousands were Irish, but in my mind they weren't truly Irish.' He looked at her. 'There's nobody as smug as a bigot. Bigotry is a warm safety blanket. I wasn't even much of a bigot: I just went with the flow. I'd nod along in pubs down the Dublin docks when strident voices bellowed out hatred of the Brits and talked about a united Ireland with every bullyboy Orangeman up North kicked back to Scotland.'

'If you were a Republican you certainly hid it when we were here,' Catherine said, surprised.

He nodded. 'That was the whole point. And in truth I was never much of a Republican, at least not after the Provisional

IRA got into their stride, setting off twenty-two bombs across Belfast on Bloody Friday or murdering drinkers in Birmingham. But back in 1970 it was soft-focused idealism. We saw civil rights being denied in a sectarian state up North, with protesters beaten up. It was easy to get swept up in it. On my first trip when I was alone here I was living out the fantasy of being a man of action. I always envied people from big families with uncles and aunts and cousins. I was so desperate to feel I was part of something bigger than myself that I let men manipulate me in 1970 into feeling I belonged to a wider Republican family.' He looked across the table. 'I lost you, thanks to my own stupidity. We can sit here all night, Catherine, but I've nothing really to say. I don't know why you bothered searching for me.'

Catherine looked out at the street where crowds thronged towards the Menin Gate. Why had she come? It was too late for reconciliations: there was too much pain to navigate. Yet she couldn't let go.

'I'm not sure why I'm here either,' she replied quietly. 'I've spent days looking at monuments to fallen soldiers and yet I can't recall a single name on them because I was trying to make sense of the person I really came looking for.'

'Me?'

'I think I came seeking the ghost of the teenage girl I once was, because if any town can accommodate all the ghosts on earth surely it's Ieper. And yes, I was looking for you after seeing photos on Facebook and half hoping not to find you. I figured if I spent a week here without finding you, I could finally mark you down as among the missing and move on with my life. Because you've not left much trace over the decades. I've contacted social services across England, sheltered housing associations, homeless hostels even, but never a trace. I mean, in this day and age how can a man just disappear?'

He shrugged. 'It was easily done here a century ago. One wrong step and you found yourself in mud, so thick there was no way out.'

'I'm not discussing a century ago.'

'A man can still dig his own grave by taking one false step. It was safer for your mother that I vanished and you knew nothing if men came looking.'

'Is that your excuse?'

He shook his head. 'I'm too old for excuses. Have I grand-children?'

This question threw her. It felt like a diversionary ambush, opening up wounds she still struggled to steel herself against.

'You had one,' she replied. 'Megan. A granddaughter. Meningitis. Eight years old.'

He slumped forward. When he looked up his face seemed even older, devastated. 'I'm so desperately sorry. Are you married?'

'I was. It's hard for any marriage to survive such a loss.'

He nodded. 'The empty place at the table, the ghost always present by its absence; that's what your great aunt Eileen called it.'

'I never knew either of your aunts.'

'The only family I had really, apart from my mother: my da didn't count. Aunt Kate died from throat cancer before you were born. During her last years she lived on tea, Woodbines and novenas. A wizened little bird: indestructible until she keeled over. Maybe it's good you don't remember Aunt Eileen. We brought you to see her when you were small, but her mind was gone. She was like a child lost in a big hospital bed. I used to keep a photograph of them both on the hall table.'

'I remember,' she said. 'Taken in a photographer's studio. Such young faces but dressed in black like far older women.'

'My aunts raised me,' he confided. 'My mother loved me dearly: she just wasn't able for life. In one of my earliest memories

I must have been around four years old. My aunts bought me a paper bag of Lemon's boiled sweets and I felt so happy walking between them. But they brought me into a building with high walls and women sobbing. There was one woman smoking in a corridor. But not a cigarette. She was using a rolled up strip of newspaper, trying to suck smoke into her lungs. Another woman in a bed opened her arms wide for me to run to her. But I just got scared in that ward of sad women, all watching like I was somehow meant to light up their day. I was scared by the smells and sounds, the brass bedsteads and peeling paint and I turned away, sobbing and begging my aunts to take me out of there. The woman's face in the bed caved in with disappointment. She was my mother. That was my first and my abiding memory of her.'

'You never talked about your mother.'

He shrugged. 'And sound like a whinging eejit? Men didn't talk down the docks, least of all about things eating you up. You communed in silence with whiskey in quiet pubs and your quietude marked you out to men with discreet propositions.' He looked at her. 'I don't mean sexual propositions.'

'What do you mean?'

'I had all the attributes needed to work on the docks. I kept my mouth shut and my eyes peeled. I saw how stuff came in, the little trickledown bribes greasing the wheels: how a few bob made some excise men go missing from their post; how shoes might discreetly fall off a pallet; how smuggled whiskey bottles clinked in a sailor's bag. A man who made it his business not to see things could do well for himself. You could even get ladies of the night being sneaked onto ships who were happy to reward one favour with another. But women were never my weakness. Gambling was. Your mother was a simple countrywoman. She never understood the docks where my aunts raised me. I didn't bet on horses for the thrill of winning, but for the thrill of bringing something home for her. Other wives needed to buy things on hire purchase: two shillings a week and the debt never paid off. I loved to come home with a new frock or a record player in a wooden case on her birthday or a Little Miss Echo doll for you. Do you remember the tape recorder inside that repeated everything you said? You owned one before they even went on sale in Dublin. Every second docker had a doll hidden under his donkey jacket, liberated from that first consignment.'

'I remember a Casper the Ghost doll,' Catherine said. 'It mouthed phrases every time you pulled its string.'

'It probably said more at home than I did,' her father replied. 'I could talk with strangers, but I was lost in my own house. In 1970 I had a bad run on the horses. A moneylender loaned me cash to try and bet my way out of debt. You can imagine how that went. I'd always warned your mother never to get into hook with moneylenders. Yet there I was, up to my oxters in debt to a bowsie who threatened to break my legs if I missed a repayment.' He paused. 'That's when I was approached: a trip to Ieper, all expenses paid. No moneylender wanted trouble with the IRA. Certain men had a quiet word and my debt was written off. Moneylenders have a conscientious objection to having their own kneecaps shattered. By making one trip to Flanders I could be a debt-free foot soldier fighting for Irish freedom.'

'Why would the IRA send you?' she asked. 'What would you even do here?'

'I was perfect to send. I was no activist, so the Special Branch had no file on me. When I started down the docks as a boy in 1945 I remember being told to turn a blind eye to Flemish men slipping down gangplanks at night. Members of the VNV avoiding retribution from the Allies.'

'Who were the VNV?'

'The Flemish National League. Fantasists or nationalists or fascists who bet on the wrong horse during World War
Two, thinking that if they collaborated with Hitler he'd unyoke
Flanders from Belgium. Hitler played them for fools and annexed
Flanders as a German province. After the war some felt it wise to
avoid facing their Flemish neighbours who hadn't collaborated
with Hitler. The Catholic Church and the IRA ensured that a few
VNV members could discreetly disappear in Ireland. The IRA
had also supported Hitler, sharing the same wishful thinking that
he'd let them run a puppet United Ireland if he triumphed.'

Her father glanced at the only other drinkers in the brasserie who were paying their bill, anxious to get a viewing spot
at the Menin Gate.

'You tell me you lost your child and all I do is blather on
about things from decades ago.' He paused. 'I'm lost for words to
say how heartbroken I am for you. I want to howl with pain for
your loss, Catherine, but all I can do is cry inside.'

'I've cried enough for us both,' she said. 'Grief is a knot so
deep inside me that no scream can expel it. Last night at the
Menin Gate I wasn't aware I was crying until a woman touched
my arm and asked, "Who did you lose here?" I felt like telling
her to mind her own business. Ieper should be a place where
you're left alone to grieve. I was crying for my daughter and crying for myself. Now continue your story.'

'It's not really my story,' her father said. 'When the Northern
Troubles erupted the IRA were totally unprepared. By 1973 the
Provos were wooing Colonel Gaddafi in Libya, who supplied
proper weapons to supplement the guns that Whitey Bulger
shipped out of Boston in coffins. But in 1970 they were scrambling around, desperate to scavenge bomb-making material
from anywhere. That's when the Flemish nationalists – who had
reinvented themselves as entrepreneurs in Ireland – told their

Republican contacts that Flanders was awash with unexploded First World War bombs. Some locals were adept at defusing them and burning off the unexploded gunpowder before they sold the shell casings as scrap metal. The IRA needed someone inconspicuous to track down any locals scavenging for old shells who might want to earn extra cash by stockpiling the explosives they extracted from the metal cases. It seemed the ultimate irony: explosives fired by the British in Ieper might end up used against British soldiers in Belfast.'

'Is that why you met those men in the German cemetery at Langemark?'

'Let's say that my wallet was lighter leaving Ieper, though on my second trip here – the one with you – my heart wasn't. They could have sent some ideologically driven revolutionary who would use terms that might impress the PLO or Gaddafi in his tent. But that guff wouldn't wash with ordinary lads scavenging shells in the fields here. I spoke a language they understood: not about armed struggle but about ready cash. And I knew how to make things disappear off ships docking in Dublin, be it a consignment of Little Miss Echo dolls or a quantity of unstable, antiquated explosives. I was known only for my ability to grease palms. I was so good at making things disappear that, when the time came, I even made myself disappear.'

'You became like a different person the moment we arrived in Ieper,' she said.

He nodded sombrely. 'I was uneasy in my soul. I made my first trip in 1970 as a naive idealist, recruited to help Northern Catholics fight against injustice, just like the Irish lads buried here were recruited to help poor Catholic Belgium. I asked no questions when I plotted how to smuggle gun powder onto a cargo ship in Antwerp to be whisked away on the Dublin docks. I might have felt the same in 1972 if the bomb-making material I sourced had only been used against military targets. But innocent civilians started dying in indiscriminate bombing campaigns. Four in an attack on a furniture showroom in Belfast – two of them babies sharing one pram. Dozens left crippled in a Belfast restaurant. I watched the news each night, seeing forensics experts pick through rubble and limbs looking for fingerprints. They wouldn't find my fingerprints but to me my fingerprints were on every bomb that went off. Many Flemish lads who happily sold me explosives in 1970 felt the same two years on. This was no lark anymore, it was murder. The IRA were no worse than the Loyalist paramilitaries: evil bastards who murdered seventeen Catholics in McGuirk's Bar in Belfast. Loyalist killers rarely talked revolution: they talked sectarian murder. The IRA responded tit for tat, but it wasn't what I'd signed up for. However in 1972 negotiations with the PLO broke down and Gaddafi was still pontificating in his tent, so pressure was put on me to return here and reopen a supply route. Any explosives I might find were ancient and mightn't even still work, but the bomb makers wanted anything they could get their hands on.

'You hid any IRA sympathies well on our trip,' Catherine said.

'I was no sympathiser to murder,' her father replied. 'I was a marked man under instructions. The young men forced to clamber out of trenches here knew they had to take their chances in a hail of machine-gun fire or face certain death from an officer's bullet for disobeying orders. In 1972 I didn't know who the IRA might send to track my movements and put a bullet in my head if I didn't succeed. Or, worse still, hurt you because it was they who insisted on you accompanying me. A father and daughter looked less suspicious. I didn't know if British intelligence were on to me. I just knew I had to go into St George's Memorial Church and memorise the name of every regiment commemorated there in case I was questioned. I had to chat to British women to make myself seem flirtatious. Then, as the evening wore on, I'd chat to Flemish women and mention local men I did business with two years before. I never talked politics. I'd mention a business opportunity if they knew anyone scavenging scrap metal. I kept you in my sight to ensure nothing happened to you and you couldn't be used as leverage. I got the IRA their explosives. Not as much as in 1970 or as cheaply. It was harder to smuggle this time but I had enough contacts to ensure the consignment reached Dublin. When we were in Ieper I did what I had to do to keep us safe. Then when we got back to Dublin, I did what I had to do next, for your sake and your mother's sake, because I had become the IRA's man on the docks. Their requests came thick and fast. Every week a different man appeared at my shoulder as I walked through East Wall and whispered the name of another ship, telling me to ensure that the coast was kept clear, any cops and customs men occupied elsewhere.'

Her father took a drink. She saw his hand shaking. 'Do you know what a Yankee is in horse racing?' he asked.

Catherine shook her head.

'An accumulator bet. You pick four horses to win four races. If all four win it means you've won six double bets, three trebles and a fourfold accumulator. A successful Yankee was like winning the lottery. I'm a lousy gambler but one afternoon, four months after we came back from Ieper, my Yankee came in – good odds on every winner. The bookmaker wasn't bothered by the huge pay-out as other punters watched the banknotes piled up. Bookmakers called such payouts "the loan", knowing that gamblers like me can't resist giving it all back, making outrageous bets to try and recapture that euphoria of winning. If I'd stayed in Dublin I'd have blown that money in weeks and hated myself afterwards. I hated myself enough as it was, every time I heard about another bombing. I was only a cog. I wasn't responsible for no-warning bombings or bombs prematurely exploding because the young lads they sent out were shaking so much. But I was responsible for you and your mother's safety and I was putting you at risk. I didn't plan it in advance but I knew that if I hesitated I'd enter the boozer and buy a huge round for every punter in that betting shop. You were at school and your mother in that big house in Clontarf she cleaned on Thursday afternoons. I went home and put my winnings under her pillow. I just kept the price of the boat fare to Liverpool and enough for two night's accommodation. I packed a shoulder bag to attract no attention. I left no clue as to why I was going. When they came looking for me it was better for your sakes to know nothing. I got drunk on the night crossing and lost every penny in a card game because I'm a lousy gambler. I stood in Liverpool at dawn, penniless, and I knew it was no one's fault but my own. I also knew I could never set foot in Dublin again. I was on my own.' He drained his glass and checked his watch. 'Now you know all there is to know. I'm not seeking forgiveness or charity from you, so you've had a wasted journey, although it's good to see you. I'm not sure I'll have the strength to come here again. So, if you don't mind, I'd like to stand for one last time at the Menin Gate when the Cloth Hall clock strikes eight.' He rose with difficulty. 'Goodbye, Catherine.'

'But I don't understand everything,' she protested. 'I don't understand why you keep coming back to Ieper.'

'I come to remember,' he said. 'Now you must excuse me or I'll be late.'

'Remember who?' she asked. 'Tell me.'

'What's there to tell?' He seemed breathless although he'd only just stood up. 'Why can't you let me be?'

'I'm trying to understand my life,' she replied. 'It's five to eight: we'll make it to the Gate if you lean on my arm.'

His earlier confident stride was gone. He looked drained. Out on the street he was silent, focused on hurrying along the cobbles towards the crowds at the Menin Gate. Only when they drew close did his pace slacken, relieved that the clock had not yet chimed.

'It's funny what this reminds me of.' His voice was infused with sudden gentleness. 'I keep thinking about when I was four and felt so happy walking along with my two aunts, unaware of where they were taking me. Maybe it's because you look so much like your great aunt Kate. Not just your face, everything about you. You'd have liked both aunts but you'd have loved Kate. Especially now that you've been touched by grief. You'd have had so much in common.'

'Did she lose a child?'

He shook his head. 'Kate never had a child to lose.'

'Then how could she know my pain?'

They reached the fringe of the crowd. He slowed to catch his breath.

'Kate understood how the weight of grief never goes away. She and Eileen both did, though they never spoke about their loss. They got on with raising me when my mother was unable to, after my father disappeared off to sea, unable to face up to his responsibilities on land. I knew how hurt you'd feel at being abandoned because I was abandoned by him as a child. The only consistency in my life were those two spinsters – that's how people described them – growing old together, keeping the tiny house they shared spotless; the back bedroom always ready for me when my mother was taken into Grangegorman Asylum. They took turns to scrub the front step as if keeping it spic and span for a homecoming, for a loved one about to turn the corner.'

He surveyed the crowd, looking for any gap to squeeze through. 'I don't think they even spoke about their grief to each other. They shared it in silence like they shared everything.' He looked at her. 'I'm not minimising your grief, Catherine. Losing a child is surely a pain like no other. But it's a public pain, obvious for everyone to see. You had a funeral for Megan, sympathisers and cards and flowers. At least the world recognised your grief.'

'Do you think that made it easier?' she asked. 'Neighbours turning up with unwanted pots of Hungarian goulash; mothers with daughters in Megan's class avoiding me; strangers offering trite condolences when all I wanted was to be left alone to curl up and cry.'

'What if there were no condolences?' he asked. 'No sympathisers, no one you could speak to about your pain. A pain you couldn't even bring yourself to mention to your sister, despite her grief being as deep as yours.'

'I had no sister.'

He nodded solemnly. 'You were an only child, like me. That's why I prayed you would have three or four children in the happy life I hoped you were leading. I'm so sorry for you and, if I'm honest, sorry for me too. I wanted our family line to go on, even if my grandchildren knew nothing about me. But it's just you and me: the last of the line. Take my hand just this once and follow me.'

Catherine realised he had been gathering his strength for this moment. As he pushed through the crowd his stride assumed a military bearing, his tone officious as he called out: 'Wreath layer coming through.' The crowd glanced at his military blazer and parted automatically, though the space was so cramped they barely had room to pass. Some moved respectfully, others resentfully, unsure if he was the wreath layer or an official escorting a wreath laying relative. Soon they stood underneath the high barrel-vaulted archway, every inch adorned with names of the missing. Crowd barriers sealed off a space where the buglers stood and tonight's genuine wreath layers gathered – two young sea scouts, several unidentified women and four old soldiers in uniform.

Her father was breathing heavily after getting them to within two rows of the crush barriers. Up on the Market Square the fun fair was continuing, but the pop music did not travel this far. There was absolute silence as the clock began to chime eight times. The buglers from the local volunteer fire brigade sounded the Last Post and someone stepped forward to recite the Exhortation for the Fallen. Catherine found herself joining in with her father in responding: 'We will remember.' She remembered standing here at sixteen, allowing him to hold her when overcome by sadness. Back then her sadness was a vague sorrow for strangers far removed for her. But tonight she was close to tears as she found herself remembering Megan and her mother and two close friends lost to cancer: people who had never set foot in Ieper but whose presence was summoned up by this simple ceremony. A Welsh school choir began to sing as people laid their wreaths. She watched her father gaze up at the densely packed columns of chiselled names.

'You used to pretend your uncle's name was so high up I couldn't read it.'

'I might have two uncles up there.' His voice sound as soft as a ghost's. 'I just didn't realise it back then.'

'What uncles?'

'The uncles I never had,' he said. 'That doesn't make them less real. I never put it all together until I was sitting alone in my Council flat, asking myself, like old men do, where did my life go wrong? And it came to me that Ieper was the place where my family went belly up. Not back in 1972 when my actions cost me the only family I had left, but long before that, when this area was reduced to mud and barbed wire and shell holes. I lost my wider family here: the family I missed out on because they were never born. Both my aunts were engaged to be married: young women looking forward to bright futures that were wiped out by gas and shells. They never spoke about their loss because such women never mentioned such things, especially after Ireland got independence and nobody wanted to remember the thousands of Dubliners who died here. My aunts were casualties of Ieper, though they were dead before I realised it. "My poor James," Aunt Kate would say softly after a glass of sherry at Christmas. "My poor James." He'd been a cooper, making wooden barrels in the Guinness brewery. I don't know his surname. I never asked. Aunt Eileen could never bring herself to even mention her fiancé's first name. There was a secret around Aunt Eileen and I didn't ask. Maybe she got pregnant and miscarried. I just know that he was a shop assistant and they had planned to marry when he next came home on leave. After her death I found a photograph of him in uniform, along with an engagement ring, wrapped in a silk scarf. I can't look up their military records because I don't know their surnames. People looked down on my aunts, made fun of spinsters who couldn't get a man. Never believe nostalgia about the past, Catherine; people were nasty and snide. Dublin women never talked about their grief at having a sweetheart killed at Passchendaele, except to themselves. I was such a quiet child, like a mouse in the corner, that I sometimes caught glimpses of a grief they only expressed in guarded whispers.'

He paused and Catherine realised that she had never seen anyone look more lost.

'I feel so old, Catherine. I'm not looking to be part of your life. I'm just explaining why I'll keep coming here while I have enough strength, why I wear a blazer and stand to attention. It's nothing to do with Britain: forty-five years there and that country still feels foreign to me. I'm honouring no army either. I've no time for armies – secret or otherwise. I'm honouring two aunts who raised me and never got a chance to stand here. I'm honouring the two Dublin lads they loved, who may well be among the missing listed here. But I don't even know that because I lack the names to find their graves if they have any, so here's the only place I can go to remember them. I'm mourning the cousins I might have had if war hadn't denied them the chance of being born. If those two young men had made it back from Ieper there would be more than just you and me left in this family. When I brought you here I thought we had no connection to Ieper. But Ieper is where the future ended for the aunts I loved and the family we never had. Stand with me for another minute, Catherine, till the buglers sound 'Réveille'. Then you should go your own way.'

The Welsh school choir had finished singing. The final wreath was laid. As the firefighters raised their bugles again Catherine saw her father tremble, looking so exhausted she did not know how he would make it back to whatever cheap hotel he was staying in. She turned towards him, like she had done, forty-five years ago when she was sixteen. There were no tears this time: she had no tears left. All her tears had been cried in private, like her two great aunts. Catherine and her father didn't speak because there was nothing to say. They just held one another, arms wrapped around each other until the last note of the 'Réveille' sounded, until the curious onlookers filed away, until the wreath layers stopped posing for photographs and the space underneath the Menin Gate emptied so that they were the only two souls left.

Acknowledgements

Like their author, and like many another Irish XI before them, these eleven stories have undergone varied journeys. 'The Lover' first appeared in *The Faber Book of Best New Irish Short Stories, 2006–07*, edited by a great champion of Irish writing, David Marcus. The author would like to record a precious memory of having the privilege of going to meet him in Wynn's Hotel in Dublin to discuss some edits to the story, and finding this elegantly dressed elderly gentleman patiently waiting on the front steps, smiling shyly in greeting. Early – and much shorter and very different – versions of 'The Last Person', 'What Then?', 'Supermarket Flowers' and 'The Rivals' were all first broadcast on BBC Radio 4, as was 'One Seed of Doubt', under its original title of 'The Unknown'. All are published for the first time at their proper length here and the author expresses his thanks to the producers who commissioned these stories. 'Martha's Streets' was also broadcast on BBC Radio 4, before being published in the anthology, *New Dubliners*, published in the USA by Pegasus Books and in Ireland by New Island Books. Certain passages of this story were later developed in the novel, *An Ark of Light*, written some years later. 'Coming Home' was first published in the anthology *Flame Angels*, edited by Polly Nolan (Mammoth Books, UK) before being rewritten as a play for BBC Radio 4, entitled *The Fortunestown Kid,* and then reclaiming its prose form when rewritten in this final version for the anthology *Silver Threads of Hope* edited by Sinéad Gleeson and published by New Island Books. 'The Keeper of Flanagan's Hotel' once anchored the midfield of the collaborative novel, *Finbar's Hotel*, which was devised and edited by the present author and crewed by Roddy Doyle, Jennifer Johnston, Joseph O'Connor, Anne Enright, Hugo Hamilton and Colm Tóibín, who all contributed individual chapters. The novel was published in the UK by Picador, in Ireland by New Island Books and in the USA by Harcourt Brace. The author's own chapter made its first bid for independence as a radio play, *The Night Manager*, produced by BBC Radio 4. It is published here for the first time as a stand-alone work of fiction in an expanded and revised form. 'Coffee at Eleven' was first published in *The Irish Times* in a shorter, early version which was entitled 'A Visitor'. 'The Unremembered' was commissioned by Vlaams-Nederlands Huis deBuren in Brussels as part of their citybooks series (www.citybooks.eu). The full text was published in Dutch in their book entitled *citybooks Ieper*, while abridged versions of the text were released as podcasts in German, French and English. The author expresses his thanks to Marianne Hommersom and Willem Bongers-Dek of deBuren and to Piet Chielens, coordinator of the In Flanders Fields Museum in Ypres. The full text is published here in English for the first time. The author would like to express his thanks to the Arts Council of Ireland who awarded him the Anthony Cronin Award, in part to buy time to complete this short story collection. Sincere thanks also for their wisdom and advice to Mary Stanley, Stephen Reid and to everyone at New Island Books, most especially Edwin Higel, who has guided that company forward, through good times and bad, since its inception in 1992.